SWEET MAN IS GONE

A MAXX MAXWELL MYSTERY

Sweet Man Is Gone

Peggy Ehrhart

FIVE STAR
A part of Gale, Cengage Learning

GALE
CENGAGE Learning

Detroit • New York • San Francisco • New Haven, Conn • Waterville, Maine • London

GALE
CENGAGE Learning

Set in 11 pt. Plantin.
Printed on permanent paper.

LIBRARY OF CONGRESS CATALOGING-IN-PUBLICATION DATA

Ehrhart, Peggy.
    Sweet man is gone : a Maxx Maxwell mystery / Peggy Ehrhart.
    — 1st ed.
        p. cm.
    ISBN-13: 978-1-59414-668-8 (alk. paper)
    ISBN-10: 1-59414-668-3 (alk. paper)
    1. Women singers—Fiction. 2. Women blues musicians—Fiction. 3. Blues musicians—Crimes against—Fiction. 4. New Jersey—Fiction. 5. Manhattan (New York, N.Y.)—Fiction. I. Title.
PS3605.H746S93 2008
813'.6—dc22   2008010786

First Edition, First Printing: July 2008.

Published in 2008 in conjunction with Tekno Books and Ed Gorman.

Printed in the United States of America
1 2 3 4 5 6 7 12 11 10 09 08

To my band mates in The Last Stand Band

I would like to thank Denise Dietz,
my Five Star editor, for all her help.

CHAPTER 1

Jimmy walks like he always hears music. Here he comes now, strolling toward me with his gig bag slung over his shoulder. He's not a big guy, but he's sexy as hell, with smooth olive skin, dark hair, brown eyes that just about make me melt—and his faded jeans fit like they were made to order.

If I hadn't sworn off guitar players, I'd be totally in love. But the thing is, I've had my fill. After the last one, Sandy, I told myself never again. Anyway, Jimmy's always been totally businesslike with me. Anybody in music—anybody with any sense, I mean—knows what a mess it is if you start falling in love with your band mates.

Jimmy catches sight of me and his face breaks into the lopsided grin that makes him all the more adorable. He pushes a strand of hair off his forehead and says, "Whew, hot out there tonight." There's a touch of the South in his speech, and he calls himself Jimmy Nashville, but he's always been vague about where he's from. "Anybody else here yet?" he says. "Or am I the first one?"

"Neil's in the bathroom."

Jimmy pantomimes someone smoking a joint.

I sling my bag onto the floor to make space for him on the ratty sofa. Every Manhattan rehearsal studio I've ever been in looks like the Salvation Army did the decor.

He sinks down next to me and leans his gig bag against the wall. "No sign of the blues brothers?"

9

"Not yet."

"Good. I could use a little peace and quiet."

"Rough day?"

"Woman problems."

He flashes me the lopsided grin. What is it with these guitar players? Jimmy's got at least six women on the string. And Sandy—my old boyfriend—well, the less said about that the better.

"Anything new in the world of music?" Jimmy nods toward the TV mounted on the wall and tuned perpetually to some music channel. Just now the Rolling Stones are talking about their upcoming tour, or at least Mick Jagger is talking about it. Keith Richards is squinting at the camera and messing with his hair.

"Think we'll still be gigging when we're their age?" I say.

"Sure. Lots of blues guys hang on forever. I plan to still be at it when I'm ninety."

"Me too," I say.

"We'll be like those guys Bart claims he's raising money for." Jimmy points past the Coke machine at a poster that's been up for a couple of weeks. "Blues from the Heart," it reads. "A Concert to Support the Pioneers of the Blues." It shows an ancient black guy sitting on a broken-down porch with his guitar.

"How come you say *claims?* Don't you think Bart's on the level with that?"

"I better keep my mouth shut," Jimmy says. "Bart can be a scary guy and I don't want to get on his bad side."

Around the corner, the elevator shudders to a stop and the doors clank open. It's Michael or Dom, I'm thinking, maybe both. But the next thing I know, coming into view is—oh, shit—Stan Dunlap, all six feet six of him, loping along with his guitar case dangling from his hand. The last person I want to run into.

He catches sight of me and halts in mid-step, forehead

puckered, mouth open, guitar case swaying at his side. Is he going to turn around and scurry back to the elevator? No, he arranges his mouth into a not very cheerful smile and advances. "Maxx," he says in a strangled voice. "Long time no see." Under his dark brows his eyes look nervous.

"Yeah. It's been a while." Do I look as uncomfortable as I feel?

He pauses in front of me, is silent for a long minute, and finally comes out with, "Hot night." He sets the guitar case down and uses both hands to prod his abundant hair into place.

I notice he's staring at Jimmy, staring so hard Jimmy's almost squirming. "Yeah," I say. "It must be at least ninety."

"So, uh, how's the band?" He turns his face back toward me, trying to sound casual but not succeeding.

I nod, feeling totally awkward. "Making it." He nods too, but he doesn't say anything, so I go on. "Working once a week, sometimes more." He nods again, but still doesn't say anything. "We'll be at the Hot Spot down in the Village Saturday," I say. He nods. He's a huge guy and my neck is starting to hurt from looking up at him. "How're *you* doing, Stan?"

He arranges his mouth into another smile, a more genuine smile, and says, "Good. Real good. Have you heard of the Blue Dudes?"

"You're in another blues band?" I know I sound amazed, and sure enough, he looks hurt.

"The blues is my main influence," he says, defensively. "You know that."

I do, but his idea of blues and my idea aren't the same thing. That was part of the problem.

He checks his watch and stoops for the guitar case. "I've got to get in there," he says. "They'll be wondering where I am. The band has a big road gig this weekend. One of those casinos up north." He takes a few steps and the guitar case narrowly misses my knees.

"Good luck," I say.

He takes a few more steps, still looking at me but moving toward the door. "Thanks," he says. "Those gigs pay good money, and it looks like it could turn into something regular."

Suddenly, one of the tech guys appears in the doorway. I say, "Stan, watch out," but it's too late. Stan collides with him. The guitar case swings crazily around, bangs into the Coke machine, and plops on the floor with a thud. Stan grabs the tech guy to steady him. He's apologizing like crazy and the tech guy is swearing.

I sink back into the sofa, trying not to laugh, at least not too loud. Stan gets the tech guy calmed down and disappears through the doorway.

"I can't believe Stan's in another blues band," I say to Jimmy when I'm sure Stan's out of earshot. "Says they've got a casino gig this weekend. Did you hear him?"

"So that was the notorious Stan," he says. "No wonder he was giving me the evil eye."

"Understandable, I guess. Sorry I didn't introduce you, but I was a little flustered. This is the first time I've run into him since . . ."

"Since you fired him?"

"I didn't really fire him. We had a discussion. It wasn't working out, and he knew it. He just doesn't have a blues soul—"

"Hey, hold on a second." Jimmy lifts a hand as if to call for silence. On the screen, a talking head is observing that something is a great loss to fans of some generation or other. "I guess she really did die," he says, half to himself. "I thought that guy was putting me on."

The talking head is replaced by the fleeting image of a woman in a fringed skirt and a cowboy hat, then by a run-down brick building that looks really old. Over the sound of a honky-tonk piano, a female voice moans, "Let me cry you some more tears."

The talking head comes back for a minute, then the screen is filled with cheerful people wearing bellbottoms and platform shoes. The camera zooms in on the cover of a CD with "Swinging Seventies" scrawled across it, and the bellbottom people do a cheerful little dance.

"Who died?" I say.

"Nancy Lee Parker."

"Who's that?"

"Oh, she's . . . I wouldn't even know about her except this crazy guy's been hassling me. She was . . . how to explain it?" He stares down the hallway as if looking for inspiration. As he stares, Michael and Dom turn the corner. "Here come the blues brothers now," Jimmy says. "We can get started." The sofa creaks as he pulls himself to his feet.

"A crazy guy's been hassling you?" I say, but he doesn't hear me—or at least he doesn't answer.

Michael's dressed for the heat in a tank top that shows off his skinny shoulders and arms. Dom is bouncing along, his comfortable little tummy straining at the buttons of a Hawaiian shirt that includes every color of the rainbow and then some. His shaved head gleams under the fluorescent lights. They're not really brothers. Jimmy calls them that because they argue all the time, which is what they're doing now.

"I don't know why we have to have these practices so late at night," Michael is complaining in his annoyingly precise voice.

"You stay up late when we have a gig, bud," Dom says in the booming voice of a New Jersey jock.

"I get paid for a gig. I don't get paid to practice, and it cuts into my sleep. Why can't you change your work schedule so we don't have to do this in the middle of the night?"

"I been there all of two months, and I'm makin' good money.

I'm not gonna go complainin' about my schedule."

"Can't you trade shifts with somebody?"

Dom ignores him, pats Jimmy on the shoulder, kisses me on the cheek, and says, "How ya doin', guys?"

I kiss him back. Jimmy says, "Not bad. Good to see you, man. Keeping cool?"

"I'm always cool," Dom says. "I'm Mister Cool."

Michael's mouth settles into a tight line, and he strides past us without saying anything. He plants himself by the Coke machine and stares at the Blues from the Heart poster like he's never seen it before.

"I'll see if they've got our room ready," I say.

Around the corner, a guy I've never met is on duty at the desk, a dark, hairy guy coping with the heat by wearing nothing but a pair of jeans and a leather vest. Neil's lounging in a mangy armchair with his eyes closed. A bunch of guys with assorted tattoos and facial piercings are perched on the folding chairs strung out along the back wall. One of them whistles at me.

In my mind I'm still a skinny chick nobody'd look twice at, but I got my nose fixed before I went off to college—not that I stayed there long—and I went blonde when I hooked up with my first band. And it's amazing how a push-up bra can help you fill out a T-shirt.

"Hey, who're you?" The hairy guy leans across the desk and gives me a toothy smile.

"Maxx Maxwell," I say. "What's happening with our room?"

He peers at the schedule in front of him. "Nine p.m.?" I nod. The smile becomes toothier. "I'm Tony." He sticks out his hand. It's warm and sweaty. "You're a singer, I bet," he says.

"How'd you guess?"

"The chick's always the singer."

"I'm a *blues* singer," I say, as a voice in my head asks if he'd really know the difference. "Is the room ready?"

He pokes a tech guy leaning against the wall, paging through a comic book. "Throw those head-bangers out of G. Their time's up and Maxx Maxwell needs her room."

We follow the tech guy into a narrow corridor with doors along each side. It feels like a low-budget motel, except there's music behind each door, a tasty funk groove on the left, "Take Five" on the right, a band trying to be the Allman Brothers down at the end.

Studio G's door is open. Actually there are two doors. The rooms are supposed to be soundproof, though they never are, so there's an inner door and an outer door, like on a submarine. And the walls are hung with panels of spongy gray foam. Three kids with gig bags over their shoulders troop past me into the hall, followed by a guy tucking a pair of drumsticks into a backpack.

Neil settles in behind the keyboards, looking like he doesn't quite know where he is or what he's supposed to be doing. Except he must know because he observes his usual ritual of slipping his sneakers off, kicking them into the corner, and launching into some incongruous Bach thing.

The tech guy is twiddling with the sound board. He looks up. "How many mikes?"

"Just one."

"You?" When I nod, he says, "Give it try."

I toss my bag on the floor and step up to the mike. "Check," I say. "Check, check," and my voice bounces back at me from the monitors. I sound like a female Darth Vader. "Back off the reverb," I say.

Behind me, Dom is thumping his way around the drum kit, punctuating his thumps with cymbal crashes. Jimmy is making minuscule adjustments to the knobs on his amp while he coaxes one sweet lick after another out of his guitar. A vision of Sandy rises up before my eyes, smiling at me over his Stratocaster as his fingers toy with the strings. I try to ignore it.

Michael has his back to the rest of us. He's unrolling his cable and plugging it into his amp. I can tell by the way he's holding his shoulders that he's still in a bad mood.

Minutes pass as he fusses with his tuner, then with the knobs on his amp, thumping one string at a time while he listens with an ear to the amp and a furrowed brow. Finally he says, "Okay, I'm ready."

"Let's go through the set list for Saturday," I say. " 'Every Day I've Got the Blues.' Jimmy, you start it."

He looks up from his guitar and flashes me the lopsided grin, catches Dom's eye, and counts off. A few bell-like notes ring from his amp. Dom comes in on the snare, and Michael's bass starts its steady dance. Jimmy's left hand inches its way up the neck of his guitar, while the fingers of his right hand pluck bits of sound from the strings, a sweet bit here, a nasty bit there.

I step up to the mike and take a deep breath. " 'Every day,' " I sing, " 'every day I've got the blues.' " I close my eyes and toss my head back. The spotlight mounted on the ceiling makes the inside of my eyelids glow red. Jimmy's fills are like echoes of my voice. It's almost like a duet.

The sound of the band surges around me. I can almost feel it—Dom, Michael, Neil with a carefully placed chord here and there, Jimmy with his melting blues lines.

In my mind, I'm sixteen again and I'm standing in front of the mirror in my bedroom in Ardendale, New Jersey. I've got the radio on, and I'm singing along with Madonna, feeling my voice grab every note just right. Across the hall my honor-roll sister is putting the finishing touches on one of her prize-winning science projects. She always had the science, and the grades, and the boyfriends, but singing was the first thing I had that was really mine. The blues came later, though—much later.

I sing another verse, the part about how nobody loves me

and nobody seems to care. When I get to the end of the verse, Neil takes over. He hunches over the keys till all I can see is hair and fingers. He's reaching for the high notes at the very end of the keyboard, punching out a quick jangle, like something you'd hear on an out-of-tune piano in a honky-tonk joint.

Jimmy's solo starts where his last one left off, way up the fret board. Notes hop from sweet to nasty and back again, so fast his right hand is a blur. I glance over at him. I can't help it. He's bent over the guitar with his eyes closed and a secret smile playing around his mouth. A piece of hair straggles over his forehead. He looks up, nods at Dom, and Dom finishes it off with a flurry of cymbals.

We run through the rest of the tunes for the Hot Spot gig and spend a little time on some new stuff. Just when my throat is about to give out, the lights blink to tell us we've got five more minutes.

"Mind if I sing one?" Jimmy says.

"Not at all." I nod gratefully and head for one of the folding chairs scattered along the edges of the room.

"Ever heard this?" Jimmy reaches for the mike stand and drags it closer to where he's standing. He catches Dom's eye. "One. Two. One, two, three—" He steps up to the mike and starts to sing. " 'I wonder who's gonna be your sweet man when I'm gone . . .' "

Like a lot of white-guy guitar players, he doesn't have much of a voice to speak of. But he looks so vulnerable leaning into the mike, with those big dark eyes, like he means every word. I know I'm staring, but I can't help myself. I'd go for him in a minute, except—I grit my teeth—I've been down that road before and it sucks.

Jimmy's in mid-solo when the tech guy opens the door. He watches from the doorway, till Jimmy's done and the song wraps up. "Nice chops, man," he says. "You do all that without a pick?"

Jimmy nods.

Meanwhile, Michael is actually complimenting Dom on his drumming.

"You sound pretty good yourself, bud," Dom tells Michael, "for a guy that's up past his bedtime."

Amazingly, Michael laughs.

"I love that tune," I say to Jimmy. "Sounds like you've been listening to Muddy Waters."

"You got it," he says with a grin.

" 'Who's Gonna Be Your Sweet Man When I'm Gone?' "

He's busy winding one of his cables into a neat round, but he looks up and, for a second, his usual vibe, pleasant but business-like, turns into something else. Don't tell me he's got a thing for tall blonde singers who'd be skinny if they didn't wear a push-up bra, and he's been fighting it off as desperately as I've been fighting off my attraction to guitar players.

"Would you miss me if I was gone?" he says, looking at me so intently that I feel a little shiver.

"Yeah," I say, when the shiver passes. "I would. I really would."

He smiles. "I'd miss you, too," he says.

I watch him tuck his cables into his gear bag, still smiling a little to himself.

Neil breaks the spell by asking me what time the sound check is Saturday.

I have high hopes for this band. Sandy and I were living on the music, living good, but I couldn't hang around with a guy I couldn't trust. After I broke up with Sandy, all I wanted to sing was blues. End of story. Not because the blues is sad, but because it's about being down and climbing back up. And if you have to get in people's faces and make a lot of noise in the process, go ahead and do it. So this is a blues band, and it's all mine, and whatever we have to do to survive—well, that's what we'll do.

We straggle out to the desk. It's brighter out here and we're all blinking like we just came out of a cave. Tony plants a sweaty hand on my arm. "Was everything okay?" he says.

"Fine," I say, easing my arm out of his grip. "Everything was fine."

"That'll be eighty bucks."

The guys and I split it five ways.

The place is as busy as it was when we showed up—maybe even busier. Guys are still sprawled on the row of fold-up chairs against the back wall, and another band that just finished up is trooping down the corridor to pay.

We pick our way through a knot of guys standing around the Coke machine, smoking and flicking ashes into the trashcan. I'm talking to Michael. Neil is plodding along silently. Jimmy and Dom are trailing behind us—at least I think they are. We're halfway to the elevator when a woman appears at the end of the hall. She's wearing tight jeans and a cropped top with a few inches of well-toned belly peeking out below. Her hair is a carefully careless mixture of deep red and reddish-gold. It's Monique, one of Jimmy's many girlfriends. She's Swedish and looks like a supermodel.

"You're . . . still . . . here," she pants in her musky voice. "I'm so glad I caught you. Where's Jimmy?" Despite the amazing body and the temptress voice, she's got the face of a little kid, round cheeks and a tiny upturned nose with a sprinkling of freckles across it.

"He's, uh . . ." I turn around. "I guess he's still back by the office."

"I was in the neighborhood." She's fanning herself with her hand. "Whew," she says. "Hot out there . . . too hot to rush around." She's still panting. "How've you been, Maxx? You look great."

"Everything's fine," I say. "The band's really tightening up, thanks to Jimmy."

She smiles. "He's an amazing guy, isn't he?"

"How're *you* doing?" I say. "How's the music?"

"I've got a great gig at a place called Lemon's—a nice restaurant on the Upper West Side. Every Sunday and Monday. Have you been there?"

"No."

"It's in the eighties, between Broadway and Amsterdam." She peers past me down the hall, her forehead crinkling in puzzlement. "What's he doing? You're sure he didn't leave?"

"I hope not. I've got to check if he wants a ride Saturday."

She's still peering down the hall, looking conflicted. "I'd look for him, but I don't want to run into my ex. He practices here, but I forget what night."

"Messy breakup?"

"Not really. We're still friends, but it would be awkward if he saw me with Jimmy. I feel kind of sorry for the poor guy." But then she shrugs and says, "Oh, well. I'll take my chances." She hurries toward the studio and disappears around the corner. Neil and Michael have disappeared in the other direction, headed for the elevator. I hear it squeal. Michael sticks his head around the corner. "Want us to hold it for you, Maxx?"

"I have to talk to Jimmy."

Three or four minutes pass, and I still don't see Jimmy. Dom wanders by, says goodnight, and heads for the elevator. More minutes pass. And more. But finally, Jimmy and Monique appear at the end of the hall. She's got her arm tucked around his possessively, and she's smiling at him, bending down a little to make eye contact.

"Hey, Maxx," Jimmy says. "We need to talk about Saturday."

"Sound check's at eight," I say. "How about if I swing by at seven?"

"Good deal." He gives me a super-nice version of his grin, a version that makes his eyes crinkle up and a little dimple come and go in his cheek. "See you then."

We start toward the elevators, but we've only gone a few feet when a voice behind us says, "Wait a minute, pal. We were having a conversation."

We all turn. It's a guy, dark like Jimmy and kind of good-looking. But he's much taller and he's got a slow, intense voice, not deep but compelling all the same. So even though he's not talking especially loud, there's something menacing about him.

"It's not very polite to walk away," he says, with maybe just a hint of a southern accent.

Jimmy looks serious but not angry. "I really don't see what you want from me," he says, pleasantly enough, looking up at the guy. "I've told you that already, lots of times."

"You don't understand, do you?" the guy says.

"I do, man. I really do."

"No, you don't," the guy says, his voice slower and even more intense. "You don't understand at all." He turns and walks back toward the studio.

"What on earth was that about?" I say. "Is that the guy you said was hassling you?" Monique is still hanging on his arm, looking like she never wants to let go.

Jimmy shakes his head. "I feel sorry for him. Really, really sorry."

When we get out on the street—Feedback's down on 30th, between Seventh and Eighth Avenues—Jimmy and Monique head east. I head west, hurrying past a block of shops, then one of tenements, till I come to an ancient Bonneville. It's seafoam green, like the old Stratocaster color, with one dark-green door.

It's shaped like a boat and it's the ugliest car on the street. It's mine.

I struggle briefly with the driver's side lock, which is stuck as usual, give up and climb in the passenger side, which doesn't lock at all. I slide across the seat, settle in behind the wheel, and drive back to New Jersey, wondering what the story was with that tall guy.

CHAPTER 2

"Blues doesn't fill a club," Boris kept saying. He's the Hot Spot's manager. Okay, so a blues joint doesn't need the doorman and the velvet ropes. And the night I got turned onto the blues, there were only a couple of people in the place. But that was Atlantic City. Who'd go there for blues?

This is Manhattan. "We'll fill it. We'll fill it," I kept saying, back when I thought that was my only worry.

So tonight's our first gig at the Hot Spot. No cover but a cut of the bar. And it's right in the heart of the Village, so a foot in the door would be great for the band.

But half of New Jersey is backed up at the tollbooths, waiting to cross the George Washington Bridge. I'm inching forward, windows open because my car doesn't have AC, breathing hot air heavy with exhaust fumes, on my way to pick up Jimmy and then head down to Bleecker Street.

I've got the classic rock station on, and the Rolling Stones are competing with the hip hop the guy next to me is blasting from his oversized speakers—and I'm glancing into the rearview mirror from time to time to watch my makeup drip away. Usually I try to dress up nice for a gig, but it's hard when it's so hot. Tonight after staring in my closet for about twenty minutes, I settled on red leather shorts and a red sequined halter, and I've got my red spike-heeled sandals in my bag.

Finally I reach the tollbooth, where I hand six bucks to a lady wearing a rubber glove. Eight lanes merge into three, and in a minute I'm out over the river. At the end of the bridge, I swing around onto the West Side Highway. It's a straight shot downtown now, with the river on my right and New Jersey beyond in a haze of heat. I take the exit at 95th and head east. Within a few blocks, a neighborhood of grand, stone-faced apartment buildings turns into one where guys stand on the sidewalk in front of bodegas, listening to salsa on boom boxes.

And something is going on. The street that skirts the side of Jimmy's building is clogged with cop cars, an ambulance, and a crowd: salsa guys, chubby Hispanic grandmas, slender brown kids who've found something interesting to look at.

The crowd is jammed up against a chain link fence with razor wire on top, filling the sidewalk and spilling out into the street. The fence protects a concrete-covered yard that separates Jimmy's building from the building next door. People are jostling and bobbing to get a better view of whatever's on the other side of the fence.

I try to edge my car past the ambulance, but one of the cops holds up a warning hand. I shift into reverse and creep back toward the corner. I turn the corner and scan the curb past a collection of cars in not much better shape than mine. I slip into the only available spot—available because it's by a hydrant. I'll just be a minute, I tell myself. I don't bother to roll up the windows because the lock on the passenger side doesn't work.

Making my way through the crowd, I notice that a gate in the chain link fence is open, and a cop is standing at the gate with a stern look on his face. A few more cops and some ambulance people are hovering around something in the middle of the yard.

I can't resist a look, even though I'm in a hurry. I slow down and stand on tip-toe to peer over the heads of the people between me and the fence. The thing everybody's interested in seems to be a person lying on the concrete, a very still person. I can't see much because leafy, tree-like weeds grow along the fence, and beyond the fence two ambulance people are crouching by the person with their backs to me. Another ambulance person is standing off to the side, talking to a cop. A stretcher is lying at the edge of the concrete patch.

"What happened?" I ask the guy next to me, a wiry brown kid with a gold chain around his neck.

He checks out my legs then says, "The guy fell . . . or something." His accent gives the statement a musical lilt.

"From where?"

"Up there." He points at the side of the building, craning his neck back to look as far up as he can.

"He was on the roof?"

"No, he came out of a window. Up there. See?"

Lots of people have their windows wide open on this sultry summer evening, and lots of the windows don't have screens, so it's hard to tell where the kid's pointing.

"Did you see it happen?" I say.

"No." He waves his brown hand in a small circle. "The people here—they were talkin' about it."

Now the ambulance people have stood up. One of them heads for the stretcher; the other one heads toward the gate.

I can see the body now, and for a minute I just feel cold. Then the whole scene stretches away from me, like it's not real. People are talking, but it's the background noise in a movie. I'm floating a few feet above the sidewalk, watching a story unfold. The breeze is stirring the leaves of the huge tree-like weeds springing up along the fence. The evening sun is glinting off the razor wire.

The body sprawled out on the concrete is Jimmy.

"I know him," I hear myself shouting. I push through the knot of people. "I know him," I repeat. A few people step aside, almost respectfully. "I know him," I say to the stern face of the cop guarding the gate.

He looks at me, still stern. "Stand over here." He gestures like he's directing traffic, pointing me to a spot along the wall of the building.

The ambulance person is hurrying back through the gate. He carries a folded white cloth. I step away from the wall so I can see what's going on. The other two ambulance people are gently lifting Jimmy onto the stretcher. I don't want to look but I'm staring. He's wearing black cowboy boots, a smooth-fitting T-shirt that says "Austin, Texas, Home of the Blues," black jeans, and a black leather belt with a big silver buckle.

The folded white cloth turns out to be a big white bag. The ambulance people ease Jimmy into it, starting with his feet. Finally, his face is gone too. If I was the kind of person who cried in public, I'd be crying, big gulping hysterical gasps. Instead, I'm feeling numb.

"You knew him? Did you say you knew him?" Standing beside me is a woman who has to be at least eighty, but she's wearing spike-heeled sandals, iridescent purple leggings, and a tight purple shirt. Her hair is jet black and it's teased into an impressive crest on top of her head.

I have to lean down to talk to her. Without the heels and the hair, she'd be about four feet tall. "He was the guitar-player in my band. We were supposed to play a gig tonight."

"What?" She cocks her head toward me. I repeat myself. "I knew him, too," she says, shaking her head, her expression mournful. "What a tragic, tragic thing."

"You live in this building?" I say it louder than I normally would.

She nods. "He and I were neighbors. Such a sweet man. Always had time for a friendly word." Her narrow lips are outlined in brilliant red. She shakes her head again. "Who could have thought he was so unhappy? But he was an artist, of course. Artists have depths the rest of us can't understand." Her voice is barely more than a hoarse croak.

"He was unhappy?"

"He must have been. Otherwise why would he—" she pauses dramatically and gestures toward the patch of concrete, now empty "—do this?"

"You think he jumped on purpose?"

"What else could it be, dear?" She fastens a claw-like hand on my arm to pull me closer. Her nails are as brilliantly red as her lips. "The same thing happened to my late husband—well, one of them anyway. I'll never forget the day. He was a musician, too."

"He was?" I barely know what I'm saying.

"Sensitive. Just like Jimmy. I can never resist a sensitive man. And I'll bet you can't either."

I'm nodding. I can't help it. Why am I talking to this creature? She's one of those people who pulls things out of you, things you wanted to hold onto and save till they turned into something you could sing about.

"Miss, excuse me," says a cop at my elbow. "What was your connection with the deceased individual?"

The cop looks like Dom—stocky and tough, with his hair shaved off. At least, the part of his scalp that isn't hidden by his hat looks bare.

"He was the guitar player in my band," I say, swallowing hard, trying to keep my voice steady. "We had a gig tonight. I came to pick him up."

The cop leads me over to a cop car where another cop leans out the window with a pad of paper in his hand and takes my name and address.

Five minutes later I'm making my way downtown, wishing I had a cell phone to call the club, wondering what to do about the gig. I'm dazed enough to run a few red lights and sit patiently at the green ones until somebody behind me honks. *Jimmy dead?* I keep thinking. *That doesn't make sense. Jimmy killed himself? That really doesn't make sense.*

But another part of my brain is dealing with practicalities. It's Friday night. People are expecting a show. I fought for this gig and the band needs the work. We can't cancel out. Neil can play rhythm, take more solos. Could I possibly dig up a sub for the second set?

Down in the Village, I squeeze my car into a place at the corner of Houston and Lafayette. I sprint up to Bleecker and dash past the clubs, Italian restaurants, shops with windows full of gauzy Indian scarves and ethnic jewelry. I dodge around knots of people drifting along the sidewalk.

The Hot Spot's windows are papered with the flyers of bands who've played there. The taped music spills out as I haul the door toward me and step inside.

"What's going on?" Michael pops off a bar stool, raising his careful voice in an unaccustomed shout to cut through the music and the roar of people trying to talk over it.

He points to the stage, where a band is setting up. I look closer. Who's that guy with the ponytail? It's nobody I know. The band isn't my band. Neil and Dom are peering at me from their bar stools, Neil looking more alert than usual. The woman on the stool next to Dom has turned around, too.

Michael shouts, "Where's Jimmy? Did he know about this?"

"About what?"

He pulls me a few steps toward the bar, as if in search of a quieter spot. "We show up and the manager tells us that we're not supposed to be here," Michael says, talking directly into my ear. "He says somebody called from the band and canceled out. He had to scramble to get these guys." Michael jerks his thumb toward the stage. "He's pissed as hell."

"What are you saying?"

28

Michael starts to lean toward my ear again, but then he shakes his head and pulls me further toward the door. I motion to Dom and Neil. A few seconds later we're out on the sidewalk, standing in the glare of a neon beer sign.

"Somebody called the club and said we were canceling out," Michael says. "What's going on? And where's Jimmy?"

I tell them.

As I talk, Dom looks at the sidewalk and rubs his forehead. Neil looks past me, the expression on his face like a kid who just found out Santa doesn't exist. Michael looks grumpy, but maybe that's his way of looking sad.

"So was it you who called?" Dom says.

"No."

"Who canceled then?"

"I don't know."

"Want a drink?"

"I sure do."

Before I can grab the door handle, the door swings toward me, and I'm staring at the woman who was sitting by Dom. "Is Jimmy coming?" she says. She has pouty red lips with lots of lipstick on them and black hair like a glossy cap.

"This is Lynn," Dom says. "She . . . she . . ." He's stuttering a little. "She was supposed to meet Jimmy here."

I guess it's up to me. I touch her on the arm and pull her past the beer sign's glare. In the shadow I can't really see her face. I tell her about Jimmy, and all of a sudden she's grabbing my hand and crying the way I wish I could cry.

Back inside the Hot Spot, I make my way past the bar, through the clutter of chairs and little tables in front of the stage, past the stage, and into the cramped hallway with three doors leading off it: ladies' room, men's room, and manager's office. The door is ajar, so I stick my head around the corner. Boris is hidden in a haze of cigarette smoke, bent over a pile of papers on his desk.

"Hey, Boris," I say. "What's going on?" We got to know each other pretty well while I was pestering him about the gig.

He looks up. He's got a doughy, pock-marked face, fine light hair cut like he shaves it off every couple months then doesn't think about it again until it starts to itch or something.

"Maxx? What's the deal?" The gravel in his voice is from the cigarettes; the accent is from Eastern Europe.

"I didn't cancel out," I say. "Who called you?"

He puts down his cigarette. "One of the bar people took the call. I wasn't here. It was early." He shuffles through the papers on his desk, muttering, "No, you're not Sex Toy" as he fingers a scribbled note.

"Maxximum Blues," I say.

"Here it is." He holds up a bar napkin. All it says is "Maxximum Blues can't make it," with some kind of a name scribbled under the message. He puts the napkin down and reaches for his cigarette.

"Did the bar person say if it was a guy or a woman on the phone?"

"This was sitting here when I came in." He balances the cigarette on the edge of the ashtray and picks up the napkin.

"I didn't call," I say again.

He shrugs. "Somebody did. So I booked another band. I had a hell of a time finding somebody at the last minute."

"I'm sorry it was a hassle for you, but the person who took the message made a mistake or something. I never called."

Boris shrugs again and reaches for the cigarette, inhales, and exhales with a long sigh. "Want to play next Saturday?" he says. "Sex Toy's singer got arrested last night."

"Next Saturday?" I can't turn it down. Never turn down a gig—that was Sandy's mantra. And the one thing I learned from him—besides never to trust a guitar player—was how to be a musician and pay the rent at the same time.

"Okay," I say. "We'll be here, somehow."

He's a tough guy with an ugly face, but somehow I end up telling him about Jimmy.

He looks unhappy while I talk, but not surprised, like maybe having people die on him hasn't been all that rare of an experience.

When I finish, he says, "This just happened? With Jimmy?" I nod. "But that call—from whoever it was—came *yesterday.*"

Like punctuation, the thud of a snare drum announces that the live music is starting.

"You're sure you want the gig?" Boris says as I turn to leave.

"Sure. Why?"

"You don't have a guitar player."

"I'll get a sub," I say, like it's the easiest thing in the world.

I'm halfway down the hallway when I turn back. "It looked like somebody signed that note on the napkin," I say, sticking my head around the corner into Boris's office. "Can you make out what it says?"

He fingers the napkin, holds it close to his eyes, then far away. "Elise," he says. "She should be working tonight."

Out at the bar, I order a shot of Jack Daniel's and a Bud. When the bartender brings it, I ask him who Elise is. I have to shout even louder than before, now that the band is playing.

"Her," he says, gesturing toward one of the barmaids who is bearing down on a crowded table at the edge of the stage. She carries a tray of draft beer in huge mugs. With her fair skin and tiny, heart-shaped face, she seems almost too delicate to handle such a load.

I swallow the Jack Daniel's in a quick gulp and take my beer bottle with me. I wait till she hands the beer around and threads her way back through the tables.

31

"Hi," I say. "Can I talk to you a minute?" She nods. "I'm Maxx Maxwell."

She nods again. "I know you."

"You do?"

"Jimmy's in your band," she says with a giggle. "I used to work at Slim's, over on Avenue A. You guys played there a couple weeks ago." She giggles again. "I thought he'd be here tonight. But you canceled out."

"We didn't," I say. "There was some weird mistake."

"There was?" She has really pale eyes. It's almost unnerving to talk to her.

"Were you the one who took the call?" She nods. "What did the person sound like?"

She shrugs. "Like a woman. Like you." She pauses. "You mean it wasn't you?"

"No," I say. "It wasn't me. And Jimmy . . ." I guess it's my duty to tell her. "Something happened to him. Something really bad."

It must be the look on my face that makes her say, "He's dead," then choke the words off with a quick intake of breath.

Before I can say more, she reacts the way the other woman did, grabbing my hand, her eyes welling up with tears, unashamedly crying. I watch her with a lump in my throat, but dry-eyed and still numb. Would I be better off if I could cry? But then, who'd manage the band?

"I told him that guy was dangerous," she moans between sobs.

"What guy?"

"That tall guy." She takes a shivery breath, turns, and dashes toward the restroom. I follow her and wait outside the door till she emerges, dabbing at her eyes with a wet paper towel.

"Tell me about the tall guy," I say, pressing myself against the wall as a couple of women squeeze past. One of them pulls open the door of the ladies' room and the other one shrugs and heads further down to the men's room.

"He was waiting outside Slim's that night," Elise says, after another shivery breath. "Just popped up out of nowhere. He went away when Jimmy told him he didn't want to talk about it—whatever *it* was. But the look on the guy's face was so desperate. I go cold all over just thinking about it."

"What did he look like?"

"I don't know. All I noticed was his face. And that he was tall."

CHAPTER 3

Julio's music wakes me before I'm ready to be awake. I can hear it through the wall, the salsa he starts his day with, rain or shine. Today it's rain, splashing in the street outside. I open my eyes. I'm lying on my side, staring at the wallpaper. Six inches from my nose is a flat bouquet of huge roses, faded to reddish-brown, a design that repeats itself all around my room. I flop over and see my clothes from the night before draped over the big chair, Mr. Rush's chair.

Then I remember. Jimmy's dead. And I've got to find a sub.

I push the sheet aside and shiver as the cool air hits my skin. The rain put an end to the heat. I pull on my Red Bank Blues Festival T-shirt and a pair of sweatpants. In the kitchen I switch on the radio to drown out Julio's salsa. The Kendall College station plays blues every morning for a couple of hours. Sure enough, a guitar noodles a handful of notes into a solo. I fill the kettle and get some water started for coffee.

While I'm waiting for the water to boil, I stare out the window. I'm eye-level with the peaked roof of the house across the street. My neighborhood is a jumble of medium-sized apartment buildings and old houses using aluminum siding to put up a decent front. Down below, the rain is running along the curb in narrow silvery-gray rivers, carrying bits of litter with it.

When the kettle whistles, I stir up a cup of instant coffee, grab my address book out of my bag, and settle into the big chair. For a minute I see that vision of Jimmy lying on the ground. Then it's replaced by a close-up of his face, strangely intent, asking me if I'd miss him if he was gone. I close my eyes and lean my head back.

When I open my eyes again, I'm staring at the phone. I open my address book and page through it. Rob? No, he moved to LA. Pete? He's got that Broadway gig now. How about Josh? He loves the blues, and he's a great guitar player. In fact, he's so great he works all the time. He's probably booked up weekends for the next year. But I decide I'll give him a try.

I punch in Josh's number, and the phone rings four times, five times, six times. Finally, a woman's voice comes on and says hello. She sounds annoyed, like I should have taken the hint nobody felt like talking and hung up after three rings.

"Is Josh home?"

"Who's calling?" Her voice is curt, almost an accusation.

"Maxx Maxwell. I knew him when I was in Sandy Wilkins' band."

"Hold on." I can hear muttered sounds in the background, male sounds, then her voice, muffled, saying, "Maxx Maxwell. She knows Sandy."

I'm staring at a square spot on the wall where the roses aren't faded, like maybe once a picture hung there or something.

My apartment is just two rooms, this one and a kitchen. I moved in right after the guy who lived here before died. His name was Mr. Rush. When I checked the place out, his son and daughter were there, a couple of pleasant, well-dressed black people, telling the landlord they'd come the next day and haul everything off to the Salvation Army. I'd just left Sandy and didn't own anything except a suitcase full of clothes and a box of records and tapes and CDs. So I asked the son and daughter if they'd mind leaving all the stuff there, and they said not at all.

I've been sitting in Mr. Rush's chair and cooking on his dishes and even waking up to his alarm clock for six months. The only things I've added to the decor are the blues calendar over the bed and the picture of my great-great-aunt Caroline on the dresser. She sang in vaudeville. I kind of identify with her. My mother calls her the black sheep of the family.

It isn't a fancy place, and every time my mother comes by, she finds something new to rag me about: the neighbors, or the building, or Hackensack in general. But it's fine for right now, half an hour from the city and cheap enough that I can survive working four nights a week at the Seafood Chalet and save my energy for the band. And when the band starts getting better gigs, maybe I'll move.

But we're not going to get any gigs at all unless I can find another guitar player, somebody who's willing to work cheap for a while because he loves the blues and believes in the band. And meanwhile, I need a sub for Saturday.

I send a little prayer out into the universe: *Josh, please come to the phone. And please say yes.*

There's some kind of muffled outburst, not Josh, but the grouchy chick, then a couple of clanks like the phone just bounced across the floor. Finally Josh comes on, cordial enough, but he sounds sleepy even though it's already ten. He probably worked last night.

"Maxx?" he says. "It's been a while. How are you?"

"Fine," I say.

"Glad to hear it. I hated to see you and Sandy break up. You guys were great together."

"That was onstage," I say. "Offstage it was different." In my mind I see myself running out of that casino, running down the boardwalk past a streaky blur of neon lights.

"Sorry all the same," Josh says. B. B. King is playing in the background. "What are you up to now?"

"I've got my own band. Maxximum Blues."

"Cool name."

"Interested in a sub job?"

"I've got a lot going on right now," he says. "Things are kind of frantic."

"It's just one gig," I say. "Saturday night at the Hot Spot."

"Blues, huh?"

"*Maxximum* Blues."

"I guess you don't mind living on beans."

"I'll find a way to make it work."

"I'm tempted," he says. "It's been too long since I played blues with a good band. But you can't imagine what my life has been like lately."

I wasn't going to tell him about Jimmy, but it comes spilling out.

"That's a lousy deal," he says when I get done. "Sounds like he was a good guy."

"I don't want the band to disappear," I say. "It was starting to turn into something. And we're trying to work up some tunes you don't hear all that often, not just the usual white-guys-play-the-blues stuff."

"Like what?"

"Stuff like, well, stuff that women do. Women like Big Mama Thornton and Bessie Smith. Do you know 'Swing It on Home'?"

" 'I wish I was an apple, hangin' on a tree'?" In the background the grouchy chick says something I can't make out.

"You got it. That's our theme song."

"Cool," Josh says, and then he's quiet for a long minute. "I'd really like to help you out. I have to check with somebody, though. I'll try to get back to you tonight or tomorrow."

I drain what's left of the coffee, and my stomach responds with a spasm. I decide I'd better eat something. In the kitchen cupboard, I discover that the bread supply is two heels and a lot of crumbs. And there's only one egg left, and it's got a crack in it.

Twenty minutes later, I'm settling onto a stool at Roy's with a copy of the *Times* I picked up at the C-Town Superette. A waitress who has oiled her hair into lustrous waves asks me what I want to eat, and I order the breakfast special with scrambled eggs and wheat toast.

By the time it arrives, I've finished the entertainment section and I'm browsing in Metro. My fork is halfway to my mouth with a bite of eggs when a headline catches my eye. "Man Falls to His Death from Upper West Side Apartment."

"A man plunged to his death from the window of his apartment Saturday evening," the article continues. "Police believe he jumped."

My eyes drift down the page.

" 'It is not being investigated as a homicide at this point,' said a police spokesperson.

"The man, whose name is being withheld pending notification of his family, fell nine stories from his apartment in a building at 105th Street and Central Park West at about 6:30 p.m., police said.

"A passerby saw him fall and ran to a nearby bodega where he asked the manager to call the police.

"Police found no signs of foul play. There was no evidence of a struggle in the apartment nor did an initial examination of the body reveal injuries unrelated to the fall."

Police believe he jumped? They think it's suicide, just what that crazy lady said.

I can only nibble at the rest of the eggs. Finally, I stick three dollars under the edge of the plate, grab the newspaper, and head out onto the sidewalk.

I'm so distracted, I walk right past the corner where I usually turn. If the police believe he jumped, believe it's suicide, they won't investigate. My guitar player is dead—*sweet man* says a voice in my head—and they won't investigate.

By the time I realize where I am, I'm halfway to the courthouse, standing in front of the Rescue Mission Thrift Shop, watching an old lady head down the sidewalk, pulling her laundry behind her in a little cart.

As soon as I step off the elevator, I see a note on my door. My first thought is that it's somebody complaining about my singing practice—like anybody in this building is ever quiet. Just now there's some kind of subdued mayhem going on behind the door of 3D, and 3F has a baseball game blasting out of his TV.

But as I get closer, I recognize the handwriting, elegant letters carefully shaped in black ink. And even if I didn't recognize the handwriting, the fact that it's addressed to "Elizabeth" would mean that it could only be from one person.

I let myself in to my apartment, toss the *Times* on the bed, and read the note.

"I've missed seeing you," it says. "Macy's has had me working extra hours all week. My fellow wage slaves are taking their vacations, and I'm filling in. Come by for a beer tonight when you get off work. I'll be up." It's signed, in that same careful hand, "Leon."

I stick Bessie Smith on the stereo and try to do a little singing, but I can't concentrate. Finally, I grab my raincoat and go out again. I walk back up to Main Street and then just keep walking, all the way to the courthouse, then past it.

What did I think happened to Jimmy? I guess I was so numb I didn't even ask myself that question. But now—yeah, what happened? It's raining on and off but I ignore it, hurrying along, trying not to remember how he looked lying there on the ground—and trying to erase that other vision of him, too.

When I get back to my apartment, there's a message waiting for me on my machine. Josh, I think, briefly cheerful. But no, it's my mother. I erase it.

I sink down into the big chair and call Aldo at the Seafood Chalet. I tell him I've got something wrong with my stomach, and I won't be in tonight. Then I climb back into bed.

"Come in, come in, come in," Leon says, sweeping the door open, smiling at me, his teeth gleaming in his dark face. He's dressed in his summer uniform, khaki pants and a short-sleeved polo shirt. He cradles a book in his hand, one long dark finger marking the page. "Have a seat."

He motions toward his tidy sofa, a throw pillow at each end and an afghan draped over the back. His coffee table, with the Sunday *Times* in a careful pile, is centered in front of it.

He strides to his desk, carefully marks his place in the book, and sets it down. "I'm at a very exciting part," he says. "I can't imagine what's going to happen next."

"What are you reading?" I say.

"It's called *Hamlet.* Ever hear of it?"

"Everybody's heard of it," I say. "You mean you don't know what happens?"

He laughs gleefully, eyes sparkling behind horn-rimmed glasses. "I'm teasing you, Elizabeth."

"I'll never understand why you read things like that for fun," I say.

"I've got less than a month till the fall semester starts. Then it's back to torts and contract law. If you think Shakespeare is tough, try law."

"No thanks."

"Some music?" he says. "What would you prefer? *Tristan and Isolde? Turandot?*"

"Anything. Whatever you like."

"Really? How about—" he hovers over his shelf of CDs "—*Lohengrin*?"

"Sure. Put it on."

"Okay. Here it comes." With a click, he flips open the CD case, balances the silvery disk on his fingers for a moment, and slides it into the player. After a few seconds of whispery scratching, the sound of an orchestra fills the room. "Beautiful," he says. "What do you think?"

"It's fine." I nod.

He turns away from the stereo. "Elizabeth? Are you all right?" He takes his glasses off and gazes at me. His dark eyes look worried.

"Why?"

"Usually you complain about my taste in music. And you remind me that your name is really Maxx—though I'll never understand why a woman would want to be called Maxx."

"Actually, I'm not all right. We don't have a guitar player anymore. He's dead."

"Dead? What happened?"

I describe turning onto Jimmy's street and seeing the cops and the ambulance, and how I felt when I realized that what everybody was staring at was Jimmy's body on the ground.

"He fell?"

"How often do grown-up people fall out of windows?" I say.

"Let me grab a couple of beers." He pauses by the CD player as he heads for the kitchen. In a moment, B. B. King's voice fills the room.

"Thanks," I call after him.

He sticks his head around the corner. "It's that one you gave me."

I hear the refrigerator open and close, the soft clink of glasses, the pop and hiss of bottles being opened. In a few seconds

Leon is back with a tray holding two bottles of Heineken and two tall glasses.

He picks up a bottle and starts to fill one of the glasses. I reach for the other bottle. "I don't need a glass," I say, lifting the bottle to my lips.

"So, what happened?" Leon says.

"The cops think he jumped. There was something about it in the *Times* this morning. A tiny article."

"The poor guy," Leon says. "Was he depressed about something?"

"No. The band was doing great, and he was excited about it."

"So you think somebody pushed him?"

"I don't know what I think. But I don't see how they could just decide he jumped, just say he jumped—and that's that. And besides, some weird tall guy had been after him, following him around and hassling him. The guy even showed up at our last rehearsal. It seems like the cops could at least ask a few questions."

"Why don't you ask them what makes them think he jumped? Call them up."

"The cops?"

"Sure."

"People can do that?"

"Well," he says, "they can try."

CHAPTER 4

"One moment." The phone clicks and crackles a few times. Then a voice that sounds like a caricature of a cop on a TV show says, "Stallings speaking."

I've never had much to do with police. Growing up in Ardendale doesn't really expose you to the darker side of life.

"I'm calling about Jimmy Nashville," I say. "The man who died Saturday? The apartment building at 105th and Central Park West?" I'm so nervous that the surface of my coffee is quivering in sync with my heartbeats.

"Yeah?" the voice says.

"I knew him," I say. "I was at his building right after it happened. I was supposed to pick him up for a gig. He was in my band." Stallings doesn't say anything, so I go on. "The paper made it sound like you think he killed himself. What made you decide that?"

"We have ways," he says, like he thinks he's funny.

"Did Jimmy leave a note?"

"No. We would've told the paper if there was a note."

"Then how can you be sure?"

"There was no evidence of foul play."

"What does that mean?"

"Just what it sounds like. Foul play would mean somebody went up there and pushed him out or somebody killed him and threw him out. And there was no sign of that—no sign that anybody was up there but him. Of course we still need the

43

autopsy results, but I don't think they'll change anything."

"Jimmy didn't have any reason to kill himself," I say, still nervous, my voice less in control than I'd like it to be. "The band was doing great, and he was excited about it."

"There's still the autopsy report," Stallings says. "But so far we have no evidence of foul play."

"If he was going to kill himself, he wouldn't do it right before a gig. Especially not a blues gig. He loved the blues."

"You can check back with me when we get the autopsy report."

"Some guy had been following him around hassling him—a real big guy, too."

"I said you can check back with me when we get the autopsy report."

"When will that be?"

"Maybe a few days, maybe longer." I hear the phone click as he hangs up.

I close my eyes and take deep breaths until I feel like I can talk around the lump in my throat. Then I try to reach Josh. Nobody answers, not even the grouchy chick, so I leave a message on his machine telling him I've got to hear from him soon enough to track down another sub if he can't do it. I try to sound upbeat while I'm saying it, but I don't feel upbeat. I debate whether to call my mother back and decide not to.

It was bad enough showing up for work when I was convinced it was only a matter of time till the band took off and I could tell Aldo's Seafood Chalet good-bye. Now, as I turn off Tonnelle Avenue after several slow miles creeping behind a truck, I gaze at the boxy stucco-covered building, grimy white streaked with rust, and a wave of gloom sweeps over me.

Aldo makes the employees park around the back, so the customers, most of which could really use the exercise, barely

have to take ten steps to get to the door. I cruise past a couple
of not very new SUVs and a pickup truck, swing right, and pull
into a place near the Dumpster.

Vinnie is out there getting rid of a few bags of garbage. He
catches sight of me, waves, and waits for me to get out of the
car. He's a little guy, barely comes up to my shoulder, with a
food-stained apron tied over his T-shirt.

"Maxx, how you doin', man? You feelin' OK? I was worried
about you yesterday."

The whole thing comes out in a burst that garbles consonants
into unintelligibility. It's like one giant word accompanied by a
huge grin that turns his eyes into cheerful slits. I've never been
able to figure out whether he's got some kind of speech impedi-
ment or just lives in a perpetual state of excitement, but he's a
cool guy, a would-be bass player, and one of the few bright
spots at the Seafood Chalet.

"Things aren't too great," I say. "Problems with the band."

"I know, man," he says. "That guy Dom, your drummer, he
was sittin' in the bar havin' a beer. Tol' me all about it. I'm
really sorry, man."

"What's Dom doing here? He lives all the way out in Clifton."

"I don' know, man, but he asked me when you'd be in. I tol'
him five o'clock. He seemed real anxious to talk to you. *Real*
anxious. Seemed kinda worried." Vinnie strides purposefully
away. "Gotta move." He tosses the words over his shoulder. "Aldo's been on my case all day. Catch up with you on my break."

I follow Vinnie in the back door, wondering what's up with
Dom and whether I really want to know.

In the break room, I pick up my special Seafood Chalet vest.
We're supposed to wear our own white shirt and black pants or
skirt. I lock my bag in my locker and head for the unisex employees' rest room, where I put the vest on and use my hair clip

to capture the stray hair that's drooping down my neck.

My fellow waitress, Carol, looks like she's about to jump out of her skin. "Get me out of here," she whispers. "Thank God you're on time. Aldo's being a total pain in the butt."

She glances around her section, soon to become my section. The Seafood Chalet was a barbecue restaurant before Aldo bought it. He never changed the decor, so people eat their red snapper and mussels in red sauce under chandeliers in the shape of wagon wheels. On the walls, cowboys spur their ponies across vast plains.

"Let's see." Carol points to a white-haired guy in a sweatsuit and a woman with really fake-looking red hair. "Their order must be just about ready." She gestures at a few other tables. "Those ones I just put in. And that guy? The one in the shiny suit? He looks like he's finally made up his mind."

The next thing I know, Dom's heading toward a table, trailed by the hostess, who's waving a menu at him. He's wearing another one of his Hawaiian shirts tonight. This one is mostly jungle tones, multi-lobed leaves like giant green hands, with monkeys peering between them.

He settles into a chair and takes the menu, then bobs up to kiss me on the cheek when I get close enough. "I got some news, Maxxie," he says.

"Good or bad?"

"You're not gonna line up a new guitar player right away, are you?"

"I'm planning on it," I say, startled. "Why? You're not going to bail out? I already called Josh Bergman about subbing Saturday."

Dom looks surprised. "Is he going to do it?"

"He's checking his schedule."

I notice Aldo glaring at me, really ferociously, from back by the kitchen door. He's one of those middle-aged guys whose shoulders narrow as their hips widen, so he's shaped like an eggplant. And at the moment, his usually florid face, with a silly mustache that outlines the curve of his upper lip, is almost the color of an eggplant.

"Be right back," I say. I take care of the shiny suit guy's order and pick up a basket of rolls for Dom.

Back at Dom's table, I set the rolls in front of him. He reaches for one, takes a big bite without buttering it. "Well, here's the deal," he says around the roll he's chewing. "I played a gig with Kenny White yesterday." He opens his menu, closes it, and looks around the room. "What's he eatin'?" He points at a guy wearing some kind of a coverall with his name embroidered on the pocket.

"Fried calamari."

"I'll have that. And a beer while I'm waitin'." He hands me the menu. "Kenny White needs a full-time drummer. He asked me if I was interested. He's kinda pressuring me to let him know, and he wants me to sit in Saturday night. So the sooner you hear from Josh the better."

"Why couldn't you be in two bands?" I say with a sick feeling.

"I can't be in two places on the same Saturday night, can I? Besides, Kenny's band is hot shit. They've actually got a manager." He raises his eyebrows. "And Bart's after 'em to play in the Blues from the Heart concert—right up there with some of the most happenin' bands on the East Coast."

"I thought Bart had that whole thing put together a long time ago. The bands are already listed on the poster."

"A couple guys pulled out, and Bart's tryin' to replace 'em."

"Why'd they pull out?"

He shrugs. "Somethin' weird's goin' on with that."

Out of the corner of my eye I notice Aldo glaring at me. "I better put your order in so it looks like I'm working," I say. On my way to the computer, I have to fend off several tables asking for their checks. "Be right with you," I say. "Be right with you," like a mantra.

I punch in Dom's beer order to the bar and the calamari order to the kitchen, get the checks taken care of, and head for the bar to get the beer, musing gloomily about the conversation I just had with Dom.

What if he quits? All I'll have left is Michael and Neil. And I was thinking of going after Josh to replace Jimmy full time—but how am I going to do that if I don't have a drummer?

I circle back to Dom's table and slip the mug of beer in front of him. He takes a swallow that leaves him with a foamy mustache. "Hey, Dom," I say, before I really realize what I'm saying, "Did you notice a tall guy talking to Jimmy as we were leaving Feedback on Thursday?"

"Tall guy?"

"Yeah. When Jimmy and Monique were heading down the hall, this tall guy came charging after them, real upset, like Jimmy was trying to escape before the guy was done talking to him."

Dom shrugs. "I didn't see anybody," he says. "Why don't you ask Monique? She was hangin' all over him. If he was talking to somebody, she must have noticed." He drains most of the beer, holds up the mug, and says, "I'm gonna need another one of these."

I hear Aldo's voice behind me. "People are looking for their waitress," he says, waving toward a couple craning their necks in my direction while they flick ashes on their empty plates.

"They don't look frantic enough yet," I say.

"What?"

"I'm going, I'm going."

I take the couple's order for one cherry cheesecake and one cannoli and punch it into the computer along with Dom's beer order. In the kitchen I pick up Dom's calamari, assemble the salad that goes with it, toss on a few extra croutons, and pick up some extra rolls, even though Aldo's limit is two to a customer.

"Think Josh would be interested in signin' on for good?" Dom says when I get back with the calamari.

"I haven't asked him yet, but I'm thinking the same thing," I say.

"If we could turn up somebody as solid as Jimmy was, somebody like Josh, I could see stickin' around for awhile." Dom picks up his fork and stabs a round of calamari. "I was lookin' forward to makin' some real money for a change. And Kenny White's band . . ."

I notice Aldo glaring at me again and edge toward the table next to Dom's, where a gray-haired lady is pointing at her empty coffee cup. I'm just as glad to get away from Dom anyway, especially while he's on the subject of Kenny White's band.

Ask Monique about the tall guy, I'm thinking as I bustle around taking orders and delivering food. Dom's right. She was probably standing right there while the tall guy was saying whatever he was saying. But how can I find her? I don't even know her last name.

I'm getting iced tea for a table of chubby middle-aged women—iced tea to go with their platters of fried jumbo shrimp—and I just know they'll put fake sugar in it. I'm draping a tasteful lemon slice over the edge of each glass when I remember: Lemon's. Monique is singing Sunday and Monday nights at a restaurant called Lemon's. On the Upper West Side, she said. In the eighties, between Broadway and Amsterdam.

Today is Monday.

As soon as my shift is over, I get rid of my vest in the break room, grab my bag out of my locker, and head through the kitchen, twenty degrees hotter than the dining room. Then I'm out the back door and over to where my car is parked in the

49

shadow of the Dumpster.

"Ho-o-o-nky, ho-o-o-nky tonk women," I'm singing to myself, "give me, give me, give me those honky tonk blues." It was playing in the bar when I picked up my last drink order of the night, and I feel cheerful, somehow, at the prospect that Monique might know something useful.

The hot air is heavy with the smell of grease from the fans that ventilate the kitchen. Their low whirring is like white noise, obliterating the sounds of traffic from Tonnelle Avenue.

"Ho-o-o-nky, ho-o-o-nky tonk women." I turn the key in the ignition and Robert Plant's voice comes blasting out of my car radio, moaning about how he wanted a woman but never bargained for the one he got.

I'm moaning along, tapping out the riff on the steering wheel. This late the traffic on Tonnelle Avenue isn't too bad. I breeze past the Starlite Motel, the U-Store It place, about twenty auto-body shops, and here's the cemetery sloping up the hill.

I take 46 toward the city. Soon I'm skimming across the bridge toward the glow of Manhattan. On the radio, Neil Young is telling me to keep on rockin' in the free world.

Lemon's turns out to be a narrow storefront, just around the corner from Broadway. A window looks out on the street, striped awning above and window boxes below. The word "Lemon's" is dashed across it in an elegant swirl.

Inside, Monique's voice is dipping and swooping through "Come Rain or Come Shine," and the guitar player's staring at her like he's hypnotized.

CHAPTER 5

Monique has turned the song into a miniature drama, the desperate story of a chick who'd do anything for her man. One minute her face is twisted like a huge sob is about to erupt, and her eyes are squeezed shut. The next minute they're open, but kind of stunned looking, and her fingers are reaching for something that they can't quite catch.

Despite the clingy bright-pink dress, she's not the gorgeous Monique who could pass for a supermodel anymore. She's some chick who's lived a hard-luck life and never had anything to care about but this guy.

I want a beer really bad, but I can't take my eyes off her. Is she always this intense, I'm wondering, or is it just because Jimmy's dead?

Finally the guitar player, a stocky, stolid-looking guy perched on a stool off to the side, wraps things up with a soft flurry of chords plucked out of a boxy Gibson. Monique's voice subsides and her face turns back into Monique. But she stands there for a minute, like she doesn't know where she is, like she has to pull herself back from somewhere else, back to this room full of upscale types lounging in squashy chairs and drinking white wine.

"Thank you," she says at last, in that musky voice that goes so weird with her little-kid face. "We'll be back next Sunday and Monday. See you then. And stop by tomorrow for a great Brazilian combo featuring Paulo Soreiro." She turns and says something to the guitar player.

She heads to the bar, and I follow her, wait while the bartender fixes her up with a double scotch on the rocks, then order a Bud. She drinks off half her drink in the first swallow, lets out a huge sigh, and drinks some more.

A few seats down from where we're standing, the guitar player has settled onto a bar stool and is sipping at a beer. He lifts his hand in a half wave of greeting.

Do I know him? Yeah, he does look vaguely familiar, maybe from the studio. So many guys hang out there that they all blur together after a while.

Monique turns, and I catch her gaze. She looks puzzled at first, then recognizes me and smiles so cheerfully that all of a sudden I have a horrible thought: *Could she possibly not know Jimmy's dead?* I edge through the crowd standing around the bar. "Singing's thirsty work," I say. "That was a great performance."

"Thanks. What brings you here?" She's still smiling. She's got teeth that look like something right out of a tooth-bleaching ad and a little dimple that kind of flickers at the corner of her mouth.

"I didn't know how else to reach you." I guess I must look like I've got something pretty dire on my mind because all of a sudden the dimple vanishes and she takes a quick breath like a little backwards cough.

"Is something wrong?" I nod. "Something to do with Jimmy?" Her face is turning back into the face of that miserable chick who sang the song.

"You didn't see the article?" Her head twitches like she wants to shake it but somehow it's frozen. "We better go back here," I say, grabbing her arm and pulling her toward a couple of squashy chairs in a corner just past the edge of the bar.

"What happened?" she says, hesitating to sit, like if she

doesn't I won't answer and everything will be okay.

I'm trying to find a way to say it, but every time I start, something clogs my throat.

"He's okay, isn't he?" She grabs my arm. "I saw him Saturday . . . uh, for a little while. We had plans for Sunday, but then something . . . I mean, it turned out he was going to be busy. I knew he had the gig with your band Saturday night. I was going to come, but—" Her voice is twisting into a little squeal. She shrugs, and one of the narrow straps holding her dress up slips off her muscular shoulder. "Sunday I stopped by his place, but he wasn't there . . . but sometimes he isn't. I know he's got other things . . ." She absent-mindedly reaches for the strap and pulls it back into place. If she wasn't so tall, those shoulders would look really weird. She's about the strongest-looking chick I've ever seen.

Other girlfriends, says a voice in my head. Is that what she means, or can she possibly think she was the only one?

"Monique," I say, easing her into the chair. "He's dead."

She doesn't scream or anything. She just lets her head sag into her lap and starts shaking and gulping.

I'm patting her on the back when I look up to see the guitar player staring down at us.

"What's going on?" he says.

I'm about to answer when Monique looks up. Her face is all pink and kind of shiny because she's been rubbing tears into it. "It's okay," she tells the guy between gulps.

"You're sure?"

I can't tell whether he desperately wants to stay or desperately wants to leave, but there's definitely something weird going on.

"Yes," she says with a frown and a shake of the head that makes her carefully streaked mass of curls bounce.

"She's okay?" He looks at me.

"Not really," I say, "but I'll take care of her."

"How about some water or something?" I say after the guy is gone.

"I could use another drink," she says.

When I get back with a double scotch and another Bud, she makes me tell her all the details. She's working on the scotch and blinking every once in awhile like she's determined not to start crying again.

"He wouldn't kill himself," she says when I get all done. "The cops didn't know him. Otherwise they'd—" Her mouth starts to quiver.

"Remember when we were at Feedback Thursday night?" I say.

"I felt so close to him that night. We stopped off for a beer and talked and talked." Her voice cracks and gets really small. She leans forward to set her empty glass on the table in front of us and lowers her face into her hands.

"Remember the tall guy who followed Jimmy down the hall when we were leaving?"

"The guy that was so pissed at him?" She pulls her hands away and looks at me like I just said something that cheered her up.

"Yeah. Was he talking to Jimmy when you showed up?"

She shakes her head. "He clammed up right away when I got close. At first I didn't even realize I was interrupting something."

"Jimmy didn't say anything to you later about what was going on?"

"I mentioned it but he changed the subject right away—like it was something he really didn't want to talk about." She pushes her hair back from her face and gives a huge sigh. "You think that guy did something to him?" she says suddenly.

"I don't know what I think. But I *know* Jimmy wouldn't kill himself."

While we've been sitting there, the place has emptied out to the point that we're almost the last ones left.

"Need a ride somewhere?" I say, as Monique starts to pull herself to her feet.

"I'll walk. I . . . it will feel good to just walk." She takes an unsteady step.

"You sure? It's awfully late."

"I can take care of myself."

We head toward the door together, Monique stumbling a little on the way.

"Say," Monique says as I reach for the door handle. "Will you give me your phone number? So we could . . . in case . . . I mean, we both knew him." She pauses, and an odd look comes over her face, kind of lonely and hopeful. "Maybe we could get together some time."

"Sure," I say.

Outside, people are still strolling here and there, trendy Upper West Side people, slowed down by the humid remains of the day's heat. I walk toward Broadway and turn right at the corner, heading toward my car.

I don't go home, though. Maybe the tall guy showed up at the studio Thursday just to hassle Jimmy, but maybe he hangs out there all the time.

I drive down to 30th Street, where I luck into a spot about ten steps from the door. Usually you push a button downstairs, and they buzz you into the lobby, but a burly black guy is on his way out and he holds the door for me.

Up on the sixth floor, it's the usual scene, even though it's about two in the morning—guys standing around the trashcan in the hall and smoking, guys pulling out their wallets at the desk and asking each other what sixty-nine divided by four is, the facial piercings crowd lounging in the folding chairs arranged against the back wall.

Tony's at the desk, counting out change with the phone balanced between his ear and his shoulder. He's wearing a tank top that shows off his hairy shoulders. "I'll get Bart to call you back," he's saying into the phone. "Don't yell at me. I don't know nothin' about it."

He deposits a pile of ones in an outstretched hand and slaps the phone down onto the desk with a flourish. He looks at me and a smile replaces his frown. "Maxx Maxwell. You okay? You look tired."

The phone rings, but he ignores it. "Fuckin' Blues from the Heart," he says. "Let Bart clean up his own mess. I don't get paid to have people yell at me."

"What's going on?"

"More people droppin' out," he says.

"Why?"

He folds his hairy arms in front of him on the desk and leans toward me. "Bart's a fuckin' crook," he says. "I know stuff about him you wouldn't believe." He presses his full lips in a tight line and rocks back and forth knowingly. But suddenly he stops and slaps his forehead. "Hey! I'm forgettin'. Sorry to hear about that guy in your band."

"Thanks," I say. "I guess word has kind of traveled through the grapevine."

"I heard about it when I came to work tonight. It's like a family here, you know? You wouldn't think that to look around, but it is. A fuckin' family." He leans toward me. "But it's late. What brings you down here anyway?"

I describe the tall guy, describe the fragmentary conversation, ask him if he remembers seeing the guy last Thursday or noticed a couple of guys arguing around the corner in the hall. All the while he shakes his head no.

"Tall guy?" he says. "Thin? Dark hair?" He waves his hand in a gesture that takes in the guys lounging against the wall, the smokers around the trashcan just visible through the door, even a troop of kids emerging from the narrow corridor that leads to the studios. "What do you see?" he says. "Tall guys, thin, with dark hair. They're all over the place. Why you askin', anyway?"

"Just curious. It was somebody Jimmy knew, I guess. And the guy was arguing with him just a few days before Jimmy died."

It's nearly two-thirty by the time I see the bridge ahead of me, hanging over the river, its outlines picked out in lights. By three I'm turning into the parking lot behind my building.

I pull into a space next to Leon's car, a tidy gray Toyota, slip out of my car, and head for the front of the building, where a few bugs are buzzing in the light over the door. I let myself in and head up the stairs.

I twist my key in the lock, push the door back, and yes, the message light on my answering machine is blinking. Before I do anything else, even take off my shoes, I push the "play" button.

"Hey, Maxx. It's Josh," says a cheerful voice. "About the gig Saturday—" Great, I'm thinking. I've got a sub. One problem solved.

But the cheerful voice continues with, "Give me a call," and leaves a number. Shit. Too late to call him now.

All night Dom's voice echoes in my brain, bragging about Kenny White's band. Toward dawn it's replaced by my mother's, warning me that dropping out of college to do music isn't a good career move. "Oh, be quiet," I mutter.

I'm surprised when Julio's music jolts me awake because I feel like I haven't slept at all.

CHAPTER 6

"Please say yes, Josh. Please say yes." I whisper it over and over again as the phone rings two times, three times, four times. One of my hands holds the phone and the other holds the remains of my first cup of coffee, but I'm too focused on those distant rings to take a sip.

Am I going to get his machine and spend the rest of the day jumpy as a nervous cat while I wait for him to return my call?

Just when I expect his recorded voice to cut in, somebody picks up the receiver and a woman's voice says, "Hello?" At least I think it's a woman. It's so flat and expressionless, I can't exactly tell.

"This is Maxx Maxwell," I say. "Is Josh there?"

"Why?" says the voice, making the word as confrontational as one syllable can be.

"I need to talk to him about a sub job for Saturday."

"He can't do it," she says. "Didn't he tell you that already?"

"No," I say, feeling my heart speed up. I lean over and put the coffee on the floor so I won't spill it. "He just said to call him back."

"Well, he can't do it."

"Can I talk to him anyway?" I say.

In the background I hear footsteps, and a male voice says, "Is it for me, Beth?"

"You're not taking that gig, are you?" the woman's voice says menacingly, not to me but like she doesn't care whether I can hear it or not.

There's a brief scuffling sound, like maybe they're fighting for the receiver, and all of a sudden Josh is on the phone. "Maxx?" he says, cheerfully enough.

"I got your message last night," I say, trying to sound cool and professional, even though my heart is now pounding away like an overenthusiastic drummer. "Uh . . . it doesn't sound like things are going to work out."

"What did she tell you?" His voice has an edge of morning grogginess that makes him sound sexy. Then, "Hold on a minute."

Whatever happens after that happens far enough away from the phone that mostly all I can hear is my own breathing. After a few minutes, Josh comes back on.

"What time's the sound check?" he says.

My heart gives a lurch then calms down. "You can do it?"

"I can't think of anything I'd rather do right now than play the blues."

"In that case, want to sit in when we practice Thursday night?" In the background a female voice is screaming something unintelligible.

"I'm there," he says.

"Feedback Studio. Nine o'clock."

I celebrate by heading out to the kitchen to stir up a fresh cup of coffee. But while I'm waiting for the water to boil, I look over at the refrigerator. I've got a flyer for one of our gigs stuck up there with a magnet. It's a photo of the band, lined up all in a row, and there's Jimmy with his guitar slung over his shoulder, hair a little messy, with that lopsided grin on his face. Sweet man. I turn the water off and make a beeline back to the phone.

The scrap of paper with the cop's number on it is still sitting on the table by the big chair. I perch on the edge of the chair and punch the number into the phone. A crisp male voice answers, "Police station."

"Detective Stallings," I say, trying to sound official.

"One moment," the voice says.

The phone crackles, and the silly TV cop voice says, "Stallings."

"It's Maxx Maxwell."

"Yeah?" he says warily.

"You said I could call about the autopsy report on Jimmy Nashville. Do you have anything yet?"

"Maybe this afternoon," he says.

"Do you have the apartment all sealed up? You know, with that yellow tape and everything?"

"Why?"

"Just curious."

"It's not being investigated as a homicide, you know."

"Yeah, I know, but is the apartment sealed up?"

"No," he says. "It's not."

"Would it be okay if I went inside?"

"You have a key?"

"No—but I'll think of something." I hang up before he can answer.

I trade my blues festival T-shirt for cut-offs and a halter top, pull my hair up with a clip, and put on some lipstick. On the way out the door, I grab my sunglasses.

Half an hour later I'm backed up at the bridge with the tail end of the commuter traffic, listening to the Kendall College radio station's morning blues program.

"Born Under a Bad Sign" and "Hoodoo Man" get me through the tollbooths and out on the bridge. A haze hangs over the city, over the Hudson too. It's already hot.

I take the West Side Highway down to the 95th Street exit, and a few minutes later I'm at Amsterdam, heading north. Sweat is trickling down my back, down my neck, into my eyes. Cars are honking; cabs are swerving around them. Here's a furniture truck blocking two lanes while drivers trapped behind it breathe fume-filled air rising hot from the asphalt.

I cut over at 100th and take Manhattan up a few blocks. There's a parking place on the corner, right in front of a bodega, and I grab it. A couple of neighborhood guys are loitering under its awning, drinking beer out of bottles with paper bags pressed around them. It's a relief to climb out of my hot car. The guys check me out. One of them says, "Lookin' good." I give him a smile and a little wave. Like I said, I lived a long time as a chick nobody would look twice at.

People from the neighborhood wander past me, a black lady with her hair set in multi-colored rollers, a skinny white guy with a nose ring, a couple of little brown girls trailing after a woman who looks like their grandmother.

I stare down the block toward Jimmy's building. The sun's higher and brighter, but otherwise everything looks just like it did three days ago, minus the cops and the ambulance and the big crowd of people on the sidewalk, spilling around the parked cars and into the street.

I take a deep breath and start toward the chain-link fence. Here's where it happened. The tall weeds are the only bright spot; everything else is asphalt, sidewalk, a string of cars whose colors long since dimmed, no-color bricks—and spots of Jimmy's blood dulled to rust on the little patch of concrete. I try the gate. It's locked. Nothing's back there anyway but weeds, bits of litter, birds pecking in the dust at the edge of the concrete.

I continue around the side of the building. Now I'm standing in front, where I was supposed to pick him up. Here, behind a set of glass doors, is sort of a foyer with a bank of buzzers on one wall. On each side of the doors is a concrete urn trailing strands of ivy.

I haul a door open and step inside. I'm scanning the labels

on the buzzers, wondering which one is the super and how I can get him to let me in Jimmy's apartment, when I look up to see the tiny, crazy woman from Saturday pulling on one of the doors with all her might. I push it toward her and step aside to let her in.

"Thank you, dear," she says. "Those doors are heavy. They get heavier every year. I can't believe how long I've lived in this building. All my friends are in Florida where it's warm. Of course it's warm here today." She glances at me. "Oh, it's you again. How are you doing? Remember me? Jimmy's neighbor?" She's all in red today, shimmery red leggings and an off-the-shoulder blouse cinched at her waist with a wide belt. "Not such a happy occasion when we met." She grabs my arm. "How are you, dear?"

Her hand moves up my arm until she's clutching my shoulder, pulling me down so we're face to face. Her features are twisted into a worried expression which, combined with her heavy makeup, gives her the look of an actress in a tragic role. I can feel her fingers sort of digging into me. "It takes a long time," she says. "Then just when you think you're okay, you realize you're not. I buried four husbands. Of course, I wasn't married to any of them anymore when they died. But I went to their funerals for old time's sake." She releases me to root around in a huge straw bag decorated with red and yellow fish, pulls up a set of keys, and sticks one in the lock on the inner door. "Come on up with me. I'll make some coffee." She grabs my arm again. "Do you drink coffee?"

"Sure," I say. "But what I really want is the super. Which one of these buzzers is him?"

"Oh, he's useless," she says. "What do you want him for?" She pushes the door open and pulls me into the lobby with her.

"I want to get into Jimmy's apartment."

"Why didn't you say so? I can let you in."

"How?"

"I have his key. I wouldn't give it to just anybody, but you look honest."

"How'd you get his key?"

"He lived right next to me. Didn't I tell you? When he was on the road, I'd look after his mail for him, things like that. Sometimes the mailman just leaves parcels out where anyone can take them. The super's useless. But I said that." I follow her across the lobby toward the elevators. She pushes a button. "These elevators are very slow," she says. "What do you think I should do with Jimmy's key? Give it to the super? They'll change the locks before they rent the place again, I suppose. At least they should. I wouldn't want to move into a place other people might have a key to. Of course, the new tenant could just hire a locksmith—" She grabs my arm. "By the way, I'm Helen." She holds out her hand.

"Maxx," I say, giving her bony fingers a light squeeze.

"That's a funny name for a girl," she says.

With a desperate squeal, the elevator bounces to a stop and the doors creak open. We step in and she pushes the button for the ninth floor. The elevator starts its halting ascent. She steps back and squints at me. "You're a pretty girl too. Very pretty. You should wear more makeup. Dress better. That outfit you had on Saturday wasn't bad—I'd like a pair of those red leather shorts myself. But today—" She looks me up and down and shakes her head sadly.

"It's a million degrees out," I say, "and I just drove over here from New Jersey."

"New Jersey? That's where you live? Why?" She knits her penciled brows.

"Too expensive here, and everything that isn't expensive is rent-control and nobody wants to move out," I say.

"I know," she says.

The elevator squeaks a few times and shudders to a halt. Slowly, the doors part. She glances suspiciously at the joint between elevator floor and hallway, steps over it, and teeters for a minute on her high heels. We proceed down the hall until she pauses in front of a door marked 98.

"This is his apartment," she says. "Come on. I'll get you the key."

She pulls me along with her to the next door, unlocks it, and ushers me in. I have the confused image of being in something like a very crowded antique shop.

"I keep it in a special place," she says, disappearing into an adjoining room.

I hear a drawer open. In a few seconds she's back, handing me a key.

"Remember, I wouldn't give it to just anybody," she says. "But go ahead, dear. Then we'll have our coffee."

I've never been inside Jimmy's apartment before, so I don't know what to expect. I feel nervous as I turn the key in the lock. Nervous but kind of thrilled, almost like I've come up here to meet *him*. And the very first thing I see after I step inside makes me feel like he's actually here.

One of his guitars is still plugged in. It's leaning against the wall, with the cable in a tangle on the floor and his pick lying on the amp—like he was playing and he just stepped away for a minute to take a little break.

The cops have come and gone. They won't care or even know if I take the pick. Then I'll have something to remember him by. I snatch it up and tuck it into the pocket of my cutoffs.

Something of Jimmy's—and yes, okay, I did have a crush on him. I finger the pick as I look around. Jimmy's pick. But why does that seem weird? A thought is nagging at the corner of my mind.

Straight ahead are two long windows, almost floor to ceiling, with a table and two chairs centered between them. On the right there's a desk, shelves, music equipment, a door that might be a closet. On the left is a sofa.

Everything is very tidy. Like the cop said, it doesn't look like people were fighting in here. On the other hand, there isn't much furniture, and no knickknacks or anything much to get broken—not like Helen's place. If somebody forced Jimmy to the window and pushed him out and a chair got knocked over or something, that person could straighten things up in a hurry before he took off.

And Jimmy was really a little guy—he was just so self-confident that you didn't notice. Even a normal-sized guy could overpower him easily, and that guy he was arguing with at Feedback was more than normal size.

I walk to the windows, open one of the shades, and look down. I can see the patch of concrete where he landed. Something in my stomach ripples. Jimmy *couldn't* have stood here, looked down like this, and jumped on purpose. But if you were going to push somebody out one of these windows—during an argument, say, or maybe even by sneaking up when the person wasn't expecting it—the window would have to be open all the way.

The window frames have layers of paint on them. Sometimes windows like that stick when you try to open them. I unlatch the one I'm standing in front of and give it an experimental push. It slides right up, smooth as you could want. And on a floor this high, there's no screen. I look down again, then I close the window and turn away.

Would he have had the windows open? Probably. There's no sign of an air conditioner, and you'd die in here on a hot summer day with no ventilation.

I take another glance around then wander into the bedroom, still fingering the pick and trying to put words to that strange nagging thought. Here's his bed, a double bed, two pillows side by side. I feel a momentary throb. What would it have been like to lie in this bed with Jimmy?

Of course, I wouldn't have been the only woman to have that experience. And as if to drive the point home, here's a tube of lipstick on the night table. I check the color. It's a deep, rich red, the color I like. And from the looks of the case, the owner buys her makeup at the dollar store, just like I do. Who does it belong to? Monique? Would she wear this color with that pale skin of hers? I can't remember if she even wears lipstick. How about that full-lipped woman with the glossy hair who burst into tears when I told her Jimmy was dead? Or maybe that barmaid?

I wander back into the living room. With the shade open, the room is brighter. I can see things. But what am I looking for? I don't know. I open the door that might be a closet. Inside is an amp and three or four guitars zipped into gig bags. I finger the pick in my pocket and the thought gnaws at the corner of my mind. It's like the pick is trying to tell me something, but what?

The desk is a jumble of CDs, papers, even a little pile of pocket change. Here's his guitar tuner, a copy of *The Village Voice*, a couple of credit card receipts, a few packages of guitar strings, a snapshot of Jimmy performing, a real close-up where you can see his fingers right on the strings.

Fingers on the strings. That's it. I pull the pick out of my pocket and stare at it.

Jimmy never used a pick. He always said if Albert King didn't need one, he didn't either. This is a strange pick too, a gaudy multicolored thing and about the thickest one I've ever seen.

The thought makes me sick. It looks just like the picks Stan used to use. I fired Stan, and Jimmy took his place. Maybe Stan came up here determined to get Jimmy out of the way so he could get his job back.

I check the knobs on the amp. Everything's been turned way up high—bass, treble, reverb, the works. The settings Stan liked.

Maybe the tall guy didn't have anything to do with Jimmy dying. Maybe it was Stan. He's a tall guy, too—a tall guy with an obvious motive.

I tuck the pick back in my pocket. Wait till Stallings hears what I've discovered. But first, the people on this floor must have heard something, with that amp turned up so high. And maybe they heard voices, too. Maybe they heard an argument. Maybe the cops were in such a hurry to decide he killed himself that they didn't even bother to ask.

Somebody knocks on the door, and my heart gives a guilty thump. Should I hide? I'm wondering, when a familiar voice says, "Coffee's ready, dear, and it's going to get cold."

I take a final glance around and head for the door. Helen leads me back to her apartment and sits me down on a love seat upholstered in gold brocade. A small table made of dark, polished wood has been draped with a lacy cloth.

"Do you take anything in it, dear?" she inquires as she totters toward the kitchen on her high heels.

"No, thanks."

"I don't either. I have to watch my figure, you know."

She returns bearing a tray that holds two cups of coffee in delicate china cups.

"Were you in your apartment Saturday when . . . when Jimmy went out the window?" I say, before I sip the coffee.

"No," she says. "I was out all day. Saturday is shopping day for me."

"So when I met you down on the sidewalk you hadn't been inside the building yet?"

"No. What a shock to turn the corner and see all that commotion. And then to find out it was poor Jimmy. He reminded me so much of my first husband—"

"How about the other people on the floor? Has anybody been talking about what happened? Did anybody hear anything going on in Jimmy's apartment?"

"No, dear. I don't really mingle that much with my neighbors. Most of them aren't my type of people. But the rent is affordable, and my fourth husband liked to live it up, so when he died there wasn't as much money left as I would have liked. Of course, I keep my eyes open. I wouldn't mind finding another man . . ."

Half an hour later, I'm still sitting in Helen's apartment, squirming with impatience. She's talking about her divorce from husband number two, the artist. I finally manage to escape by looking at my watch and gasping, "Oh my God, I have to be at work in half an hour"—even though I don't.

Out in the hall I wait until Helen has closed her door. Then I knock on the door across from Jimmy's. I hear shoes tapping across a bare floor. The door opens to reveal a stocky, pleasant-looking black guy, maybe forty or so. I tell him I'm a friend of Jimmy's, ask him if he knew him, if he heard what happened.

"Who hasn't?" he says with a rueful laugh. "For a while people even forgot to complain about the weather." He pauses. "Oh," he says, "Ruben. Ruben Kelly." He sticks out his hand. I take it.

"Maxx Maxwell," I say. "Were you here that afternoon?"

"Yeah," he says. "Things were pretty noisy for a while, too."

"They were? Like what?"

"Jimmy tended to be a pretty considerate guy with the guitar practice, so I don't know what he was up to. I could hardly hear myself think."

"Loud music?" I say. He nods. "What time was that?"

He screws up his mouth. "Late afternoon. I wasn't really looking at the clock."

"Was it near the time he went out the window?"

Kelly shrugs. "When was that? Six o'clock? A little later? I was in here watching TV, didn't find out about Jimmy till the next day."

"There would've been sirens."

"You hear sirens around here all the time." He shakes his head. "I was sleeping on and off, had the TV on . . . can't really say exactly what happened when."

"How about some of the other people on the floor? Did anybody say whether they heard anything weird?"

"No," he says, scratching his chin. "But you could do almost anything up here on a Saturday night and hardly anybody'd know." He nods toward Helen's door. "I'm not sure Helen hears so good."

"She was shopping, anyway," I say.

"Figures." He pauses, then nods toward the door on the other side of Jimmy's. "That guy's the one who told me about it, but he wasn't here when it happened. He's a maitre d'—works a long shift Saturday and Sunday. I think he heard about it from Helen."

"How about the people on each side of you?"

"That one's vacant," he says, twisting his head to the left. "And this one—" He jerks his thumb toward the right. "His wife lives in Boston, and he flies up there weekends to see her. Long-distance marriage." He grins. "Maybe that's the secret. My ex-wife . . ." The grin fades, and he shakes his head. "My ex-wife, yeah—that reminds me. There was one more thing last Saturday."

"What was that?"

"Somebody went tearing out of Jimmy's place . . . after the music, quite a while after the music, and slammed the door so hard I thought a bomb had exploded or something."

Back outside again, I walk south, along Central Park West so I don't have to pass the spot where Jimmy died. I turn at 100th

and pass a Laundromat, a grocery with fruit in bins on the sidewalk, a hair salon with photos of braids in the window, and another bodega. This one sells cold beer, hot coffee and lottery tickets. My car is a couple blocks north, but I don't go back to my car.

Instead, I stick my head in the door of the bodega and ask the woman behind the counter where the police station is.

"Next block," she says, in a soft, Spanish-accented voice.

CHAPTER 7

The police station is a no-nonsense structure of buff bricks with heavy glass doors in a bland facade. As I pull back one of the doors, I'm replaying the conversation I had with Elise, the barmaid at the Hot Spot. I thought she was talking about the tall guy when she described the guy hassling Jimmy outside Slim's the last time we played there. But no, it was Stan, of course. And Stan's the one who called the Hot Spot and canceled the gig—or at least got some lady friend to do it for him.

Inside, the place is like a giant refrigerator, air conditioning cranked up to the max.

"Help you, miss?" It's a black cop, spiffy in his starched collar and tie, regarding me from behind a pane of glass. There's a microphone arrangement so we can talk to each other.

"Is Detective Stallings in?" I say.

"I believe he is," he says, cordially enough.

"May I talk to him?"

"That can probably be arranged. What's on your mind?" He seems like a nice guy, nicer than I thought a cop would be.

"I knew the man that died Saturday night—on 105th? I was there right after it happened. I was supposed to pick him up for a gig. He was in my band."

"He was a musician? What did he play?"

"Guitar. He played blues guitar." I can't tell from the look on the cop's face whether he thinks it's silly or cool when white

71

guys play blues.

"Hang on." He swivels around, picks up a phone, and talks into it. I can't hear what he's saying because of the glass. After a couple of minutes, he puts the phone down. "Detective Stallings will be right out," he says.

I stand there for a while, fingering the pick in my pocket, going over in my mind what I want to say. I'm starting to get goose bumps from the air conditioning. Eventually, a door opens and a guy looks out, a jowly guy with ruddy skin, wearing a sports jacket in a weird shade of green. He beckons toward me and holds the door. I follow him into a hall. It's just as cold back here, maybe even colder. Too cold to be wearing nothing but cut-offs and a halter top.

"Are you the person who called a couple times?" he says, his voice grumpy.

I nod. "I'm Maxx Maxwell."

"Walter Stallings," he says. "Why are you here?"

"I think I discovered something important," I say as I trail him down the chilly hall. "Something that the police who went over Jimmy's apartment didn't notice."

"Hang onto it till I'm sitting down," he says over his shoulder. "I can't take much excitement anymore. I'm supposed to retire this year, and I want to survive till then."

He opens a flimsy door and motions me into a little office formed from wooden partitions where he gestures toward a chair pulled up to the edge of his desk.

He settles himself into a chair behind the desk, leans back, and rests his chin on his collar. It turns into two chins, a little one above and a bigger one below.

"So you got inside the apartment," he says. "How'd you manage it?"

"His neighbor has his key. You guys were done in there, right? That's what you told me."

He nods, but the raised eyebrow says he's not really going along with this. "So what's your discovery?"

"Somebody who wasn't Jimmy was in there playing the guitar, and whoever it was left his pick, a really thick pick. Jimmy didn't use a pick." I pull it out of my pocket. "It could have had fingerprints, but I touched it before I realized it couldn't be Jimmy's."

"That's it?" I nod. "Don't go into police work," he says.

"But everything on the amp was turned way up, like some crazy heavy-metal guy had been using it. And the neighbor across the hall said he heard real loud music that afternoon. Jimmy didn't play that style at all. But I know somebody who did."

Stallings frowns. "Are you trying to do my job for me?" he says.

"No, but this is so obvious. I fired a guy—and I hired Jimmy to take his place. And the guy I fired liked thick picks and extreme amp settings—"

"There were no signs of a struggle."

"Jimmy wasn't a huge guy, and he doesn't have air conditioning, so the windows were probably already wide open. And this guy had a motive . . . a really strong motive."

And he also has an alibi, I suddenly remember. I feel my face growing hot even though it can't be more than about fifty degrees in here.

Stallings stands up. "I have a lot of work to do this afternoon."

"But someone . . . you have to . . ." Have to what? I look at the pick and put it back in my pocket, feeling like an idiot. The conversation I had with Stan last Thursday night about his road gig with the Blue Dudes is replaying in my head. He said they were booked at a casino up north somewhere. He couldn't have been on his way up north with the Blue Dudes and in Jimmy's apartment pushing him out the window at the same time.

Stallings starts to step out from behind his desk.

"Did the autopsy report come in?" I say, just to say something.

"Not yet. Maybe tomorrow."

As I walk back to my car, I picture Stan up there with Jimmy, in front of those huge windows. One good shove is all it would take. Such a tempting scenario. Maybe Stan didn't have an alibi. Maybe the gig got canceled. Maybe I didn't hear the day right. Maybe the gig started really late. Sometimes those casinos have music round the clock. Once people are in there under those fluorescent lights, the whole point is to make them forget about time.

I check my watch. Stan's probably down at Manny's right about now.

Back at my car, I ease myself onto the hot upholstery, turn the key in the ignition, and discover that my car radio has been taken over by an alien force. A voice with a western twang is singing about lonesome heartaches while a bow skitters over fiddle strings in the background. I lean across the passenger seat to open the window and get a little cross-ventilation. What happened to the classic rock station? Then I remember that I had the Kendall College station on. They play a grab bag of everything, depending on what the DJ likes.

The song ends with a decisive fiddle lick and a cymbal crash. Now the DJ is talking about some upcoming country music event. But I'm not really listening because I'm trying to merge onto the West Side Highway and wondering what I'm going to say to Stan. A coward with Ohio plates is ahead of me on the ramp. He starts to shoot out into traffic, then loses his nerve and slams on his brakes. I stop with about an inch to spare between my front fender and his rear, and give him a good blast on the horn.

This gets him moving again. I'm sailing along too, trying to switch into the middle lane, when the DJ says something that pulls my attention back to the radio and makes me almost sideswipe a delivery van chugging up beside me.

He's talking about the same person Jimmy was so interested in the other night, Nancy Lee Parker, the C&W singer they were profiling on the music channel.

He feels a personal sense of loss, the DJ is saying, and anybody who had discovered this overlooked artist will feel the same. Her death last week wasn't unexpected, but it was a blow to her fans nonetheless.

At first there's no sign of Stan when I walk into Manny's. Proof, says a voice in my head. He left town after he pushed Jimmy out the window. I look around, just to double check.

In the corner, a guy with white man's dreads and a really amazing tattoo on his bicep is hunched over an amp, cradling a Stratocaster on his lap and spinning out dense waves of distortion-laced sound. On the wall behind him hang rows and rows of electric guitars, every finish from smooth baby-blue enamel to violent purple sparkle glaze. Aside from the dread-lock guy, the place is empty.

But here comes Stan, making his way from the back of the store with a carton of guitar strings. He's wearing faded jeans with a hole in one knee and a T-shirt that manages to be oversized even on his tall body.

"I found the D'Addario Heavies," he says to the dreadlock guy. "How many sets do you want?"

"Ten," the guy says.

"Sure thing. Charge?" The guy nods and the dreadlocks rustle on his shoulders. Stan turns toward the counter, sees me, and drops the box of strings. "Aw, shit." He's down on his knees in a flash, scooping up the little plastic envelopes and dumping them back into the carton, glancing back and forth between his task and me, pushing his hair off his face every time he looks up again. As he tucks the last pack of strings back in place, he says, "What brings you in here, Maxx?"

"I want to talk to you, but I'll wait till you're done with that." He seems awfully nervous, but then he's always been nervous around me.

"I *am* done." He scrambles to his feet and hoists the carton onto the counter. "Don't tell me—you need a sub for tonight, and you want to know if I'm free." He's trying to carry it off like a joke, but the earnest look in his eyes tells me he wishes it wasn't. "You still have my phone number, don't you? Or did you throw it away when you fired me?" He produces a feeble smile.

The dreadlock guy is spinning out sounds like he'd just as soon sit there all day.

"I've still got it," I say, "but I was in the neighborhood."

"What's up?" he says.

"You said the Blue Dudes have been playing casino gigs up north?" He nods. "You had one lined up for last Saturday?"

"Sure did," he says.

"How'd it come off?"

"Uh . . ." He pauses for a minute like he's searching for words, finally seems to make up his mind. "Great," he says with a decisive nod. "Really great."

"Do you mind if I ask which casino it was?"

His gaze strays toward where the dreadlock guy is sitting. "Uh, no," he says. "I guess not." His face brightens, and he looks back at me. "Oh, I get it," he says. "Okay, I'll tell. There's plenty of work for everybody." He replaces a strand of hair that has emerged from behind his ear. "The Mohegan Sun in Uncasville. Ever been up there?"

"No. The casinos I played were in Atlantic City."

"This is much nicer," he says. "*Much* nicer." He draws the

word out like a leisurely guitar lick. "It's a bit of a haul, but not too bad."

"What time did you start?"

"Oh, the usual . . ."

"Which would be?"

"Uh, just the usual. Eight. I guess it was about eight."

"Do you know the name of the person who does the bookings there?"

He shakes his head. "No," he says. "One of the other guys in the band takes care of all that." He's smiling now, quite cheerfully. "So you're . . . ah . . . things are working out good now with your band?"

"Well, I don't know if you heard, but the guitar player—"

"My replacement," he says, still quite cheerful. "You can say it."

"He's dead."

"He is?" Stan's eyebrows shoot up to his hairline, and his mouth drops open. He looks like an actor who doesn't trust his audience to get subtleties.

"He ended up on the ground nine stories down from the window of his apartment."

"Oh my God," Stan says. His hands spring from his sides and lock convulsively in front of his chest. "When did this happen? Was he pushed? What do the police think?"

With every question, his hands twitch.

I tell him what I saw and what the cops are saying.

"So you *do* need a sub," he says.

"We've got someone," I say. "It's all taken care of."

On the way back to New Jersey, I keep thinking about Stan's reaction—like he was trying to be surprised about something he wasn't surprised about. But what does he have to cover up, if he was really at the Mohegan Sun?

77

★　★　★　★　★

It's about two when I pull into the parking lot behind my building. After forty-five minutes in my car, I'm as hot and sweaty as if I just stepped out of a sauna. I hurry around the front of the building and up the stairs, shove my apartment door open. No phone messages.

I peel my clothes off and drop them on the floor. As the cutoffs fall, I hear a clink and realize I've still got Jimmy's apartment key. I pick it up and put it on my dresser.

I can hardly wait to jump in the shower, but first I sit down with the phone and track down the person who does bookings for the Mohegan Sun.

"Yes," she says, in a pleasant voice with a hint of New England flatness in it, "We did book the Blue Dudes last Saturday night. They went over very well. We'll probably have them back."

"What time was the first set?" I say.

"Eight o'clock. They played at eight o'clock in the Wolf Den."

Jimmy went out that window at six-thirty, no earlier. The Mohegan Sun is in Connecticut. It's got to be two hours from Manhattan—even further.

I throw my clothes back on and run down to my car.

Julio is strolling through the parking lot as I rummage in my glove compartment for a New York State map. He always has time for a chat, so I pretend like I don't see him, grab the map, and head back upstairs.

I spread the map out on the kitchen table and study the crisscrossing red and blue lines. Uncasville is two inches from Manhattan on the map. Boston is four inches. It takes at least four hours to get to Boston. Stan couldn't have pushed Jimmy out the window at six-thirty and gotten to the gig by eight.

When I get home from work, I've got another note from Leon

waiting for me.

"Knock on my door," it says. "I'll be up."

Inside my apartment, the message light on my machine is blinking. Hopefully not Josh changing his mind. I hold my breath and push PLAY. An all-too-familiar voice says, "Hi, Liz. It's mom. Give me a call." I erase it.

I get rid of my work outfit as fast as I can, grab two cans of Bud from the refrigerator, and head next door to see Leon.

He greets me with his usual smile, pulls back the door, and waves me in with a hand that holds a section of the *Times*. Behind his horn-rimmed glasses his eyes look serious. "Are you okay?" he says. "I was worried about you today."

"Want a beer?" I say, handing him a Bud.

"Not to be snobbish," he says, "but I've got some Heineken in the refrigerator. Mind if I drink one of my own?"

"Go ahead," I say and settle onto my end of the sofa. The elegant sound of violins intermingled with piano drifts from the stereo. On the coffee table a copy of *Macbeth* has been flipped over to hold the place.

In a few seconds, Leon emerges from the kitchen carrying a bottle of Heineken and two glasses.

"I'll drink out of the can," I say.

"If you insist." He pours himself a glass of beer and raises it to me in a toast. "So what's new?"

"I called the cops," I say. "I asked them what made them think Jimmy killed himself."

"And?"

"Basically they said because it didn't look like anybody else killed him. They're doing an autopsy—I guess they have to—but really it's like they've already made up their minds. So I went there."

"Where?"

"To Jimmy's apartment. A neighbor let me in. The craziest

old lady you'd ever want to meet."

"You don't know my mother," he says with a laugh.

"Somebody had been up there playing Jimmy's guitar. Whoever it was turned all the knobs on the amp way up and left a pick behind, a really thick one. Jimmy didn't play with a pick, and he hated that distorted amp sound. But the thing is—Stan, the guy I fired and replaced with Jimmy, always turned everything on his amp way up, and he loved those thick picks. So I went to the police station and told the cop that's supposedly working on the case, and the fucking asshole didn't even care. He acted like it was all a big joke."

"Elizabeth. Your language."

"Then I realized Stan can't have done it because he's in another band now, and they had a gig at a casino in Connecticut on Saturday night, and I called the casino, and it's really true—they were there. One weird thing though—when I told Stan that Jimmy was dead, he acted so surprised it seemed fake."

Leon laughs a surprised laugh. "Ms. Detective, huh? Have you been watching reruns of *Murder She Wrote*?"

"You think this is funny, but it's not."

"I don't think it's funny. Your friend died."

"And I'm afraid my band is going to die, too. It's hard to find people to play blues. Either they don't understand it so they can't make it sound real, or maybe they sound great but they can't afford to pass up gigs that pay better. Jimmy was totally into the band, and now he's gone." I feel my throat getting tight.

"He was a white guy," Leon says, puzzled. "And you're white. *I* should love the blues, but I love Beethoven."

"When something grabs you inside, there's not much you can do about it."

Doretta's face rises before my eyes, mouth shaping an urgent cry, and my spine tingles like it did that night.

CHAPTER 8

I don't sleep very well, despite drinking my two cans of Bud with Leon and one of his Heinekens, then having another Bud when I get back to my apartment. Thunder wakes me just when I've finally drifted off into a confused dream about Doretta.

I get up and peer out the window. I see patches of lightning at the edge of the sky like explosions on a distant battlefield. The thunder finally rumbles off toward the Delaware Water Gap, but I lie on the bed for a long time afterwards, filling out the memory that the dream awakened.

The neon blur of the boardwalk is behind me. My heart is fighting to get out of my chest, and my mouth is dry from panting. I can't run anymore, and soon, after I've limped two or three blocks, I'm shivering in the chilly March air.

It's a street of shabby wood-frame flats, the Atlantic City the tourists never see. A doorway beckons, only because maybe it's warm inside. A neon beer sign says it's a bar.

Stale beer smell, empty stools, a few shadowy figures bent over drinks—and in a small clearing amid the empty tables, a band. It's not like the band I just ran away from, though, and I feel self-conscious in my fancy dress.

A scrawny white guy is twitching chords out of a cheap guitar, and a black lady who probably outweighs him by a hundred pounds is singing into the mike. Except it's not like any singing I've ever heard before. Her voice sweats and begs and squeals and brags and whispers. Amazed, I sink into the first chair I

81

stumble upon.

"I love my baby, but my baby don't love me." Her voice shades from a shriek to a moan in a wave of sound that pulls me right along with it. "I love my baby, but my baby don't love me." Now she rears her head back and lets her voice throb. "I'm going to cast my troubles down into the deep blue sea."

The tune is right up my alley too, because I've finally had it with Sandy.

"You from one of the casinos?" she says later, taking in my dress with a glance. I nod. "Wanna sit in with the band?"

"No, it's not my style. I mean, I love it, but—"

"Go ahead, honey. Give it a try."

"No, really . . ."

But I want to. I really want to.

At last the room becomes light, and Julio's music starts its cheerful throb. I pull myself out of bed and head for the shower, eyes burning and feeling as wired as if I've been out partying all night.

I left Jimmy's apartment too soon yesterday, I realize, as I let the hot blast of the shower massage my back. I was so excited about finding the pick that I didn't look hard enough at everything else.

I park in front of the bodega again, hurry past the chain link fence and the tall tree-like weeds that divide the sidewalk from the concrete yard where Jimmy landed. As I turn the corner, a cheerful-looking Hispanic guy is on his way out and holds the door for me without a second thought.

Ruben Kelly is waiting for the elevator when I step out on the ninth floor. He gives me a big smile and asks me how I'm doing today. I tell him I'm doing fine. He tells me to take care of myself.

Okay, what would Ms. Detective do? I ask myself once I'm inside Jimmy's apartment. My gaze lands on the wastebasket, tucked between the side of the desk and the wall. I didn't notice it the last time I was here, but detectives on TV are always looking in wastebaskets. I walk over to it and lean down to peer inside. It's almost full with what you'd expect—junk mail, crumpled papers, tissues, even a few old socks.

I take the copy of *The Village Voice* off Jimmy's desk, open it out on the floor, and dump the wastebasket onto it. Out come junk mail, papers, tissues, and a pair of old socks, followed by a cassette, sliding out and landing with a little plop, and a tube of lipstick that rolls across the room. I crawl after it and fish it out from under the sofa. It's that deep red color, like the one on the night table.

I pull myself to my feet and stick my head around the bedroom door. The lipstick on the night table is still there.

I return to the pile of trash on the *Voice*. I pick the cassette up. It's a homemade tape with a handwritten label. "Nancy Lee Parker," it says, "Thinking of You." Then, underneath, in parentheses, "The Last Album."

Nancy Lee Parker? That person again.

I put the cassette aside and start un-crumpling some of the crumpled papers. Most of them are just more junk mail. But here's a whole pile of papers—ten or twelve sheets—folded and twisted and bent into a "V" shape. I untwist them and sort through the pages. They are songs, neatly typed, one to a sheet, with chords written above the words here and there. I smooth them out as best I can. The top one is called "Whiskey for Breakfast." I let my eyes wander down the page.

> *I'm cookin' for myself now*
> *Eatin' pork and beans*
> *Findin' my own socks*
> *Washin' my own jeans*

83

Mama don't care for me no more
Mama don't care for me no more
No, mama don't care for me no more.

There's another verse, in the same vein. It's kind of a country song, I guess, like those songs you hear on the radio where guys think it's the woman's job to cook for them and wash their clothes. I skim a few more pages—lots of heartaches and lost love.

I set the songs aside and check out more of the crumpled papers. I'm reading a notice about some repairs scheduled for the elevator when I hear a tap at the door. I catch my breath. My heart gives a little skip then goes to double time.

A voice says, "Is that you Maxx? Ruben said a friend of Jimmy's was here."

It's Helen, the crazy lady. I dump the stuff back in the wastebasket, all except for the songs and the cassette, and I stick the wastebasket back between the desk and the wall. As the tapping continues, I grab the songs and the cassette and head for the bedroom. When I was having coffee with Helen yesterday, she only got as far as her divorce from husband number two. No telling how long it will take her to bring me up to the present, and I've got to work on some stuff for the band this afternoon.

I hurry through the bedroom and slip behind the bathroom door. While I'm standing there waiting for my heart to calm down, I suddenly remember. I've got the key now. She can't get in without it.

I sit on the toilet seat and again read "Whiskey for Breakfast" and some of the other songs. Jimmy never mentioned that he wrote songs. And, anyway, would he have written songs like these?

I ease my way out from behind the door and stick my head around the corner. No more tapping. Helen seems to have gone away. I stick the songs and the cassette in my bag and take another look around the bedroom. Is it my imagination or has somebody been using the bed since I was here yesterday? It's not as tidy as it was before. One of the pillows is sort of poked out of shape and the blanket is rumpled, as if somebody pushed it aside and then hastily pulled it back into place.

Or did I just not notice it before?

I peel back the sheet and blanket. Nothing. Nothing under the pillow, either. I look around the room. Does anything else look different? How about that lipstick? I could have sworn the one that was on the night table before was in a cheap tube like the 99-cent stuff from the dollar store. This one looks classier.

I pick it up and check the color. It's a weird salmon color, not that deep red like the one that was here before. And it's from the Body Shop. The red lipstick in the wastebasket must be the one that used to be on the night table. Who's been in here? And why did they care about what color lipstick was on the night table?

Before I leave, I switch the amp on, wait a minute for the tubes to warm up, grab the guitar, and stroke my thumb across the strings. A hoarse, metallic burst of sound surges through the apartment, more like a jackhammer than a guitar. The tone Stan always went for.

He couldn't have pushed Jimmy out the window because he was on his way to Connecticut Saturday night, but he must have been up here during the day. I'll bet he could tell me something useful if he wanted to. I check my watch. He should be down at Manny's right now.

But as I'm on my way to my car, I remember that Stallings said the autopsy results might be in today. I continue on down to 100th Street, hurrying past strolling black ladies and muscular Hispanic guys in sleeveless undershirts and gold chains.

Bracing myself for the blast of frigid air-conditioning, I haul back the heavy glass door of the police station and step into the reception area. Today the cop behind the pane of glass is a lady cop, olive-skinned with a heavy face and oily ringlets bleached reddish gold.

"May I help you?" she asks in lightly accented English.

"Detective Stallings, please?"

"What is it about?"

"Tell him Maxx Maxwell is here," I say. "He knows me already."

I'm shivering by the time he comes out. Shivering and rubbing my arms.

"Chilly?" he says, his voice unsympathetic. I nod and follow him down the hall. "The autopsy report came in," he says without turning around. "I guess that's what you're here for."

"You said you'd give me the results."

In his office, he drags a chair to the edge of his desk and waves me into it. Rummaging through a pile of papers, he extricates one and smoothes it out in front of him. He blinks a few times, then pushes the paper further away. "Can't see anymore," he mutters, pulling the paper closer then pushing it away again. "No drugs in his bloodstream," he says. "No signs that he struggled with anyone, no skin under the fingernails or anything like that. No evidence of any injuries before he went out the window." Stallings looks up. "That's about it. No reason to consider it a homicide. Besides, his neighbors say he's been depressed."

"They do?"

"Well, one of them said he was sensitive."

"That's not the same thing. And, anyway, how can you know if injuries happened before he went out the window or after?"

"Forensics. Maybe he landed a little bit nearer the building than they usually do when they jump, but that doesn't prove anything. Don't you watch the cop shows on TV?"

"Not often enough, I guess."

"We have ways."

"What ways?"

"Trust me."

As I'm heading out the door of the office, Stallings says, "Uh, hang on a second," in a hesitant voice that doesn't sound like him at all.

I turn around. He's still sitting behind the desk, but leaning forward now, with a funny look on his face I don't recognize. "You're keeping the band going?"

"Yeah. I'm trying to. Why?"

"I used to play the drums," he says. "A long, long time ago."

My car has turned into an oven. I roll down both front windows and open both doors. After three or four minutes, it feels a little better, but the seat still scalds the backs of my thighs. I slide way forward so only my rear end is touching the seat. I turn the key in the ignition far enough to make the radio come on and pop the cassette from Jimmy's wastebasket into my tape deck. I want to hear what Nancy Lee Parker sounds like.

A guitar sketches out a lick with a mournful twang, repeats it, and repeats it again. Then the singing starts: "I'm sitting here, it's gotten late, I'm smoking, I'm alone . . ." Her voice has a hoarse edge to it, sexy and kind of human. I like it. Did Jimmy like it? If he did, why was the cassette in the wastebasket?

A black woman is pushing a stroller along the sidewalk. The stroller has a white kid in it. I watch them pass. Then I pull myself upright on the seat, close the doors, and start the car. Easing myself out of my parking space in front of the bodega, I head north on Manhattan, turn right, pass the spot where Jimmy died, turn again, and make my way down Central Park West.

I'm momentarily distracted by the mob of people trying to

cross at 96th, until a fiddle bow skitters over the strings and catches my attention. The fiddle sketches out a wistful solo, then Nancy Lee Parker comes in again. "You headed for a barstool, sat yourself on down. I was wonderin' where you came from. A better part of town?"

It's not really a powerful voice, and she doesn't have much range, but she's got a nice lilting twang. It's a good country voice for sure.

I take Central Park West downtown, stopping and starting at almost every corner as a bus lumbers ahead of me, spewing out exhaust. The song ends with a cool guitar lick and a flourish on the drums.

At Manny's, Stan is helping a kid with a stud under his lip figure out what kind of guitar strap to buy, the paisley one or the one with skulls. I wait while the kid makes up his mind and Stan writes up the purchase. He doesn't catch sight of me till the kid walks away.

He smiles cheerfully and says, "Looking for a sub after all?"

"No," I say.

"Just joking." He laughs. "I've got my hands full with the Blue Dudes." He scoops up the remaining packets of guitar strings from an open carton on the counter and turns away to tuck them into a display behind him. He's got kind of a pirate look going on today, with a bandanna folded into a triangle and tied rakishly over his hair.

He pushes the empty carton aside, hefts another up off the floor, and goes at it with a box cutter. "How'd things go with the Mohegan Sun?" he says. "Did you score a gig?"

"Not yet," I say. "We're still sorting out what to do about a permanent guitar player."

"I could give you some other leads for gigs—" He's looking

at me earnestly, meanwhile slicing busily away with the box cutter.

"Stan," I say. "Watch what you're doing. You could—"

"Yikes!" His finger flies to his mouth.

"Are you okay?"

He inspects his finger, now glistening with saliva. "Just a slight nick," he says. "Mostly I got my fingernail. Shouldn't try to do two things at once. My mom always told me that." He puts the box cutter down. "What brings you around today?"

I take a deep breath and blurt out, "What were you doing up in Jimmy Nashville's apartment last Saturday?"

"What? Who?" He looks totally startled, but I don't know if it's because he's amazed that I've found him out or because he thinks I've lost my mind.

"Jimmy Nashville's apartment. You were up there on Saturday, weren't you?"

His face is frozen, open mouth, raised brows, the wild hair escaping from the bandanna like a cartoonist's version of surprise. "Who's Jimmy Nashville?" he says at last. Then, "Are you okay, Maxx?"

"Of course I'm okay. And you know perfectly well, Jimmy Nashville is the guitar player that we got after you left, the guy who died last weekend. We were talking about him when I was here yesterday."

"I didn't know that was his name," Stan says. "Are you sure you're okay? What makes you think I was there?"

"His amp. Somebody turned all the knobs way up, just like you do. And Jimmy's neighbor said he heard loud music."

"Lots of guys play like that," he says scornfully. "Lots of people happen to like that sound."

"Somebody left a pick there, a big thick one like those ones you use."

"Lots of guys like thick picks," he says. "Look here." He

reaches over to where a fishbowl filled with picks is sitting on the counter, grabs a handful. "Thick picks. Tons of them."

I feel myself blush. "Never mind," I say. "Forget this conversation."

"No," he says. "What are you up to anyway? You think I did something to the guy?"

"You were on your way to the Mohegan Sun when Jimmy went out the window. I was just wondering if you were there earlier, and if anybody else was there too, or if he talked about somebody he was expecting."

"I wasn't there. Why would I go there? Look." He thrusts the handful of picks at me. "There are millions of these in the world. Millions."

Back at my car, Nancy Lee Parker is in mid-song when my engine coughs itself to life. She's singing about how lonely the city is when you don't have a guy you can call your own.

The West Side Highway is bad considering it's only the middle of the day, not rush hour. Things are complicated by a breakdown in the right lane. As I try to peer around the van in front of me to see why nothing is moving even though the light is green, a mournful fiddle lick signals the beginning of the next track.

Half of my brain is listening to the tape. The other half is drifting here and there, wondering why the tape was in the wastebasket, and who wrote "Whiskey for Breakfast" and the other songs, and if somebody has been in Jimmy's apartment using the bed since he died, and even if the owner of the salmon lipstick is the one who threw the red lipstick in the wastebasket. And whether Stan is the worst actor in the world or one of the best.

Half an hour later, I can finally see the George Washington Bridge, blurred by a slight haze of heat, hanging over the river.

And then my stomach growls, and I realize I'm starving.

On the tape, Nancy Lee Parker is mournfully telling somebody that she'd rather share him than have him gone for good. The guitar player, probably some crafty Nashville session guy who has broken more than a few hearts himself, is skillfully weaving a delicate line around her voice. The song ends with the guitar noodling a sad little tune while Nancy Lee hums a few lines. Then the tape goes silent. Even allowing for the fact that C&W is all about hard times, romantic and otherwise, this has to be about the most depressing stuff I've ever listened to. And I start to wonder if Nancy Lee Parker had a good reason to be depressed.

The first thing I do when I get home is run into the bathroom and splash cold water on my face and neck. I'm too hungry to take a shower before I eat.

I towel myself off and head for the kitchen, where I pop open my second-to-last can of Bud and check the cupboard to see if I've got lunch. There's one can of tuna in the cupboard and those two heels in the bread bag from Sunday, one big and one little. I grab the mayonnaise out of the refrigerator and mix up a bowl of tuna salad, sprinkle a little salt and pepper on it, and plop a good-sized scoop of it on the biggest heel, balancing the little heel on top.

Before I take a bite, I go into the other room and put the Nancy Lee Parker tape on my tape deck. While I eat, I scan the list of song titles on the j-card. The first song, the one about being alone, is "Nights You Don't Call," and things go downhill from there, the depressing titles all printed out in those careful capital letters.

The list continues onto the back. Remembering the haunting song I listened to before the tape turned into silence somewhere along the West Side Highway, I put the sandwich down, slip the j-card out of the plastic case, and turn it over. The last song on the list is called "I'd Rather Share You Than Have You Gone for Good." There's more writing though, at the very bottom of the card, something that's not a song title.

It's in the same capital letters, but larger and darker and kind of uneven, like maybe the person writing it was really mad at whoever the message was aimed at. It says, "This shouldn't be her last album, but it is—and all because of you." The last word is underlined with a savage stroke.

As I read the words, I feel a jolt. Were they meant for Jimmy?

Down below, the mail guy is trudging along in the sun. He's just finished with the row of aluminum-siding houses across the street, and he's heading for the big apartment building on the corner. A DPW guy is coming down a driveway. He drops two bags of trash at the curb. The mail guy stops. Now he and the DPW guy are talking. The mail guy laughs.

The tape is still playing, but I'm not listening. I'm staring at the message on the j-card. Should I call Stallings and tell him about it? He'd probably just laugh at me.

Now Nancy Lee Parker is singing about growing up fast when your man walks out on you. Did Jimmy walk out on her? Is that why this was her last album?

But if the woman in the fringed skirt on the TV screen the other night was Nancy Lee Parker, she'd have been about sixty when she died last week, at least a generation older than Jimmy. Old enough to be his mother.

Who could I ask about country and western music? Somebody who could tell me all about Nancy Lee Parker and why this was her last album and what Jimmy Nashville could have had to do with it.

Danny. Of course. I'll ask Danny.

CHAPTER 9

I zigzag over to Main Street, dash past the West Indian grocery and the Laundromat. Danny's standing in front of his shop, smoking. He looks like a small, blond version of Elvis posed under the hand-painted sign that turns the letters of the words "Vintage Vinyl" into musical notes staggered across a staff in a fragment of a melody. He catches sight of me and calls, "Hey, gorgeous! How ya' doin'?" I look over and wave. A pickup truck passes, and I dart across the street. "Comin' to see me?" he says with a smile.

"You guessed it."

"Check out what I got." He takes an eager step toward the door and beckons me to follow.

Once we're inside, he gestures toward eight or ten cardboard boxes lined up on the floor and says, "Look!" Each box is filled with forty-fives, still in their paper sleeves, and LPs, arranged in neat rows. "A guy just sold me his whole collection from the 50s and 60s. I can't wait to go through them."

He backs toward the cluttered counter where he usually sits and stubs out his cigarette in an ashtray shaped like a warped record. "So what's up, gorgeous? How's the world been treatin' you? Aldo still gettin' on your nerves?"

"Most definitely." I pull the Nancy Lee Parker tape out of my bag and show it to him. "Ever hear of her?"

Danny squints at the tape through a haze of leftover smoke. "Nancy Lee Parker? Doesn't ring a bell." He reaches for his cigarettes, gets another going, and reaches for the tape. "What kind of music is it?"

"Country and western. They've been talking about her on the radio—that Kendall College station. She just died."

"The tape looks homemade. Is it a demo?"

"I think somebody recorded it off an album."

" 'The Last Album' it says here. How many other ones were there?" Danny takes a drag on his cigarette.

"I don't know. Maybe not many. Otherwise we would have heard of her, like Patsy Cline or somebody."

He reaches behind the counter and pulls out a thick reference book. "Interested in covering some of her tunes or what?"

"Not really the band's style. She's got a cool voice, though, and I like the way she puts the songs across."

He opens the book and leafs through it, finally pointing to a spot on one of the pages. "She'd be right here, but she's not. Maybe it doesn't go back far enough." He closes the book with a decisive snap and takes another drag on his cigarette. "C&W isn't really my strong point, you know. But I'll ask around. And in the meantime, why don't you call the radio station?"

On the way home, I remember I'm almost out of food and beer. I don't feel like walking back to Main Street for the beer, but I stop off at C-Town Superette and grab a loaf of bread, some eggs, and a few cans of tuna.

The kid who answers the phone at the Kendall College radio station doesn't have a clue what I'm talking about.

"Somebody there must know about Nancy Lee Parker," I say. "Somebody was talking about her yesterday morning. Who is it that does the C&W program?"

"I'm not into C&W."

"But do you know who does the program?" I say, hearing a grouchy edge creep into my voice.

"Not really. If you want to find out about this Nancy whatever her name is, why don't you go on the Internet?"

"Because I don't have a computer," I say.

Thank God it's a quiet night at the restaurant. No big family groups, and Marie's back so I don't have to cover her section too. But the down side is that I have plenty of time to think about Nancy Lee Parker and her sad songs and her messed up career. And thinking about that makes me think about my career and how my band was going so great until somebody killed Jimmy and now it looks like it's going to hell.

I drive home in kind of a daze, hardly aware of where I am or what I'm doing, almost startled when my headlights pick up the motley assortment of cars in the parking lot behind my building and come to rest on the yellow-beige bricks of the building's back wall as I slip into my usual parking space.

I make my way around to the front of the building, noticing the heavy hum of the air conditioners protruding from the occasional window, feeling the warm air stir with an even warmer breeze as I pass under the ones on the first floor.

As I turn the corner, I almost collide with a tall, dark form. Or rather, I almost collide with a plastic garbage bag. The tall, dark form is Leon, and he's bearing the garbage bag before him like a trophy.

"Housecleaning," he says with a smile. "Garbage gets pretty ripe in this weather. I've been so busy at work I've been falling behind on my chores. I'd advise you to either hold your breath or back up."

I back up. "Can I use your computer, Leon? I need it to do some research."

"Maxx the Blueswoman doing research?" he says in a teasing voice.

"What's so weird about that?"

"You told me you dropped out of college because you thought it was a waste of time."

"I need to find something out on the Internet. What about it? Mind if I drop by?"

"I'd like nothing better than to encourage your scholarly impulses, but my computer's in the shop." He lowers the bag of garbage to the ground. "How about a beer, though? I'll get rid of this and meet you upstairs. I can't wait to hear the latest installment of your mystery."

"I went back to Jimmy's apartment, and I found something pretty interesting."

"More interesting than the guitar pick?" he says with a laugh.

"I know Stan didn't do it. Like I told you, he was playing a gig at the Mohegan Sun."

Leon shifts the garbage bag to his other hand. "I'll see you in a minute," he says and heads down the sidewalk that leads to the back of the building.

"Sorry for the mess," Leon says, handing me a bottle of Heineken and waving toward a pile of newspapers on the coffee table. "I've been too busy at Macy's to keep up with them." He settles onto his end of the sofa and pours his beer into a tall glass. "What's this interesting thing you found?"

I hand him the j-card. "Turn it over and read the last line," I say, then take a long swallow of beer.

He squints at the card, brings it closer to his eyes, sets his glass of beer on the coffee table, and retrieves his glasses from his desk. " 'This shouldn't be her last album, but it is, and all because of you.' " He looks up. "Where'd this come from? And whose last album shouldn't it be? And who's the 'you'?"

"It's part of this," I say, holding up the cassette. "It was in Jimmy's wastebasket. The cassette is a homemade recording off an album of songs by a C&W singer who died last week.

Somebody named Nancy Lee Parker. But I don't know who the 'you' is, except that the tape was in Jimmy's wastebasket, so maybe it's him."

"Hmmm," Leon says, nodding with furrowed brow. "Did you say anything to the police?"

"No. The detective just laughs at me."

"So what do you know about Nancy Lee Parker?"

"Not much. That's what I need the Internet for. I only know she was old. So it's not like she was his girlfriend and they broke up and she was so depressed it wrecked her career." I tilt my beer bottle to my mouth, take a long swallow, and set the bottle on the coffee table. "But that's not all I found." I pull the songs out of my bag. "These were in the wastebasket, too."

He reaches for the pile of crumpled papers. "Songs?" he says, shuffling through them.

"Yeah. Most of them are kind of lame, but the one on top is funny."

"Did Jimmy write songs?"

"Not that he ever mentioned. And even if he did, I don't think he would have written songs like these."

"Which one was on top?" Leon asks, shuffling through the papers again.

" 'Whiskey for Breakfast.' "

He pulls out a page and sets the rest on the coffee table next to the pile of newspapers. " 'I'm cookin' for myself now,' " he reads. " 'Eatin' pork and beans. Findin' my own socks.' " He looks up. "Who found his socks before?"

"Mama," I say. "Keep reading."

In a few seconds he looks up again. " 'Mama don't care for me no more'? This is the one you thought was funny?"

"Funny ridiculous, I should have said. Why do guys assume their girlfriends want to take on the role of their mothers? Of course she doesn't care for him anymore. She got tired of looking for his socks."

"Maybe it's not about his girlfriend," Leon says. "Maybe it's really about his mama. And maybe she's the one drinking the whiskey for breakfast."

"Why would somebody write a song about that?"

"Lots of people might," he says, still gazing at the page. "Some people have really sad lives. Maybe it has something to do with Nancy Lee Parker. Drinking whiskey for breakfast could mess up a person's career pretty fast." Suddenly, he looks up. "Say, they've got computers at the Hackensack Public Library. As far as I know, anybody who wants to can use them to surf the web."

"The Hackensack Public Library? Where's that?"

He rolls his eyes. "Right up on Main Street. You've probably walked past it a million times."

As soon as I climb in bed and close my eyes, I'm back in Atlantic City, sitting in that shabby bar.

"You're sure you don't want to sing?" Doretta's eyes are searching my face like she's looking for something.

"Not tonight . . . no, I just . . ."

The guitar player's been watching me with a wary half-smile. Now he turns away and says something to the drummer that makes them both laugh.

Next I'm running again, back in the direction I came from. The car's not where Sandy parked it before the gig, and when the cab drops me off in front of the apartment building, the car's not there either. But did I really think Sandy'd be home just because I called him on his story about the late-night errand that "really, babe, really" didn't have anything to do with the chick sniffing around him between sets?

Up in the apartment, huddled into a ball on my side of the bed that seems way too big without Sandy, I can't sleep. How did the tune that Doretta was singing go? The only line I can remember is, "I love my baby, but my baby don't love me." I sing it, experimentally. But with my voice wrapped around the words, it sounds too sweet, like some cheesy pop song. How do you get your voice to reach out and worm its way into somebody's soul?

Awake, I switch on the stereo and run through every radio station I can find. Nothing sounds like Doretta. Nothing at all.

Chapter 10

Thursday I wake up with a start as soon as Julio's music cuts in. Tonight's the rehearsal with Josh. I close my eyes, and cross my fingers, and send a desperate plea out into the universe: let the band make a good impression on Josh—no silly squabbles between Michael and Dom—and let him say yes when I offer him Jimmy's spot.

My wishes don't always come true, though, so I feel kind of sick as I pull myself out of bed and get ready to head over to the library.

It turns out to be a building I always thought was a church, perched on the corner right after the Indian Imports store, set off by a tidy square of faded late-summer grass and a few aggressively pruned bushes. It's squat but massive at the same time, shaped out of dark brown stone, rough-hewed, with deep windows that look like they don't let in much light.

Inside, besides all the books, is a long table with a row of computers, identical gray plastic pods cocked obediently toward the intent faces of the un-identical people arrayed on chairs before them. I ease myself into a chair next to a guy with a really impressive growth of dreadlocks tied in a bundle at the back of his neck.

I gaze at the screen, finger the plastic doodad on its plastic pad, make the little arrow dance around among the shapes and symbols displayed in front of me wondering which one will lead me into the Internet and what I'll do once I'm there. I click on a few things at random and watch in alarm as the screen goes blank then fills with new symbols and shapes.

Finally I lean toward the dreadlock guy. "Uh, excuse me," I say. He turns away from his screen and looks at me. He has a long thin face, almost scholarly, despite the hair. "Can you give me a hand with this?"

"What do you want to do?" he replies in a low, careful voice that, if you heard it with your eyes closed, you'd imagine was coming from a college professor.

"I'm trying to research a country and western singer named Nancy Lee Parker."

"May I?" He half stands and reaches for the plastic doodad with a slender brown hand. The screen goes blank briefly and is suddenly filled with a confused jumble of pictures and text.

Half an hour later I know that Nancy Lee Parker is sorely missed by her fans and that altogether she made four albums, and *Thinking of You,* which came out in 1962, was indeed the last. I know her career started in 1958 when the first album came out and that after 1962 she stopped performing because of personal problems. But I don't know what those problems are, or were, and I'm no closer to understanding what Jimmy might have had to do with her death than I was before.

"Maybe there's a book about her," the dreadlock guy says, piloting the plastic doodad around on its plastic pad, clicking a few times, and making the screen offer him a little rectangle where he can type in the words "Nancy Lee Parker."

Nothing comes up.

But eventually I find myself sitting at a small table at the end of a corridor whose walls are floor-to-ceiling shelves of books. And I'm paging through a pile of books with titles like *Cavalcade of American Music,* and *Roots to Rock,* and *Country to the Core.* And she's actually in some of them, and one even has a picture of her in a fringed skirt and a cowboy hat, standing behind one

101

of those clunky old-fashioned microphones and smiling a smile that the black and white photo makes look like it's shaped with black lipstick. She's gazing adoringly at a guy who, even in a dorky cowboy outfit, has to be one of the handsomest guys I've ever seen. He's got a guitar around his neck. Poor Nancy Lee Parker.

My stomach growls, and I realize I haven't eaten anything all day.

I'm hurrying along Main Street toward Roy's when Danny pops out of his shop.

"Hey, gorgeous," he says. "I found something for you. C'mon in."

Inside, he hurries behind the counter, stoops, and comes up with an LP. "I stuck it down below here so nobody'd ask to buy it," he says. "Those boxes of stuff I showed you the other day had more than just rock and roll in them."

He displays the front of the LP with a flourish. It's a Nancy Lee Parker album, *With Love from Nancy Lee,* number three if I remember right from my Internet research. The cover shows her head, framed by a huge heart exactly the same color as her lipstick.

"For you," he says, handing it to me. "Compliments of the management." He flicks the ash off his cigarette. "Great stuff," he says.

"You listened to it?"

He nods. "So cheerful. That's why I like the fifties. People were happy then."

"Cheerful? The tunes on that tape I showed you are about the most depressing stuff I've ever heard. Something awful must have happened in her life after she made this one but before the other one. I'd love to know what it was. Do you know anybody who's into C&W the way you're into rock and roll?"

"C&W?" says a harsh-faced woman browsing through Danny's bargain bin. "You like C&W?"

"Are you a fan?" I say.

"Sure am." She nods enthusiastically.

"Ever hear of her?" I pass the album cover to the woman.

She knits her brow. "Doesn't ring a bell." She looks up with a smile that softens her rough features even though the teeth it reveals aren't that great. "I'm into line dancing," she says. "It just makes you forget everything." She hands the album cover back. "Have you ever been to Willy's? In Lodi?"

"What's that?"

"Willy's Western Wear. He's got the clothes and boots and everything. And the music. He's got a whole room full of music."

"How do I get there?"

She gives me directions, and ten minutes later I'm zooming along Essex with the windows open and my hair blowing all over the place. Essex is a pretty significant thoroughfare, two lanes in each direction. The traffic moves so fast that if you don't know exactly what you're looking for, you can zip right past it.

Lots of gas stations, carpet outlets, used car lots, crowded rows of storefronts that always seem to include a pizza joint. I'm just about to decide the C&W woman was wrong about where Willy's is, or else I blinked once too often and missed it—signs are announcing I'm about to enter Maywood, when here it is, tucked away between a craft shop and a place that sells and services lawnmowers. "Willy's Western Wear," the sign says, and the Ls in "Willy's" are shaped like cowboy boots.

I lurch into the parking lot, ignoring the EXIT ONLY sign and my rear-view mirror glimpse of the startled look on the face of the driver behind me. I pull up in front of the store, next to a pickup truck with a bumper sticker that says "You can take the boy out of the country, but you can't take the country out of the boy." In the store window are a couple of mannequins that look like they're waiting for the caller at a square dance to tell them to do-si-do.

The store smells like leather and sounds like a honky-tonk. Standing behind the counter, near a display of string ties, is a pot-bellied balding guy dressed in a western-style shirt and crisp unfaded blue jeans. The music is coming from a turntable set up on a shelf behind him. All around me are racks and racks of western-style shirts and jeans, flouncy cotton skirts, shelves of cowboy hats, and a truly impressive selection of boots. Against the side wall is a display of cassettes and CDs.

The guy behind the counter—I guess he's Willy—has a round, rosy face and twinkling blue eyes. He looks like somebody's grandpa. "How are you doin' today?" he says, sounding like Hackensack is about the furthest west he's ever gotten in his life.

"Do you have anything by Nancy Lee Parker?" I say.

The smile disappears. "Poor Nancy Lee," he says. "People are paying attention to her again, now that she's gone."

"Would it be over here?" I point at the rack of CDs.

"Nope." He shakes his head. "None of it's been released on CDs."

"A friend gave me a couple of her albums. I really dig her voice, and I'd love to hear more."

"Yeah? Which ones do you have?"

"*Thinking of You* and *With Love from Nancy Lee*. I guess she only made two others."

He nods mournfully. But then his face brightens. "You've got 'em on vinyl?"

"*Thinking of You* is a tape somebody made—I guess somebody that had the vinyl. The other one's vinyl."

"What kind of shape?"

"I don't know. It plays okay."

He slips out from behind the counter, beckons me toward a

door in the back wall, and opens it. "Come on in here."

We step into a room that looks like a record library, walls covered floor to ceiling with shelves holding row upon row of LPs.

"Wow," I say.

"They're not for sale," he says. "My wife put her foot down a couple years ago, so I have to keep them here." He shrugs. "What can I say? I love the stuff. And when I'm gone, she'll be able to sell it all for a fortune on eBay, but she doesn't see it like that."

He bustles toward a section of shelving and extracts four LPs. "Here's Nancy Lee," he says. "I've got the whole set. Mint condition. This was the first one." He shows me the top album.

The cover shows the face of a dark-haired woman with carefully shaped brows and a carefully lipsticked smile. She's wearing a cowboy hat and has a narrow scarf knotted around her neck. It's *Dreaming Country.* I recognize the title from my Internet research.

"And here's number two, *Roads to Travel.*" He holds it up. It's got the fringed skirt picture from the music channel on the front. "Then here's the one you've got on vinyl." He holds up *With Love from Nancy Lee.* "And then there's *Thinking of You.*" He produces it with a flourish. "This one is worth a fortune. Look at that cover—the shape it's in. Looks like the album just came out yesterday." The cover shows her leaning dreamily on one elbow, her hand cupped under her cheek.

"C'mon back into the store," Bill says. "Let's hear some."

Out in front again, he extracts the LP from *Dreaming Country* and exchanges it for the record on the turntable. In a minute, that familiar voice, not really beautiful but totally human, fills the store. He lays the other albums out along the counter.

"What happened to her anyway?" I say. "She sounds happy enough here, but *Thinking of You* is about the saddest thing I've ever heard."

He nods mournfully. "She fell in love."

With that gorgeous guitar player in the picture, says a voice in my head, and my heart sinks.

CHAPTER 11

"What's so bad about falling in love?" I say, even though I already know the answer.

"It wasn't bad at first. They got married—people did that in those days. She was on top of the world."

"Then what?"

"The SOB—pardon my language—left Nancy Lee and took up with another woman. After that it was downhill all the way. Booze." He shakes his head sadly. "Drugs."

"Drugs? She looks so wholesome."

"Sleeping pills mostly," he says. "Not that stuff the rock stars take. But mostly booze, lots of booze. Such a waste." He looks sadly at the album covers. "She was so pretty once. Later she didn't look so good." He picks up *Thinking of You* and sort of cradles it in his arms.

"Who was the guy anyway?"

"Ever hear of Bill Jenks?"

"Not really."

"He was a big C&W star, right up there with Hank Williams, Merle Travis, those guys. And it ran in the family. His dad was one of the founders of the Grand Ole Opry."

"Do you know if Nancy Lee ever had any connection with a guy named Jimmy Nashville?" I say.

He scratches his head. "Nashville? Like the city?" I nod. "He's got the right name. Nashville's where she lived all her life. But no. *Jimmy* Nashville? Doesn't ring a bell."

A few customers have entered the store. One of them, a red-headed woman already decked out in western wear from head to foot, approaches the counter. She's carrying several cowboy-style shirts. While Willy is helping her, I glance over the song titles on the two albums I don't have. There's nothing called "Whiskey for Breakfast." Why would there be? She was cheerful then. But I'm wondering whether any of the other songs I picked out of the wastebasket are Nancy Lee Parker's. I pluck my notebook and a pen out of my bag and copy the titles down.

As Willy finishes up with the cowboy-shirt woman, I think of another question for him.

"Who was the woman Bill Jenks left Nancy Lee for?" I ask.

He snorts in disgust. "Actress. From up around here, New York. Met her when he was touring. Turned his back on his own roots."

On the way home, my brain sorts through this new information about Nancy Lee Parker, trying to somehow make it fit with the message on the tape: "This shouldn't be her last album, but it is—and all because of *you.*" But who's the *you?* Is it really Jimmy?

It could be Bill Jenks. Obviously, if he hadn't taken up with an actress and deserted poor Nancy Lee Parker, she wouldn't have gotten into drugs and drinking and her career wouldn't have been destroyed.

But it could be the actress. A glamorous home-wrecker. If she hadn't lured Bill Jenks away from Nancy Lee Parker, Nancy Lee's career could have lasted for decades.

What if Jimmy made the tape for somebody else? Like Bill Jenks or the actress? And that person got pissed off, showed up at Jimmy's place, and tossed the tape in the wastebasket and Jimmy out the window?

Why didn't I ask that guy in the store if Bill Jenks and the woman he deserted Nancy Lee Parker for are still alive?

I zoom into the emergency entrance of Hackensack Hospital like I'm having a real emergency, circle the parking lot in a quick U-turn, and in a second I'm heading west again.

The Nancy Lee Parker LP is still playing as I enter the store. Willy is kind of whistling along with it as he stands dreamily behind the cash register. He gives me a puzzled look. "Forget something?" he says.

"Is Bill Jenks still alive?" I say. "And what about the woman? The actress?"

"Sad story, isn't it?" he says, like he's not surprised at all that I came back for the details. "Bill Jenks died a few years back. Lung cancer. He was a heavy smoker. It kind of went with the life."

"And the woman?"

"She's still alive, last I heard."

"Did she stay in Nashville after he died?"

"Don't know that either."

"And they were married all that time?"

He nods. "All that time."

"What was her name?"

"Something . . ." He squints. "One of those actress names. Sylvia, Loretta, something like that."

"Did they have any children?" I suddenly think to ask.

He shakes his head. "Sorry."

"How about Bill Jenks and Nancy Lee Parker?"

"One."

"Boy or girl?"

"That I don't know."

On the way out, I stop by the display of cassettes and CDs against the side wall. A CD catches my eye. On the cover, a tall handsome man with an acoustic guitar hanging around his neck is leaning against a rail fence. He's wearing a cowboy hat, a shirt with pointed pocket flaps, and narrow pants that flare over the tops of his cowboy boots.

"Bill Jenks" the cover reads. *Thirty Years of Country.*

He looks even better here than in the picture where Nancy Lee was gazing at him like he was a god. If he got rid of the cowboy hat, replaced the silly flared pants with a nice faded pair of jeans, and either cut off more of his hair or let it grow a little bit, I'd be ready to get in line too. And if he traded that clumsy looking acoustic guitar for a Strat—well, let's just say if Nancy Lee was still alive, we'd have a lot to talk about.

On my way home I stop by Mr. Kim's for a case of Bud.

The first thing I do when I get home is stash the beer in the refrigerator. I know I'm going to need a cold one when I get home from the rehearsal tonight.

The second thing I do is sit down at the kitchen table with my notebook, open to the back where I copied the song titles from the Nancy Lee Parker albums, and leaf through the pile of songs from Jimmy's wastebasket. None of the songs from the wastebasket seem to be Nancy Lee's songs.

As I'm checking through the list one last time, the phone rings. I run out to the next room, plop into the big chair, and grab it.

"Hello? Maxx?" says a woebegone female voice, more like a whimper, really. My first thought is that it's somebody from the restaurant trying to get me to cover her shift, putting on a sick act so I'll believe she's desperate.

"Yeah, this is Maxx," I say.

"It's Monique. Remember me?"

Monique? It doesn't sound like her at all.

"Are you okay?"

"Thank goodness I got you. I don't know who else would understand. You knew him too—how he was. I'm just losing it. I can't snap back. I haven't been outside for days. I haven't been out of bed—even though I can't sleep. Can you come over to the city? If I just had somebody to talk to, something to do besides think these thoughts all the time." The words come out in a quavering stream.

"God, Monique," I say. "I'd be there in a minute, but I've got rehearsal tonight."

"Ohhhh." It's a pitiful wail. "I don't know what to do. I've been trying to write in my journal—something, anything to distract my mind. But I can't concentrate. I don't know what to do with myself. I just don't feel like I exist anymore. And he's gone forever. It's not like breaking up with somebody. He's dead . . . and I'll never get him back. Never, never, never."

"Is there somebody else you can call? Or just drag yourself out and go shopping or something?"

"I can't. My credit cards are all maxed out. How do people get through this kind of stuff?"

"Just like we're doing, I guess. After a while it must get better."

"I can't eat. I feel sick, even when I only think about food. I keep remembering his voice, and how he smiled, and his little tender ways. My ex was so hard to know, so reserved. I never knew what he was thinking. Jimmy was so warm, so alive, but now he's not . . ."

I listen, trying to think of what I could possibly say that would help her. Maybe nothing. Maybe just letting her talk. So I let her talk, making sympathetic murmurs from time to time. Finally, she kind of winds down. "Can you come over to the city tomorrow?" she says at last in a tiny, teary voice.

"Sure. Do you want to have dinner somewhere?" I tell her about an Italian place on Bleecker Street where Sandy and I used to go. The NYU students all eat there, and it's the cheapest place around.

"Seven-thirty?" she says.

"Want a ride?"

"I'll meet you there. It'll do me good to get out and walk a little bit." I don't hear anything for a minute, and I think she's about to hang up when her voice comes back. "Maxx?" she says. "Just a warning. You might not recognize me. Something bad happened."

"What?" I say, but she's gone.

I leave Hackensack at eight. Rehearsal's not till nine, but sometimes parking in the Feedback neighborhood can be a real hassle. Sure enough, 30th Street is a mess, but I manage to squeeze into a place at the end of the block.

It's hot, a summer night in the city. The asphalt is giving up the heat it stored all day, and the heat is mixing with the exhaust fumes of cars speeding down Seventh Avenue in confused overlapping lanes. People are surging along the sidewalk, laughing, joking, faces suddenly bright in the glare of shop windows.

A couple of kids with gig bags slung over their shoulders are halfway through the door when I walk up. I grab the edge of the door and follow them across the tiled floor. The elevator's waiting for us.

"Hey, hold on!" calls a voice behind me. It's Josh, catching the door just before it latches. He's wearing faded jeans and a white T-shirt that sets off his swarthy skin and dark eyes.

"So how are you doing?" Josh asks as the elevator creaks its way up. "You look great."

"Thanks," I say. "So do you." With his closely cropped hair and trim body, Josh could be any age from twenty-five to fifty.

The elevator lurches to a stop and the doors clank open. "You been here before?" I say.

"Sure." He shows me his perfect teeth. "I've worked in New York for a long time." He stretches out the word "long" like a blues singer draping a syllable over three or four notes. He pauses to shift his gig bag to a more comfortable spot on his shoulder, and we head around the corner into the long hall that leads to Feedback.

Somewhere at the end of the hall an argument is in progress. Voices reach us, one voice at least, a furious voice, rising and falling, pausing briefly, cutting off an inaudible reply with a bark like a rim shot on a snare. Josh stops, laughs, and says, "Holy shit. That guy sounds mad."

The voice pauses briefly, then launches again into a furious rant, getting louder, hoarser. I pick out a few words, like "bastard" and "son of a bitch." We venture a few steps further.

Now I can see Neil. He's sitting on the sofa outside the Feedback office, head lolling back, half-closed eyes fixed on the TV. He seems oblivious to the sounds emerging from the office door. He looks up when we get closer, smiles faintly when he sees it's me.

"What's going on?" I say, between bursts of shouting.

"It's Bart," he says. The shouting continues. I have to lean over to make out what Neil's saying. "He's arguing with somebody on the phone." Neil looks tired. He has dark circles under his eyes, at least what I can see of them through his shaggy hair.

"About what?"

"The Blues from the Heart concert, I think." He points past the soda machine to the Blues from the Heart poster taped on the wall. I notice three or four more bands have been crossed off the list of performers.

Now Bart is telling whoever it is that they'll never work on any project he has anything to do with, and if they don't believe him they don't know who the fuck they're dealing with.

"Is somebody in our room?" I raise my voice so Neil can hear me over Bart's yelling.

"I don't know."

113

I introduce Josh to Neil, who acknowledges him by pushing a few dog-eared copies of the *Voice* off the sofa to make room for us to sit. The music channel is running something about Elvis. Just now he's still the young Elvis, gyrating in a plaid sports jacket.

All of a sudden Neil sighs and pulls himself upright, shaking his hair out of his face. "I'm totally bummed out," he says. "I haven't been sleeping or anything. Jimmy was a cool guy, and his playing *made* this band."

It's the most I've ever heard him say at one time. Worn out by this uncharacteristic burst of conversation, he slumps back against the sofa.

Down the hall the elevator groans and creaks. Dom rounds the corner, makes his way down the hall, and gives me a quick kiss on the cheek. I introduce him to Josh. Josh stands up, shakes Dom's hand, and says something cordial about looking forward to working with him.

In the next room, Bart screams one final assurance that the person on the other end will never work again and slams down the receiver. There's a louder clank, as if something, maybe the phone, has fallen on the floor. A voice says "Fuck." Bart comes charging through the door and rips the Blues from the Heart poster off the wall.

CHAPTER 12

Bart's a burly guy, not tall but kind of intimidating. He's got scruffy hair, like a wiry growth of sun-browned underbrush, straggling across his scalp. Maybe he once had a baby face; now deep lines from his nose to the edges of his mouth make him look permanently disgusted.

He rolls the poster into a clumsy cylinder, grabs the ends, and twists. Then he folds it into kind of a pretzel and jams it into the trashcan. For good measure, he kicks the trashcan. He turns and heads back into the office. In a few seconds we hear a door slam.

Josh nods, almost to himself. "I heard there were some problems with that concert," he says.

"People backing out?" He nods again. "Do you know why?"

"There's rumors, but—" He shrugs.

I don't press it. Josh is one of those guys who has survived in music by never getting on anybody's bad side.

"Bart's a bastard," Dom says. "He'd sell his grandmother if he thought he could get the price he wanted. Everybody knows he was going to put most of that money in his own pocket."

"Who told you that?" I say.

"Jimmy. He knew Bart pretty well."

"Last time I heard you talk about the concert, you thought it was a great idea and you thought Bart was a great guy."

"I did—but then Jimmy wised me up."

We watch Elvis gyrate until the clanking of the elevator announces that someone else has arrived. "Well, well, well," Dom says looking down the hall. "Here comes Mr. Sunshine." Michael strolls toward us, looking his usual grouchy self.

"I better make sure they know we're here," I say. I pull myself up off the sofa and head through the door into the office.

Tony's on duty at the desk again, wearing his leather vest and looking hairier than ever. He gives me the toothy smile and says, "Hey! Maxx Maxwell." He leans forward. "How've you been?"

"Hanging in there. How about our room?"

"Coming right up." He points at the tech guy, a shaggy-haired kid with an earring in his nose, then jerks his thumb down the hall. "Get moving," he says. "Maxx Maxwell needs her room." He leans toward me again. "We aim to please," he says. "Anything you need, just let me know and I'll—"

But he's interrupted by a guy who's just emerged from the corridor that leads to the studios, a stocky guy who's frowning so hard I'm wondering if he'll ever get his forehead back to normal once he calms down. While I'm wondering this, I realize he's the guy who was backing Monique up at the restaurant.

What with the frown and the fact that he's kind of bristling with energy, I'm expecting another Bart-like scene. But when he opens his mouth, the voice that comes out is surprisingly calm, with just a little tremor in it to show he's pissed off. "I can't play jazz with some kind of a rave-fest going on next door," he says. "Tell those kids in F to quiet down or I'm going to find another place to rehearse. Permanently."

"What's goin' on?" Tony says.

"Whatever they're doing in F—I wouldn't call it music—is blasting through the wall," he says, his voice rising, but only slightly. "I can't concentrate."

"They pay just like you do, man," Tony says. "And loud is kinda the ethos of the music, know what I mean?"

"No," the guy says. A muscle in his jaw twitches, and he stares at Tony till Tony starts to squirm. Finally the guy turns and heads back down the corridor.

"Creepy bastard," Tony says. "I like it better when people yell."

The kid with the earring in his nose hauls open the door of Studio G, releasing a surge of amplified guitar chords that sound like a hive of angry bees. The bees halt in mid-buzz. I hear the kid say, "Time's up." A few minutes later, four guys troop out with gig bags over their shoulders.

I step around the corner, wave at the band, and we file into Studio G. Now the room is reverberating with a metallic thudding, apparently coming from the studio right next to us. It's probably the same sound the grouchy jazz guy was hearing, and I can see why he was bugged. It's loud as hell, and just enough out of sync with whatever else is going on in there to make the whole thing sound like some crazy fusion experiment.

Nonetheless, Josh matter-of-factly gets to work tuning his guitar. Nobody else looks very happy, though. I feel my spirits start to sag.

Neil is sitting behind the keyboard with his head drooping so low all I can see is a mop of hair. He's still wearing his shoes, and he's not even going through his usual ritual of warming up with Bach.

Dom is staring in the direction of the noise and rubbing his forehead like he's in pain.

Michael's got his bass around his neck, and he's gloomily inspecting the bass amp. He notices me watching him and says, "Why do we use this place anyway? Can't we find a studio that isn't overrun with noisy kids?"

In my mind, I'm on the phone again, pleading with every guitar player I know, while one by one my other band members quit.

I take a deep breath. "It's usually okay here," I say. "Once we start playing, you won't notice it." Michael plucks a few strings, frowns, and twists a knob on the amp. Dom gives the snare a few unhappy taps. I wait a few more minutes then say, "Ready to go?" Neil is still sitting motionless.

Josh nods. He's the only one smiling.

Neil pokes a few keys and looks up. One eye peeks through his unruly hair. "I can't hear myself," he says.

"Turn yourself up," I say. "We'll just have to play loud enough to drown them out." He kicks his shoes off and tosses them into the corner. A hopeful sign. I look back at Dom.

"I guess I'm set," he says, and waves a stick in the air. The other hand continues to rub his forehead.

" 'Sweet Home Chicago,' " I say. "Let's go." Josh kicks it off with a sweet, teasing lick, two strings chiming together, a long swoop, and a flourish.

" 'Hey, baby, do you wanna go?' " I sing, and Josh's guitar answers me. Dom thumps along with a steady shuffle; Michael's bass weaves in and out. After the second verse, I nod at Neil to take a solo. He does a honky-tonk thing, pairs of notes in staccato bursts. He's hanging over the high end of the keyboard, nothing visible but hair, with fingers poking the keys so fast they're almost a blur.

Josh solos, and I sing the last verse and the chorus about "sweet home Chicago." Dom winds it up with a round of every drum in front of him and a satisfying crash on the biggest cymbal.

Josh is laughing when we finish. "Man, my ears are ringing. I feel like I'm back in my parents' garage, only there's no neighbors to call the cops." He looks over at Dom. "Nice drumming, man." The expression on Dom's face becomes a little more cheerful. "You guys sound good," Josh says. "Real good."

"So do you," Michael volunteers. His thin lips form themselves into a shape as close to a smile as they ever get.

"Cool soloing." This comes from Neil.

I feel like pinching myself. Maybe this will work out after all.

Two hours pass so quickly that I don't even have time to call "Swing It on Home." We're mid-way through "She's Into Something" when the tech guy sticks his head in the door and mouths the words "Time's up."

Josh takes it out with a solo that winds up on the highest notes on the highest strings, so many and so quick that his fingers blur.

"Man, that was fun," he says with a laugh as Dom's last cymbal crash dies away. He tugs his strap over his head and rests the guitar against his amp. The white T-shirt is clinging to his back now, damp with sweat. "It's been too long since I played the blues."

We can hear the sounds from the neighboring studio again now that we've stopped, a chugging guitar like an amplified cello and a vocal like a dog barking. But nobody's complaining anymore.

Michael is placidly arranging his cable and his tuner in his gear bag. Neil is putting his shoes back on. Dom has climbed out from behind the drums and is wiping his face and hands with a towel.

And Josh was totally into it. I'll wait for the guys to leave and ask him if he wants to join up for real.

The three of them get their stuff stowed and drift toward the door while Josh is still winding up his cables. He tucks the cables away, slides his guitar into his gig bag, and tugs the zipper up. "Cool band," he says with a grin. "No shit. That drummer really knows what he's doing."

"Say, here's a thought," I say, mentally taking a deep breath. "Would you like to join permanently? Not just be a sub?"

He raises one brow. A puff of air escapes his lips, a little sigh.

His eyes focus on something that isn't me. "You mostly play gigs on weekend nights?" he says. I nod. "Places like the Hot Spot?" I nod again. There's a bigger sigh. "I have to make more money," he says. "I'm already supporting an ex-wife and a kid, and Beth's about to move out. I'm gonna have to come up with the whole rent starting next month." Now he looks at me. "Friday and Saturday are big nights for club dates. I can make two or three hundred bucks at a pop."

"That's what we're aiming for," I say. "Weddings, parties, conventions. I know we can do it. We're just starting out—and with you, there's no limit to the great gigs we could get."

"Man, I'd love to. I'd love to play blues every night. But I can't afford to play in bars if it means turning something else down."

"Please," I say. I know I sound piteous, but I can't help it. "We really need you. And besides, it's the blues. You're a blues guy. And we will make money, lots of money. Soon."

"These women are milking me dry. I just can't do it." He looks like he wishes he could.

"You're sure?"

He nods, then looks at his watch. "Hey! I've gotta meet somebody. What do I owe you for the room?"

"I wasn't going to ask you for money," I say. "You're doing us a favor."

"I worked last night," he says with a grin. "A union gig." He digs down into his jeans and comes up with a small sheaf of folded bills. "Here." He tucks a couple of them into my hand. I stick them in my pocket without looking at them.

He hoists his gig bag onto his shoulder. "I've gotta run. See you Saturday night." And he's out the door, probably off to meet whoever he's about to replace Beth with. No wonder she's leaving. What is it with these guitar players anyway?

I slide out the bills Josh gave me. Two tens, more than his

share. I lower myself onto the big Fender blues amp. What to do next? Go home and start calling guitar players again, I guess.

Out by the desk, a bunch of guys are milling around, pulling out wallets. Dom is standing off to the side. Michael and Neil are nowhere in sight.

"Here's their money." Dom hands me some folded bills. "Michael had to head home to bed, and Neil couldn't wait to get back to his weed. So—" Dom's got a weird look on his face, hopeful but worried. "You asked him?"

"Josh, you mean?"

"Yeah."

"I did."

"What'd he say?"

"He can't afford to use his weekends playing bar gigs. Too many women are after him for money."

"So that's it?"

"Dom, he's the first guy we tried. I'll get somebody."

"What should I tell Kenny White?"

"Tell him you're in a great band, and you don't need another full-time gig."

"Josh Bergman isn't the only guy who'd like to make some money for a change."

"We'll make money," I say.

"Will there be a guitar player Saturday night?"

"Of course. Josh is going to do it. He can't tie up all his weekends because if something that pays better comes along he wants to be able to take it."

"But I can't do that?"

"Dom, you're a founding member of the band. I thought you believed in this, and in me."

"OK, Maxxie." He leans forward and pecks me on the cheek. "You're better looking than Kenny White, so . . . I'll try to string him along for a couple more days." He tries to smile.

"See you Saturday night?" He pats me on the shoulder and takes off.

I step up to the counter. Tony gives me the toothy grin. "Have a good rehearsal?" he says.

I really want to pay up and get home to a cold beer, but he's determined to chat. I listen with what I know is a grouchy expression on my face, finally pull myself away just in time to collide with a gorgeous guy: dark blond hair, tanned olive skin, green eyes. He looks almost exactly like Sandy.

"Are you Maxx?" he says.

I smile in spite of myself, and a flirty voice I hardly recognize as my own says, "Yes. Yes, I am. Why?"

"I'm looking for you." He reaches for my hand, and I happily let him take it. "I'm Ray Collins."

"Hi," I say stupidly, noticing how cool his hair is, long enough to almost skim his shoulders, not so long that he looks like a hippie throwback. I feel myself blush.

"I ran into Josh Bergman just now," he says. "According to him, you need a guitar player."

"I do."

"That's me."

"Blues?" This is a disaster, says a little voice in my head. You can't let this fantastic guy in your band. You wouldn't survive one rehearsal without falling in love with him.

"Of course." He smiles and the corners of his eyes crinkle in a heart-melting way.

"We're not making a lot of money yet."

"I love the blues," he says.

"We practice here every Thursday," I say, like an alien force has taken control of my tongue. "Nine p.m."

"Why don't I show up next week?"

"Uh, yeah. That would be good." My face feels like it's on fire.

"Then if things work out . . . Josh says you guys are gigging all the time. That's just what I'm looking for." He shakes my hand again and saunters off toward the corridor that leads to the studios.

Tony is looking at me with the woebegone expression of a guy who knows chicks will never swoon over him.

"What do you think?" I say. "Have you ever heard him play?"

"Amazing chops," Tony says with a sad smile. "I wish I could play like him."

I head for the elevator, feeling a little dizzy, my head still filled with the vision of that hair and that skin and those eyes. It's for the sake of the band, I tell myself. I can't turn down a guitar player who could be our salvation because I'm afraid I'll fall in love with him. Besides, I'll be all business, just like I was with Jimmy. Everything will be fine. I'll call Josh in the morning and thank him for the referral. This could be the biggest stroke of luck I've had in ages.

I push the button, listen to the squeals and moans as the ancient cables drag the elevator up the shaft to the sixth floor. It shudders to a stop, the doors peel open, and I step in.

From around the corner I hear a voice call, "Hold that." I fling my arm against the rubber bumper on the door nearest me. I hear the sound of hurrying feet. The voice repeats, "Hold that." The feet come closer.

And in steps the guy Jimmy was arguing with the Thursday night before he died. The tall guy.

He glances at me briefly and pushes the button for the bottom floor. I stand there in a daze as the elevator gently sways its way to the ground. Yes, it's definitely him. Tall. And thin. Dark. Good-looking in a way, but holding himself kind of awkwardly, like he's not sure what to do with his body.

"I'm Maxx Maxwell," I say, sticking out my hand. "I think I've seen you around." He looks me up and down but doesn't take my hand. "What's your name?"

"You won't remember it if I tell you, so what's the point?" he says. Like I noticed before, he's got a hint of a southern accent.

"Are you with a band that practices here?"

"I'm not in a band," he says, staring at a spot on the wall somewhere near my right shoulder.

By this time we've reached the ground floor. The doors wheeze open and he steps out, walking like he's in a hurry. I take a few steps after him, call "Wait" as he pushes his way through the lobby door. He doesn't wait, though. By the time I reach the sidewalk, he's threading his way among the couples still loitering in front of Rave and heading toward Eighth Avenue.

"Wait," I call again, and plunge into the mob to follow him. A few people look at me curiously as I elbow my way past them.

Now the tall guy is running, darting around anybody that gets in his way. I'm running, too. The air is so humid it's almost like swimming; my panting breaths are like big gulps of warm water instead of air, laced with a hint of exhaust fumes.

Thirtieth Street is as crowded as it was three hours ago. Guys in baggy pants jostle each other, watch the limber girls in midriff-baring tops prancing along in pairs.

"Will you wait for me?" I yell. "I've got to talk to you." We're almost at the corner. He'll have to stop. The light is red and traffic is whizzing past, beeping cabs, delivery vans, a guy on a motorcycle.

I reach him before the light changes, and before I realize what I'm doing, I grab his arm. He's wearing a T-shirt, so what I've grabbed is bare flesh and I'm hanging onto it with both hands, my bag slung over my shoulder.

"What the hell are you doing?" He pulls away from me, but I don't loosen my grip. People are edging away from us, but not so far away that they don't have a ringside seat for whatever's

124

going to happen next.

"Who are you?" I say desperately. "What did you have to do with Jimmy Nashville?"

"It's hard to explain," he says. "Come to the Purple Snail next Monday night. Maybe you'll find out then."

A few minutes later I'm talking to Tony again.

"A guy left here right after I did," I say. "Tall, thin, maybe in his thirties. Dark hair, not too long. He's the guy I've been looking for, the guy Jimmy was talking to. I just chased him down the street, all the way to Eighth, but he wouldn't tell me his name or anything. He just said I should come to the Purple Snail next Monday."

"Oh, that crazy guy," Tony says with a laugh. "He's some kind of a singer. The studio hosts these open-mike nights down there. He came by to put his name on the list."

"What *is* his name?"

"I don't know."

"Where's the list?"

"Over there." Tony points at a sheet of paper tacked to a bulletin board by the restroom door.

I head toward the bulletin board, almost colliding with a guy emerging from the restroom in a cloud of marijuana smoke. I squint at the list. The last name on it isn't really a name, at least not a legible one. It's just a scrawl that might be a couple of initials.

"The guy's got awful handwriting," I say. "You don't know anything about him at all?"

"Nothin'." Tony shakes his head. "But here." He grabs a flyer from a pile neatly arranged on the corner of the desk, holds it out to me, and bows as I take it from his hand.

Out by the elevator again I scan the flyer. "Open Mike Night—Singers Welcome," it says. "Purple Snail—6th Street and Avenue B—Monday Nights—8:00 p.m. till midnight," and there's a line drawing of a generic sensitive guy emoting into a microphone with a boxy acoustic guitar hanging around his neck.

My mind runs back to the day after Jimmy died when I called in sick. What did I tell Aldo then? That I had a stomach virus? I guess I'll be having a relapse.

CHAPTER 13

Where on earth is Monique?

I made it down to the Village in time to spend half an hour looking for a place to park and still get to the restaurant by seven-thirty. Now I'm sitting in a brightly lit room with lots of mirrors that make it seem like it's actually big enough for all the tables crammed into it. Most of the tables have people sitting at them, people in skinny black T-shirts and black jeans, people drinking red wine and all talking at once.

A waitress, dressed like the customers in slim black pants and a form-fitting black T-shirt, asks me if I want something from the bar. I order a shot of Jack Daniel's and a Bud, feeling vaguely awkward as all around me people chatter amiably, two, three, four to a table. I try not to think about the times I used to come here with Sandy. Time passes.

The last thing Monique said on the phone was that something bad happened and I might not recognize her. What was that all about? I glance toward the door, where a tall guy with a shaggy beard that makes him look like he just stepped out of a time machine is standing with his arm around the shoulders of a tall thin woman dressed in a gauze caftan. She looks like she came out of a time machine, too. Lurking behind them is a slender guy with a mournful face and hair so short and pale he almost looks bald.

He steps out from behind the time-machine couple and lets his gaze wander around the room. When he sees me, his face brightens. Except he's not a he, despite the muscular shoulders and the well-toned body. He's Monique.

"My hair looks like shit, doesn't it?" she says, as she slides into the seat across from me, jostling the elbow of a guy at the next table, who spills some of his wine and gives her an annoyed look.

Her hair is about an inch long all over, maybe not even that. And it's a much different color than it used to be. Actually it's not really any color at all.

"What happened?"

"I thought if I changed my hair it would help me cheer up," she says. "I was going to make it blond—like yours. But the new color reacted with what was already on there and it turned kind of purple. I put more bleach on it and it started breaking off. So I had to cut it."

The waitress comes back. I tell her I'm fine for now, and Monique orders a double scotch on the rocks. After the waitress leaves, she says, "I shouldn't be drinking anything really . . ." She looks down at the table.

"You're not pregnant!"

"No." She shakes her head mournfully. "I wish I was. Then there'd be something left of him. It's just that I went to the doctor and got some sleeping pills, and you're not supposed to drink if you're taking them. They help, I guess, but when I'm awake I still can't help thinking about what happened and what I said before he—" She stops, like she's startled at her own words. "Oh, Maxx, if only . . ." The words become fainter and fainter until she stops.

"Before he what?"

"Nothing. Nothing."

"You were with him when it happened?"

"No, no," she says. "No, of course not." She blinks like she's not sure where she is or who I am, glances around the room and a sick look comes over her face. "All these mirrors . . . I feel so self-conscious with my hair like this, and I've got to show up at Lemon's Sunday night. Nobody will want to hear me sing."

"How about a wig?"

She shakes her head mournfully. "That would look so fake."

"Is there some way you could fix the color?"

"If I do anything else to it, I think it will all fall out."

"Don't use anything with peroxide. Get some henna. It's very gentle. Believe me, I know. I could write a book about hair disasters."

The expression on her face says she's tuned out of the conversation, but the waitress arrives with her double scotch and a request for our dinner orders. Monique finishes the scotch in two gulps while I'm ordering spaghetti Bolognese. She orders a salad and another double scotch.

"Bring the drink right away," she says. "Don't wait to bring it with the food." She looks toward the bar and squeezes her empty glass till I picture myself prying shards out of her hand one finger at a time.

Find a cheerful topic, says the voice in my head. "I love those jazz standards you do," I say. "How'd you get into in that style?"

"My ex," she says with another sigh. "Jazz was his thing, and Charlie Christian was his idol. He hated the blues, hated rock, hated rock and roll, hated everything that's fun. He wanted me to get into jazz, so I did. I would have done anything for him, if you want to know the truth. I really wanted to get married, have a kid. He seemed like a good catch, as they say. Didn't drink or do drugs. Steady income, at least for a musician."

"How'd you meet him?"

"Tae Kwon Do class." She laughs. "Weird, huh? But it's great for your body." I notice again how muscular her shoulders are. "It's not something I'd have thought a guy like my ex would be into. Didn't seem to go with his personality." She pauses. "Or, you know, maybe it did, in an odd way."

"How?" The scotch arrives. She gulps down half and, before the waitress has taken two steps, calls her back to order another drink. I'm still working on my Bud.

"Oh, who wants to talk about him?" Her words are a little slurred. "I wanted to get married. He didn't. End of story." She gulps the rest of the scotch. "And then I met Jimmy . . ." Her voice trails off and her gaze wanders back toward the bar.

"My last boyfriend was a guitar player," I say. "They're . . . definitely appealing."

"What happened? I always wondered why you weren't with a guy. With your looks, you could pick and choose."

I catch a glimpse of myself in the mirror. I see a shapely blond chick with a bright, lipsticky smile. She's wearing a red mini dress and red sandals with really high heels. "So could my ex-boyfriend," I say. "My next boyfriend is going to be fat, ugly and old." And you better find him soon, says a voice in my head, before you're rubbing elbows with Ray Collins two or three nights a week.

Monique laughs—sort of. "Being around you is good for me," she says. "You don't let stuff get you down." A new glass of scotch arrives for Monique, and she takes a quick swallow. I order another Bud. "I don't have many women friends," Monique says. The words are a little slurred. "Oh, Maxx. Jimmy was just my whole life." And she's off again.

Thankfully, the food arrives.

"Let's check out what's going on at a few clubs," I say after I've finished eating and Monique seems to be done picking at her salad. "After all, this is Bleecker Street, and it's Friday night."

"Maybe I will try the henna," she says. "I liked it when I was a redhead."

★ ★ ★ ★ ★

We spill out of Terra Blues at about one o'clock.

"Want a ride?" I say.

"That's okay," she says, "I can get home okay by myself."

"Where do you live?"

"Jimmy's building."

"What?"

"I live in Jimmy's building."

"You do? Since when?"

"July. A unit opened up, and I grabbed it. He didn't want us to actually live together because of his practicing and all, so this was perfect." She looks around. "If I can just remember where I came up out of the subway . . ."

"Monique, it's the middle of the night. It'll take you forever to get the train. Not to mention that it'll be dangerous."

"I can take care of myself."

She's veering toward a lamppost as she says this. I grab her arm and haul her back. For a minute I almost think she's going to wrestle with me, and I'm pretty sure I'd lose.

"Come on," I say. "I've got to drive uptown anyway to get to the bridge."

"I'm really okay," she mumbles, sounding like she's not okay at all. I toss my arm around her shoulder and manage to steer her to my car without having her collapse. Since she's a couple of inches taller than I am, she's hard to steer.

Thankful for once that the passenger-side door doesn't lock, I keep a grip on her while I swing it open. I nudge her in and let her crumple onto the seat. I fight with the lock on the driver's side for a few minutes, but I can't get it to work. I go back around to the other side and wrestle Monique into the back seat, wishing I had worn any shoes but these spike-heeled, back-less sandals. When I get Monique arranged as best I can, I slide across the front seat and settle in behind the wheel.

As I turn the key in the ignition, "Layla" comes blasting out of the radio. It lasts as long as it takes to poke along Houston over to the West Side Highway. As soon as the final chords die away, a mellow Led Zeppelin thing starts, acoustic guitar and Robert Plant sounding plaintive, quiet enough that I can hear Monique's low snores from the back seat.

Ten minutes later I take the turnoff and swing across the Upper West Side. I cut over to the edge of the park, pull a U-turn on Central Park West, and coast into a place by a hydrant in front of what used to be Jimmy's building.

I turn around and lean into the back seat. Monique is stretched out like a little kid, one chubby cheek resting on the textured vinyl of the upholstery, a tiny dribble of saliva at the corner of her mouth.

"Monique? You're home. Can you wake up?" No answer. I lean closer. She's definitely breathing. I can hear the soft intake and exhalation of breath. I touch her shoulder and say "Monique" again.

"Umph." She twitches.

"Monique, you're home. Can you move?" I give her a gentle shake. She opens her eyes and says something unintelligible.

I slide across the seat, get out of the car, and open the back door. Slowly, I pull her upright, ease her feet onto the sidewalk, guide her into a standing position.

Keys, I suddenly think. I've got to dig out her keys so we can get in the downstairs door. I let her droop back onto the seat, grab her purse, and dig through it. Keys in hand, I pull her upright again. She swoons against me, and we make our way to the front of the building.

I have to try almost all the keys on her key chain before the lock clicks and the door springs open. The key that does the trick is a shiny one that looks brand new. That makes sense, I think, since she just moved in.

"What floor do you live on?" I ask her as we wait for the elevator. She's kind of leaning against me.

"Umm?"

"What floor do you live on?"

"Nine."

"That's Jimmy's floor."

"No, no. You're right. Seven. I'm on seven."

We ride up in silence, Monique looking a little green in the fluorescent glare of the elevator. At the seventh floor, I guide her over the elevator's threshold.

"Which way?"

She looks around like she's surprised to discover where she is. "We're home?" she says.

"Home. Which direction is your place?" She takes a few hesitant steps to the right. The next thing I know, we're standing in front of what would be Jimmy's apartment if this was his floor. "Are you sure this is you?" I say. "Come on. Try to think."

"Seventy-one," she says at last. "I live in apartment 71."

I maneuver her along the hall. When we come to 71, I do the key routine again, trying another shiny one that doesn't work and then a shiny one that does. Her apartment is smaller than Jimmy's, just a studio. A hallway leads past a tiny kitchen, opens out into one square room with one window in the far wall. Doors in the near wall must be a bathroom and a closet.

Cardboard boxes crowd the edges of the floor. The new-looking sofa, smallish and covered in an elegant off-white textured fabric, probably turns into a bed. Otherwise, there's not much furniture—just a card table and a couple of folding chairs.

I lead her over to the sofa and let her slump down onto it. I'll call her in the morning to check on her. On the way out, I switch off the light.

★ ★ ★ ★ ★

Julio's music seems to start in the middle of the night, or at least long before he usually gets himself moving. I pull myself off the pillow and gaze groggily at the clock on my dresser. It's actually a little after eight, but the room is as dark as if the sun was barely up. I flop onto my back. Through my windows I can see heavy blue-gray clouds like a thunderstorm is brewing.

Tonight's the gig at the Hot Spot, and I probably won't get to bed till three. I might as well try to store up a little extra sleep while I have the chance—and maybe the threat of rain will keep the motorcycle guy indoors and quiet. I roll over, bury my head in the pillow, and somehow before I'm even really asleep I'm back in Atlantic City.

The place is hard to find again. That first night I was running, half crazy, zigzagging, anything just to keep moving, not caring if the neighborhood was dangerous, even hoping that it was. Now I'm in a cab, telling the driver, a patient, turbaned Sikh, to slow down, let me look out this side, look out the other side, maybe left at the next corner . . .

It's that street of shabby wood-frame flats, some derelict, and the bar's on the corner, door open like it was that night, the sound of the bass almost making the cab quiver.

"Here," I say. "This is the place."

"Are you sure?" His accent gives the words a soothing cadence. His dark face looks worried as I hand over the fare.

But it's not Doretta's band. The place is jammed with guys that look like they do construction work during the week, and they're grooving out to a Led Zeppelin tune.

"Where's the band that was in here the other night?" I ask the bartender.

"They ain't comin' back," he says. "Nobody wants to hear blues."

"I do. How can I find them again?"

"Owner might have a phone number, but he's not here now."

I wake up again when an extra loud burst of music surges through the wall, horns building to a frantic climax and about twenty singers shouting "Hola!" in overlapping waves. A glance at the clock tells me it's eleven.

I climb out of bed and wander over to the window. There's still no sign of the sun, but the sky is a little brighter, like a dirty lampshade with a light bulb shining through it. From somewhere off to the west comes a hint of thunder, a low rumble like somebody dragging furniture across the floor in the apartment upstairs.

As I wait for the water to boil for my coffee, I stare at the pile of songs I pulled out of Jimmy's wastebasket. "Whiskey for Breakfast" is on top. I read through it, idly wondering why whoever wrote it didn't put in a line about making his own coffee. That's another thing guys like you to do for them. But maybe he couldn't think of a rhyme for "coffee."

I should call Boris to make sure nobody's tried to cancel the gig again, but it's too early to reach him. Then there's Monique. I should check to make sure she's okay after last night. My heart kind of sinks at the thought. I'll probably end up listening to half an hour of complaints about how depressed she is.

But after I stir up a cup of coffee, I head out to the big chair, grit my teeth, and punch in Monique's number, sighing as I anticipate the likely form the conversation will take. On the other end, the phone rings. It rings again. And again. No answer—except her phone machine.

CHAPTER 14

I start to get worried. Monique really shouldn't have been drinking if she had those sleeping pills at home. On the other hand, when I left her she was already asleep, or passed out or something, so how could she have taken any?

I get out the Comet, rubber gloves, a sponge and a bucket, and head for the bathroom, where I scour the sink, the shower and the floor. After I'm done in there, I clean the kitchen, wash some underwear, and take the rugs down to the parking lot to shake them. When I get back up to my apartment, I put the rugs back where they belong and try Monique's number again. This time somebody answers on the first ring.

"Hello? Monique?" I say.

"Maxx? I recognized your voice. What's up?" She sounds like her old self, like the cheerful person who came to meet Jimmy at Feedback that Thursday night before he died.

"I was kind of worried," I say. "You were really out of it last night and I called before and nobody answered. You didn't take any of those sleeping pills, did you, after all that scotch?"

"I didn't need them." She laughs, cheerfully enough but with a kind of hysterical edge. "I slept right through till about eight this morning. I feel better than I have in days. I was at the store looking for some henna to put on my hair. And while I was out, I went to a place that sells wigs—those real cheap ones that aren't made out of human hair, and I tried some on, and I almost bought one, but then I thought I probably wouldn't really wear it." She stops for a quick breath. "It was blond, with millions of little curls, sort of cascading down almost to your shoulders, and—" She stops again, almost panting.

"You don't have a hangover?" I say, thinking she sounds *too* cheerful, almost manic.

"A little, but compared to how it felt when I wasn't sleeping, this is great. I think maybe I'll go back and get that wig, or maybe I'll just go shopping. It feels so good to want to do things again, and it's a beautiful day. Have you been outside?"

But it looks like it's about to rain, I'm thinking to myself.

"And oh," she continues, "did you see that Etta James is singing in Central Park tomorrow? One of those SummerStage things. Totally free. All you have to do is stand in line for tickets. Should we go? Do you have to work?"

"No. I'm off Sundays. Let's do it." Etta James is one of my favorites. And besides, maybe Monique needs somebody to see her through this manic phase. She's as up now as she was down before.

"Meet me at the Beethoven statue," she says. "By the old band shell. One o'clock. The concert doesn't start till two, but the earlier you show up the better seats you can get."

I kill the rest of the afternoon listening to Big Mama Thornton and Bessie Smith, warming up for the gig by singing along with the songs I especially like. At five o'clock I make a tuna sandwich and drink a can of Bud. At five-thirty, I turn the stereo off and climb in the shower. After my shower, I blow my hair dry, put on some makeup, and open my closet.

It's too hot for suede pants. Besides it might rain, and I don't want to wreck them. I settle on jeans, the faded pair that fits the best, and a white tank top with an ad for a sparerib joint on the front. I pull on my cowboy boots and rummage in my jewelry box for my big silver and turquoise earrings.

I'm about to head out the door when the phone rings. My stomach gives a little flip because my first thought is that somebody in the band can't make the gig.

"Maxx?" says an urgent male voice.

"Yeah?"

"It's Dom."

"What's up?"

"The van won't start. The engine won't turn over, and there's no time to mess with it. I'm lucky I caught you. Can you swing by and get me?"

"Do you think we can fit all the drums in my car?"

"We'll have to," he says. "What else can we do?"

I hurry down to the parking lot. Dom lives in Clifton, about fifteen minutes west of Hackensack. It'll take five minutes, maybe longer to load the drums, and forty-five minutes to get into the city.

"Okay, let's get busy," I say, jumping out of the car.

Dom rents a little house on a street of little houses, all the yards tidy and reasonably green except for his. His scorched, overgrown grass looks like shredded wheat. He's standing on the sidewalk by his driveway, drums in their black nylon cases piled on the dead grass next to him. He's got another one of his Hawaiian shirts tugged down over his comfortable tummy and tucked into a pair of jeans. The jeans are held in place by a belt with a broad silver buckle. He's already sweating.

We plop the bass drum into the trunk, only to discover the trunk won't close on it. The satchel of hardware is as long as a small human and about as heavy. My car's not wide enough to fit it in the trunk or the back seat, so we wrestle it into the passenger side. I arrange the smaller drums and the cymbals in the trunk, and Dom slides the bass drum in the back seat and climbs in after it.

It's seven-thirty. We're going to have to hustle if we don't want to be setting up long after Boris expects us to start playing. And Michael is going to be grumpy all night if we get off to a bad start.

I'm backing out of the driveway when Dom's front door opens, and a woman steps out on the porch. She's got pale blond hair cut off short and fluffed out around her tiny face. Everything else about her is tiny, too. She's so short and slight she almost looks like a little kid. Just now, though, she looks like a very grouchy little kid.

She hurries down the steps and over to the car, peering into the windows until she locates Dom.

"So you're going anyway?" she says with a dark frown, ignoring me.

"I can't cut out on a gig," he says. "And we've got to leave right now. We'll barely have time to set up as it is."

"When will you be back?"

"I don't know. One, two."

"That's awfully late. You know I don't like being here alone at night." Her voice is kind of piercing.

"Jesus, Dora. Lay off. You know this is what I do," Dom says. "Go ahead and back out now, Maxx."

"I'm still talking to him," Dora says.

"Yeah, well I'm not answerin'. Drive, Maxx."

We leave her frowning on the sidewalk. As I shift into drive and start up the street, she's yelling something, but we can't hear what it is.

"Should I take the tunnel?"

"Yeah. I don't know what's eatin' her," Dom says as I head toward Route 46. "She's not usually like this. It started when she came to one of our gigs. Back when we still had Stan."

Dom is silent as I cruise past a spacious park where a soccer game is in progress. "Maybe she doesn't like me bein' in a band with a good-lookin' woman." He gives me a sidelong glance. "Kenny White is a guy—and he's ugly as hell besides."

"It's about time," Michael says as I open the car door and climb out. He's standing on the sidewalk in front of the Hot Spot when I pull around the corner from Bleecker. A couple of punk kids from the suburbs are inspecting the collage of band flyers in the window of the bar next door.

The air is hot and heavy and still, totally still. A rumble of thunder reminds me that it's still threatening to rain.

"Dom's van is messed up," I say. "I had to bring him. Is Josh here yet?" Michael nods. "Let's get these drums out of here so I can look for a parking space."

By the time I get rid of the car, Dom's got the drum kit put together, and he's sitting at the bar having a beer. Michael and Neil have staked out a table near the stage. I catch a glimpse of Josh, glass in hand, talking to one of the barmaids. He's all in denim tonight, jeans and a work shirt with the sleeves cut out. There's a pretty good crowd. Most of the tables are full, and people are two or three deep at the bar.

"Is the sound guy here?" I shout at Dom over the taped music. He nods. "Were you able to check the levels?" He nods again. "The mike, too?"

"Everything's set," he says.

It's nine o'clock. I go in the rest room and rub some wet paper towels over my arms and neck. When I come back out, Dom's settled in behind the drum kit, and the lights reflecting off his shaved head show a light stubble. Neil's got his shoes off, Michael is checking his tuning one last time, and Josh is coaxing sweet little exploratory sounds out of his guitar. I pass the copies of the set list around.

I step up to the mike and tell the sound guy to kill the tape,

glance around at the band and say, " 'Sweet Home Chicago.' "
Dom nods and says, "Ready to go." I nod at Josh, and he plays
the opening lick.

No matter how many times you do this, you still wonder if
anything is going to come out when you open your mouth. I
lean toward the mike and take a deep breath.

" 'Hey,' " I sing, " 'baby do you want to go?' " My voice
bounces back at me from the monitors, so I guess I lucked out
again. I repeat the line. Josh sketches out an echo to my voice,
and I come back in again.

I signal the band for stop time and Dom gives me a rim shot
on the snare. I scan the house. Nobody's leaving, and a lot of
faces are turned our way, even from way back at the bar. I catch
Josh's eye and nod at him to take a solo. He nods back and
bends over his fret board with his version of the secret guitar-
player smile. His fingers barely move but notes pour out of his
amp in a sweet breathless rush, each one perfect and clear for
an instant then edged out of the way by the next one.

Neil is next, all hair and fingers, notes chiming together,
bright as the spots of light dancing off the equipment.

Halfway through the set, I realize I'm having fun. Josh looks
like he'd be happy to play all night, and Neil and Dom and Michael are nodding and smiling too. The band sounds as tight as
it's ever been. Boris is lurking near the front door. I can't tell
whether he's digging us or not, but he's paying attention.

We wind up the set with "Swing It on Home" and take a
break. A couple of guys sitting at a table right up near the stage
watch me as I stick the mike back on the stand and make my
way to the bar, where I pick up a free Bud. Josh pushes his way
up next to me, the sweat on his swarthy skin making him glow.

"You sound good tonight," he says. "I like the way you cut
loose on 'Sweet Little Angel.' " The bartender gives him an
inquiring look, and he asks for a Coke. I talk to him gratefully,

trying not to make eye contact with the guy checking me out from a couple of bar stools away.

When another one of the barmaids claims Josh's attention, I head for the rest room where I rub some more wet paper towels on my neck.

When I come out, I climb back up on the stage and scan the house again. Sitting at the bar, so conspicuous that he must have just come in or I would have noticed him sooner, is Stan. He's a head taller than everyone around him, his face, with its dark eyes and heavy brows, a pale blur against the cloud of his luxuriant hair, a white tank top stretched over his lanky torso. He senses me looking at him and raises his glass of beer in a cheerful toast, sloshing about a third of it into his lap. Two women standing near him move away in alarm.

When the set ends, Stan is standing at the edge of the stage waiting for me.

"Good, good, real good," he says. "So that's the new guy?" His gaze follows Josh as he heads back to the bar. "He's good," Stan says. "Good tone. I like what he does."

"Yeah, he's great," I say.

"I think I've got a better idea what you want now, Maxx. I've been listening to more blues, like you said to do. Suppose I sit in tonight for a few tunes? You've got another set, right?"

"The guitar situation is all taken care of," I say.

"You're sure?"

"Stan," I say. "Please don't do this to yourself. The more times you make me turn you down, the more painful it's going to be for you. Your style is great, but it's not what I'm looking for."

His shoulders sag, and his head droops. All I see is hair. "I sound different now," he says from somewhere beneath the hair.

"But you've got the Blue Dudes, right?" He nods, or at least his hair quivers. I can't see his face. "Don't you usually gig with

142

them on Saturday nights?" His hair quivers again. "You can't be in two bands at once."

He glances up, and for the first time since I've known him, he looks angry. Without saying anything, he turns and walks away.

Forty-five minutes later, we've wrapped up the last set. Boris is handing me a wad of bills and asking me when we want to play again. I join the band at the bar and sort out the money, almost fifty bucks each. The place is still pretty crowded.

"Man, that's thirsty work," Josh says. He asks the bartender for a Coke.

"Hey, thanks a lot," I say. "You sounded great. And thanks again for putting Ray Collins onto us."

"Sure." He takes a thirsty swallow of the Coke. "Sorry I couldn't commit. I dig playing with you guys. It's just, like I told you, I can't turn down a club date to play in a bar. Too many women want my money." His gaze drifts toward one of the barmaids he was talking to earlier. She's a willowy blond with hair the color of butter, a long smooth fall of it all the way to her waist. For a second I wonder how Monique made out with her henna project, or if she went back and bought the wig. I guess I'll find out when I meet her for the SummerStage thing.

I tell Dom I'll get my car and pick him and the drums up in front of the club. And I step outside to discover the thunderstorm that was threatening all day has finally hit. The rain is falling in heavy sheets, almost steaming as it hits the sidewalk, bouncing like the drops that jump up around a rock tossed in a pond. The air doesn't smell clean yet. The rain hasn't been going long enough to wash away the heat and grime of the day, so the rain intensifies the dirty city smell.

As I hurry to my car, I enjoy the way my shirt is instantly soaked, the feel of streams of water coursing off my arms, my sodden hair. At Bleecker, I turn left, dodging the few people

143

who haven't taken shelter by pressing themselves against the facades of the clubs and restaurants that line the street. My feet, snug in my cowboy boots, are the only part of me that isn't wet yet.

I see my car, its faded green brightened by the rain, cascades of water blurring the windows. I dig my keys out of my jeans pockets as I get closer. I don't even bother trying the key in the driver's side. I pull open the passenger door and get ready to fling myself across the seat.

Except somebody's sitting there, a huge dark form with matted hair plastered against its head and bare shoulders, a soaked tank top clinging to its bony chest. I feel like I've just touched a shorted-out mike. I reel backwards, my mind blank, tottering on the heels of my boots. A quick glance in one direction then the other tells me that there's nobody on this stretch of the street except me.

Chapter 15

I've got a head start. At least I'm already on my feet. I'm splashing through the puddles back toward the bright lights of the clubs when I hear a voice behind me, a familiar voice.

"Maxx, Maxx," the voice is calling. "I didn't mean to scare you."

I keep running but look back over my shoulder. It's Stan, clumsily trying to catch up with me.

I run a little bit further, till I'm almost at the corner and can see people again along the stretch of sidewalk where the clubs start up. I stop and face him.

"I didn't mean to scare you." He says it again.

"Well, what the fuck *did* you mean to do?" The rain is so heavy and loud it's like we're standing in a waterfall.

"It was raining," he says. "I remembered that your car didn't lock. I wanted to stay dry."

"What were you even doing near my car?"

"I wanted to talk to you. I saw it parked there when I came down Bleecker Street on my way to the club." He gives me a hapless grin. "It *is* kind of conspicuous, with that one door that doesn't match and everything." He grins again. "I thought I'd wait for you, but then the rain got so heavy . . ." He shrugs.

"It's still heavy," I say. "And I'm really wet, and I want to get in my car and drive back to New Jersey and go to bed."

"But I need to talk to you."

"I already know what you want to talk about, and there's no

145

point in discussing it any more."

"I feel like I'm drowning," he says. "Can you least give me a ride home? It's only a couple of blocks." Rivulets of water are running down his face. He looks absolutely pitiful.

"Where's your car?"

"I don't like to drive it because then I lose my parking space."

"I've got to go back to the Hot Spot and get Dom and the drums. You can ride along. Maybe you can wait inside the club till the rain stops."

We splash along the sidewalk past the NYU dorms in silence. When we reach the car, I open the passenger-side door and slide across the seat. Stan slides in beside me. "Thanks a lot, Maxx," he says humbly. "I really appreciate this."

A towel would be nice, but I don't have one. I push my soaking hair off my face and shake my hands in the air. A few drops of water fly off. "So how're things at Manny's?" I say as I turn the key in the ignition and the engine sputters its way to life.

"Okay," he says. "Why?"

"Small talk," I say. "Just making small talk." Poor Stan. I guess if you devote your life to seeing how fast you can get your fingers to wiggle around a fret board, certain social skills elude you. I switch on the headlights and get the windshield wipers going.

We ride the block and a half back to the Hot Spot in silence, Stan slumped wetly against the seat. But as I pull up in front of the club, he turns toward me

"I was talking to that guy, that Josh? He told me he was only subbing for one night. Please, Maxx, please. Just give me one more chance." He looks like he's going to cry.

"No. Can't you understand it's not going to happen? I've got somebody else lined up. He's rehearsing with us Thursday, and if it works out, he's in."

"Thursday at Feedback," he says, shaking his head. "That

used to be my absolute favorite thing. Even more than the gigs. And now—"

"Stan, give me a break. I wouldn't have let you get back in my car if I thought you were going to keep ragging me about this."

"Please? If this other guy doesn't work out, couldn't I . . . please?" His voice cracks and the word turns into a sequence of gasps and choking noises. I can't tell if he's actually crying because his face is already so wet from the rain.

"What about the Blue Dudes?" I wonder if I should sort of pat him on the shoulder or something. I never know what to do when people cry. "I really don't get this," I say. "You're in a band, a band that plays much better gigs than Maxximum Blues."

He doesn't answer. He just stares at me mournfully as water drips off his chin.

"What is this obsession with being in my band? Do you know what we made tonight, Stan? Fifty bucks apiece. Is that what you want? You want to take a pay cut to prove that I shouldn't have fired you?"

"I'm not really in the Blue Dudes," he says at last. "They were trying me out."

"You're not gigging with them?"

"No." The sound comes out like a little whimper. Then, louder, "They don't think I play hard enough. They think I sound too traditional."

"How could they?" I say, half to myself, then, "You haven't played any gigs with them at all? Not the Mohegan Sun? Not anything?"

"No. Not anything." He pushes the car door open, hunches himself through it, and trudges grimly across the sidewalk toward the Hot Spot.

By the time Dom and I wrestle the drums through the rain

and back into the car, even my feet are soggy inside my cowboy boots. Dom is soaked, too, and it's making him grouchy.

"Practice as usual Thursday night?" he says with a scowl, after he settles himself in the car.

"You got it," I say. "Boris was totally into us, but we've got to keep working on the band if we want to make more than fifty bucks each."

"Got anybody lined up for guitar?"

"Of course." I turn the key in the ignition. The car coughs a few times. The coughs become a low rumble, and I ease away from the curb.

"Mind if I ask who?"

"Ray Collins," I say, liking the way it feels to say his name.

"Not that blond show-off?"

"You know him?"

"No, but I know who he is." Dom shifts in his seat. "Can't get comfortable," he mutters. "My clothes are sticking to me."

"Have you heard him play?"

"No. Have you?"

"No." I say it really quietly, hoping the sound of the windshield wipers will drown out my voice.

Dom squirms a few times. After a long silence, he says, "You're really going to pull this back together? Because Kenny White called me again. It's not like I'm the only drummer in the world, you know, and if I put him off too long . . ."

"Everything will be fine. There are plenty of guys out there who'd be happy to have the gig if Ray doesn't work out. Josh totally dug the band, and he was the first guy I asked. Only he can't afford to play blues every weekend."

All Dom wants to talk about the rest of the way home is Kenny White's band. And he reminds me every second or third sentence that he can't put Kenny off forever.

I finally get him and the drums delivered to Clifton. I poke back along Route 46, hitting every traffic light even though three a.m. is the one time of day that 46 doesn't have traffic. I've got the classic rock station turned up as loud as it will go, trying to drown out the echo of Dom's voice.

It's Sunday morning, early, barely light outside. The windows are open, and the birds are just getting started. A fresh breeze is stirring, rattling the blinds. The thunderstorm really cooled things down, at least for awhile. It'll be a perfect day for the SummerStage concert.

I haven't slept much though, or at least it wasn't restful, because I found Doretta again . . . the narrow stairs, the smells in the hallway, Doretta at the door, puzzled, her hair twisted onto plastic rollers.

"You musta been interested if you tracked me all the way up here," she says. "But you better stay with that casino job, honey. Blues ain't payin' my rent."

"I can't stay with the casino job," I say, and it all comes spilling out about Sandy.

"Well," she says at last. "Sounds like maybe you got somethin' to sing about. We got a gig this weekend at another place. Maybe you'll come on down. I'll show you a couple things."

Doretta's image fades and I roll onto my back. The sky is a dull gray color streaked with pink along the bottom edge, but now the birds have really kicked in, and it's going to be impossible to sleep any more. There's a bird outside the window going nuts, chirping his way through every scale he knows. I guess male birds do it to show off and impress the female birds. Or do the female birds sing too? I flop back over on my stomach and pull the pillow over my ears.

The next thing I know the birds have been replaced by the sound of a motorcycle engine, and the room is bright with sunshine. A groggy glance at the clock tells me it's almost noon. I must have drifted off to sleep again. And this time the sleep wasn't full of Doretta. It was full of Stan. What he told me last night is just beginning to sink in.

A long shower gets the sweat and stale beer smell still left from the Hot Spot out of my hair, but it doesn't leave me feeling less groggy. Before I take off to meet Monique, I'd better bring myself back to life with some coffee.

I pull on my biking shorts and blues festival T-shirt and head for the kitchen to get the water started. When the kettle whistles, I dump a spoonful of instant coffee into a cup, pour in the water, stir it up, and wander over to the kitchen window.

Up the street by the big apartment building at the corner, the motorcycle guy is hard at work polishing the chrome on his Harley. I'm not thinking about him, though. I'm thinking about the fact that Stan was around the night Jimmy died—not playing a gig at the Mohegan Sun like he told me before. But Stan's so goofy, so awkward and hopeless, so wrapped up in trying to get his fingers to move faster than the speed of light. Would he really kill a person?

I change into a sundress for the SummerStage concert, a vintage dress from the thrift store. It's yellow plaid with a full skirt and a halter neck and a wide belt made out of yellow plastic that's supposed to look like patent leather. I'm going to have to park on the Upper West Side and walk about ten or fifteen minutes to get to the Beethoven Statue where Monique said she'd meet me, so I don't wear my red spike-heeled sandals. Instead I pull on my spare pair of cowboy boots—the ones from last night are still soaked—and I grab a straw hat to keep the sun off.

Just as I'm nearing the end of the hallway, the door to the stairwell opens and here's Leon, smiling in a white polo shirt and well-pressed khakis. He's carrying a shopping bag from the

C-Town Superette.

"Well, you look summery," he says.

"So do you."

"What's new?"

"I found a new guitar player—a real nice looking guy, too."

"What's his playing like?"

"Uh, I'm not sure."

I guess I look embarrassed because he says, "Sorry I asked."

I make it over to the city in less than half an hour and find a place along 74th, by an old blue armchair. Somebody's put it out for the trash, somebody who lives in one of the super-elegant brownstones that line the street.

I walk up to Central Park West and cross at the light. Grand trees line the sidewalk at the park's edge. Their dark green leaves, intermingled with the occasional crinkled brown one now that it's late summer, rustle heavily in the breeze. At 72nd, I follow the road that cuts into the park, veering onto the curving path that leads past sloping lawns, yellowing here and there after a summer with not enough rain.

Cyclists zip around me from behind in their gaudy streamlined suits. Coming the other way is a smiling woman about my age being dragged forward by a dog while a little kid clings to her other hand. At the intersection between this path and another, an ice cream man has parked his wagon. He's handing an ice cream bar to a short middle-aged guy wearing khaki shorts and a polo shirt just like Leon's.

Soon I can see the Beethoven statue about fifteen feet ahead of me. It's not his whole body, just a square-ish column, with a bust of him on the top. It stands in a grassy patch shaded by a tree. The tree's branches droop over his shoulders and the leaves brush the top of his head.

I check my watch. It's ten after one. I'm not really that late. I'm coming up on the statue from the back, so I can't see Monique yet, but I'll catch sight of her in a minute, waiting for me, hopefully with her hair improved by a little henna.

I emerge from the shady walk into the bright sun and circle around in front of the statue. No sign of Monique, so I wander over to one of the park benches that line the Mall and settle down to wait for her. There's plenty of time to get in line for the concert tickets, and she should turn up any minute. Kids are skateboarding on the paved area in front of the band shell, calling to each other and laughing as their boards scrape the ground.

It's shady on my bench and there's a slight breeze. A kid is doing stunts on his bike as the skateboarders swoop and glide around him. Over by the entrance to the concert area, a line of people is starting to form.

Half an hour later I'm still sitting on my bench and watching the skateboarders and the kid doing bike stunts.

The line of people waiting to get in now stretches down to the band shell. I'm beginning to get a creepy feeling.

Half an hour late isn't that bad. I've got friends who are always half an hour late. And besides it's Sunday. Subways and busses don't run as often. Monique will show up any minute. I decide to get in line. I can still keep an eye on the statue.

I get up and walk over to the tail end of the line, where I edge up behind a guy in mirror-shades and a backwards baseball cap.

Now the line is moving, inching forward. She's forty-five minutes late, and I have a *really* creepy feeling. Monique was cheerful enough yesterday, but too cheerful, kind of manic. Maybe she couldn't sleep again last night and she had a couple of drinks and took some of those pills.

"You don't want your place?" says the guy behind me as I leave.

"No," I say. "I've got to check on a friend."

CHAPTER 16

The cowboy boots are useful now that I'm running, the yellow plaid skirt swishing around my knees, the straw hat clutched in my hand. I emerge from the park and run to where my car is waiting for me, next to the blue armchair. I'm panting, and my face is dripping with sweat.

I jump in the passenger side, slide across the seat, stick the key in the ignition, and shift into drive. The engine whines a few times then coughs itself to life. I maneuver out of the space, coast up to the red light at the corner of Central Park West, and swing left when the light turns green.

The next several blocks are stop-and-go traffic. It seems as if there's a red light at every corner. Finally Jimmy's old building comes into view, pale gray stucco, two monumental wings with vertical rows of bay windows facing the park, the entrance between the wings decorated with concrete urns dripping sprays of ivy.

I pull up in the bus stop, jump out of the car, and dash across the street, ignoring the light. A startled Hispanic guy on his way out of the building freezes as I yell for him to hold the door.

The elevator is waiting, doors open. The Hispanic guy must have just gotten out. I push the button for the seventh floor, wait while the elevator makes its creaking ascent, stopping for no apparent reason at floors three, four, and five.

At last the elevator sighs to a stop. The doors inch open, and

154

I step out into the hall. Someone is cooking with garlic and olive oil.

Monique's is the last apartment on the right. I make my way past four or five doors. Behind one, somebody is listening to a baseball game. I stop in front of 71 and tap. No answer.

"Monique?" I call. "Are you here?"

No answer.

I tap louder. Nothing. I try the knob. The door is locked, of course. It's New York City.

The super, I'm thinking. Supers have keys, don't they? But I never figured out how to track down the super in this building.

I hurry back the way I came, take the elevator up to the ninth floor, and hurry past more apartment doors until I'm standing in front of Helen's apartment. I tap. There's a little bustle inside and that familiar voice says, "Who's out there?"

"It's me, Helen. Maxx Maxwell."

The door swings inward, revealing Helen in a black satin robe and high-heeled, pointy-toed slippers garnished with drifts of wispy feathers. Her hair is twisted onto large rollers, and her face is covered with a thick film of shiny green stuff.

"I was supposed to meet Monique for the concert in the park," I say. "She's on the seventh floor, you know, Jimmy's old girlfriend—and she didn't show up. And she doesn't answer when I knock. I'm afraid something's happened to her. We've got to find the super."

"You caught me in the middle of a beauty treatment," she says.

"You don't have to let him see you," I say. "Can you just call him and tell him to come up to the seventh floor? You must have his number."

"I do." She turns and clatters toward the living room on her high heels. "But I can't guarantee he'll even be around. He's useless."

I follow her toward a dainty bureau standing between the windows, just like those long windows in Jimmy's apartment.

As she roots in the top drawer, she says, "That girl just moved in, you know. Wanted to be near Jimmy." Helen shakes her head and purses her lips. With the rollers in her hair and the green skin treatment, she looks like a strange wind-up toy going through its routines. "It's never a good idea to rearrange your life for a man. But some girls don't have anything else to live for."

I'm about to scream, "Can't you hurry?" when she pulls out a slip of paper and crosses to the phone to dial a number.

"Here," she says, handing me the receiver. "He seems to be there. Tell him what you need."

I tell the super that I was supposed to meet my friend and she didn't show up and now there's no answer when I knock and she's been very depressed because she knew Jimmy Nashville and could he please come up and open the door? In the background I can hear a baseball game in progress.

"Is probably nothing wrong," he says soothingly. "Probably she just forget."

"No," I say. "She didn't. I don't want to call the police because maybe she's just asleep—she had some sleeping pills. So please. It won't take very long. Or can I come down there and get the key?"

"I can't give you the key," he says. "Is the same key for lots of apartments."

"Please. She could be dying right now, while we're talking."

He sighs disgustedly and mutters something in Spanish. "What floor? Where are you?"

"She's in 71," I say. "I'll be standing out in front."

I say good-bye to Helen, run back down to the seventh floor, and knock on Monique's door again. No answer. I wait and wait, getting jumpier by the minute. At last I hear the elevator creak, the doors heave themselves open, and around the corner comes a short, chubby man with brown skin and a bushy mustache.

"Okay, okay," he says. "I'm here. Stand back." He leans toward the door, fits the key in the lock, and twists. I hear the lock click open. "Be my guest," he says. "My man is at bat, and I'm missin' it." He scurries back toward the elevator.

I give the door a little push and look around the edge. I can see straight down to the long window in the far wall, but not around the corner into the little sleeping and sitting area. The window is open, the lower pane pushed up as far as it will go. I can feel my heart ticking under the yellow plaid of my dress.

"Hello?" I call. "Monique? Are you here? Is anybody here?" I take a few more steps, past the tiny kitchen—no sign of her in there. The sofa bed is unfolded, made up with light-blue sheets, a pillow in a light-blue pillowcase. The sheets are rumpled, like somebody recently slept in them. Some of the boxes standing along the walls have been opened, like maybe she decided to make a little more progress toward getting settled.

The window is open so wide. Could she have jumped out? I take a deep breath and walk the rest of the way across the room. My stomach does a flip-flop as I lean out the window and look down. Monique's single window is in the back wall of the building, just like Jimmy's, overlooking the concrete patch and the luxuriant weeds.

But there's nothing down there this time, no small female body with short henna-colored hair. I turn away from the window.

The bathroom is the only room left. The door to the right of the sofa bed is slightly ajar. I can see the edge of a sink.

She's in the bathroom, in the tub. And the tub is full of water, except the water isn't clear. It's the color of blood. And Monique, judging from the ashen color of her face, doesn't have

157

much blood left inside her anymore. One of those box cutter things is lying on the bathroom floor, a squiggle of blood on the white tile forming an arabesque around it.

She couldn't go on without him, I'm thinking as I push the buttons on her phone for 9-1-1. That's what she told me. She couldn't go on without him.

I tell the operator someone's dead. I wonder if that counts as an emergency. Since she's already dead, it won't make any difference how fast the cops get here. Should I have called 9-1-1? The operator asks me the address, says she'll send the police.

I'm shaking, and my teeth are chattering. First I go stand by the window, but after a few minutes I go back in the bathroom. She slept in her bed last night, so when did this happen? I stick my finger in the water. It's warmer than it would be normally, even on a hot day. The tub must have been filled fairly recently.

I won't touch the box cutter. I already made that mistake with the guitar pick in Jimmy's apartment. I get down on my hands and knees and stare at it though, especially at the blood on the floor around it. The blood doesn't look like it's dry yet. And the box cutter reminds me of something, but my mind is in too much of a whirl to think of what.

It's creepy being in here—the body in the tub with that awful hair that she didn't even try the henna on, the red bath water, and the box cutter and blood on the floor. And then everything else just looking like a normal, tidy bathroom. Towels, light blue like her sheets, are folded smoothly over the towel racks. A box of tissue, light blue, is sitting on top of the toilet tank. A roll of toilet paper, light blue, is fitted neatly into the toilet paper holder. On the counter that surrounds the sink is a cosmetic case, printed with delicate little flowers, overflowing with tubes of lipstick and little pans of eye shadow and bottles of foundation—all that fancy Body Shop stuff.

Body Shop—like the lipstick on the night table in Jimmy's

apartment. The one that replaced the bright red stuff that ended up in the wastebasket. So that solves that mystery. Monique was the one who was going into his place and messing up the bed. I guess she had his a key. Maybe there was something special going on with her, not like all those other chicks he flirted with.

The buzzer sounds the way an electric shock feels. I jump and feel my skin tingle. The cops are here. I run to the door, which is still open. Where are they?

The buzzer sounds again, right in my ear, and I jump again. The sound is coming from a panel on the wall by the front door. They're still downstairs, trying to get in the front. I push the button at the edge of the panel and wait, my heart pounding, to see if the buzzing will start up again.

Figuring they got in okay, I head for the window to take a few breaths of fresh air, then wander back to the middle of the room where I nervously perch on one of the folding chairs. In a few minutes I hear feet outside and official-sounding male voices. There's a tap at the door. A voice says "Police," and the door hinges squeak.

I lead them to the bathroom. Their walkie-talkies squawk, and in a few minutes Walter Stallings is walking toward me down the hall in his ugly green jacket, followed by a thinner, younger, better looking cop in uniform.

Stallings catches sight of me. "What are you doing here?"

"I didn't touch anything," I say.

"You better not have, but what are you doing here?" He looks more imposing standing up than leaning back in his desk chair with a couple of chins resting on his collar and the fluorescent light turning his skin the color of Pepto-Bismol.

"She was Jimmy's girlfriend. I got to be friends with her too. We were supposed to go to the SummerStage concert in Central Park, but she didn't show up, so I came up here to look for her.

There was no answer when I knocked, so I got the super to let me in."

"Where is she?"

"In there." I point to the bathroom. He takes a few steps and I start to follow him.

"Sit down." He points to the chair I just got out of. He and the young, cute cop head toward the bathroom door.

"I think it happened really recently," I call after him. "The water in the tub doesn't feel all that cold, and the blood on the floor might still be wet. I can't be sure, though, because I didn't want to touch it."

He doesn't answer. I hear their voices, muted, bouncing off the tile walls.

Poor Monique, I'm thinking. *Jimmy dies and she's obviously one of those chicks that has to have a guy in her life or she doesn't feel real. Then she messes up her hair. Trying to cheer herself up, she said. But why did she do it herself? That dark red, light red streak thing she had going on before was a high-class salon job. Why didn't she go back to where she had that done? In a big hurry, I guess. Like she really couldn't wait to get some kind of a new look going on. But why the rush?*

An idea hits me with a jolt that makes my legs twitch. Maybe she didn't do it to cheer herself up. Maybe there was another reason. Maybe she didn't want to look like herself anymore. Maybe she didn't want to be recognized.

What if she was at Jimmy's place when he was killed? What if she saw something? What if she saw some*body*, and somebody saw her?

Then I get another jolt. I remember where I saw a box cutter. I was at Manny's, talking to Stan, and he was using it to slice open a case of guitar strings.

The cops must have called for some more cops to come because next thing I know the buzzer is buzzing and the young cute cop is hustling past me to buzz back. While he's gone I edge toward the bathroom door. I can see Stallings's back. He's half bent over, clumsily, like an out-of-shape old guy, which is what he is.

"Excuse me," I say.

"Yeah?" He straightens up and turns around, bumping his hip on the sink. He winces. "We'll get to you in a minute," he says.

"You know the guy who left the guitar pick behind in Jimmy's apartment?" I say. He nods warily. "I saw him using a box cutter a couple days ago."

"What was he doing with it?"

"Cutting open a box." Stallings rolls his eyes, but I go on. "She was afraid of somebody," I say. "See her hair? She changed the color and cut it all off right after Jimmy died. She did it herself. That's why it looks so bad. She used to be really pretty."

"It's very cramped in here," he says. "And the medical examiner is coming. Why don't you relax in the next room for a little while?"

The young cop comes back down the hall, leading a guy in a sports jacket and a lady in a navy polyester pantsuit. The lady is carrying an impressive leather case. Stallings comes out, and he and the young cop stand at the window. Stallings smokes a cigarette, leaning out the window to exhale. With his free hand, he's absent-mindedly drumming on the windowsill.

"You have a good sense of time," I say.

He turns around looking puzzled.

"You're tapping on the window sill. I can tell you have a good sense of time. You said you played the drums."

He pulls the hand away from the sill and holds it self-consciously at his side. "I was in a couple bands," he says. "But that's all over now. I'm too old to stay up late." He turns back to the window.

Finally the guy in the sports jacket comes out of the bathroom and pulls up the other folding chair near mine. I tell him who Monique was and how I knew her and how we were supposed to go to the concert today and how she didn't show up—the whole story, except for the fact that I'm sure I know who killed her. He probably wouldn't be any more interested than Walter Stallings was.

Since it's Sunday I can park almost in front of Manny's. I pull into a spot behind a van some kids are trying to stuff a huge amp into and sit there for a minute asking myself what I'm going to say to Stan if he's there.

I take a deep breath and jerk the door handle on the driver's side down. It won't open. I try again. It still won't open. I slide across to the passenger side and climb out onto the sidewalk.

As usual, the windows of Manny's are jammed with great-looking musical equipment. The window on the left is all devoted to drums, including a spectacular set with a red pearlized finish. In the window on the right are about ten Stratocasters, every color of the rainbow, looking like a lineup of swimsuit models showing off their curves.

I step inside, trading the warm glare of midday sunshine for the cool glare of fluorescent lights. Stan's usual post is over to the right, the strings-picks-pedals-straps counter. But Stan's not there. In his place is a medium-sized guy with a shaved head and one of those little Satan-like beards. Except since he's got fair skin and blue eyes, and the beard is blond, he doesn't look very Satanic.

"Help you?" he says, pulling in his stomach and looking interested. Something tells me the guys who work in Manny's guitar department don't get too many female customers.

"Is Stan here today?"

"Nope. I can help you, though. What do you need?"

162

"I'm not a guitar player," I say. "I'm a friend of Stan's. Was he supposed to be here?"

"He called in sick. I usually work back there." He points toward a display of amps.

"Did you talk to him?"

"No. Why?"

"I just wondered how he sounded."

Out on the sidewalk, the kids are still struggling with the amp. I open the passenger door of my car and slide across the seat, maneuver the car out into the road, and set off for the East Village.

Stan lives in a walk-up on St. Mark's Place. Back in the days when he was still in my band, I took him home a few times and once I even accepted his invitation to come up for a beer. I head down Second to St. Mark's, poke along all the way to Tompkins Square Park, and circle it twice before I find a place big enough for my car.

Five minutes later I've climbed the steep half-flight of steps that leads to the stoop in front of Stan's building, and I'm pushing the buzzer that says "Dunlap" next to it. I'm almost surprised when it buzzes back and the door pops open with a click.

The hallway has been painted so many times that chunks could be cut out of the walls and framed, like that art where a guy takes a canvas and goes crazy with nothing but a king-size tube of paint and a palette knife. Stan lives on the fourth floor. The stairs are steep and narrow, and they seem to double back on themselves about ten times before I finally emerge to face a dark hallway with a few dim doors arranged along it. Up here, the walls are even more interesting, fissured and peeling, the color in any spot depending on how many layers of paint have peeled off.

Stan is at the end, number 17. I'm feeling lightheaded after the climb and, now that I think of it, I haven't eaten much. And maybe I'm nervous, too. Do I really want to be here?

I'm halfway down the dark hall when Stan's door opens. I only know it's opening because I hear the latch click and hinges squeak. It's as dark behind the door as it is out here in the hall.

"Who's there?" a voice croaks.

I can't tell if it's Stan. "Maxx Maxwell," I say. I can feel my pulse ticking in my neck.

"Maxx?" The voice sighs. "You're an angel."

The door swings open wider. I hear it, but I don't really see it. Everything's still dark. Feet stumble across the floor in the apartment, and I hear the sound of something big collapsing.

CHAPTER 17

I reach the door and peer inside. I can vaguely make out a dark shape outlined against a pale rectangle. Stan's bed, as I recall, is the centerpiece of his room.

"Do you mind?" I say, fumbling along the wall for a light switch. I find a promising outcropping and push on it with my thumb.

Suddenly the room is brightened by a bare bulb hanging over the bed. It illuminates the piles of clothes on the floor, the jumble of guitars and gear in every corner, the armchair with foam stuffing exploding from a hole in the seat, the TV tray holding a box of crackers, the disorderly mountain of CDs piled by the stereo—and Stan, lying on a not-too-clean sheet in his underwear.

"No—please." His voice is a hoarse yelp. His hands grope for his face and cover his eyes. "It hurts." Then he lifts a hand and flutters it toward the window. I can see an eye now, squeezed tight shut. "Get the shade instead. Just open it a little."

I can hardly hear him. I get the lighting fixed the way he wants it and lower myself onto the edge of the devastated armchair. "Are you sick or what?" I say.

"Sick. Will you make me some tea? With honey?"

"What happened?"

He reaches behind his head and paws at the pillow until he gets it wedged against the headboard. Then he scoots back a few inches and props his head on it.

"I got so wet last night when I was trying to talk to you. Then after I left the Hot Spot, I went over to SOS for the midnight jam. Man, it was so air-conditioned in there. It was freezing. But I was depressed, and I didn't want to come home and be by myself. So I stayed all night. When I came out, the sun was already up. And my throat just about felt like it was on fire."

I have to lean close to make out what he's saying. "So you've been here all day?" I say.

"I get dizzy when I stand up. Will you make me some tea?"

"I suppose."

"With honey?"

"Where's the kitchen." He points toward a curtain. "You've got tea bags?"

"On the counter. The honey's there, too."

The kitchen is also the bathroom, it turns out. At least that's where the bathtub is. The counter is a length of plywood balanced across a couple of orange crates and the stove is a hot plate.

When I return with the tea, he pulls himself further upright and readjusts the pillow behind his back. I hand him the mug, and he inhales gratefully before taking a tiny sip, then a larger one.

"Good, Maxx," he says. "Real good."

The tea restores him to the point that in a few minutes he's fussing around with his free hand tugging a sheet up off the floor and trying to tuck it around his legs, apologizing all the while for the fact that he's not dressed. I keep a wary eye on the tea sloshing in the mug and finally stand up, take the sheet out of his hand, and arrange it across his chest.

"Thank you," he says. "Thank you. You're so kind. It was such a miracle that you came today. I always knew you were a good person, even though it didn't work out with the band."

So now what? I ease back into the chair, trying to avoid the spot where the foam is bursting out. Is he really sick, or is he the best actor I've ever met? His throat really does sound bad. Of course, a good actor could fake that. But he looks awful, kind of green, with dark circles under his eyes. And getting wet then spending the whole night at the SOS jam and getting sick from the air conditioning is definitely a Stan thing to do.

He hands me the mug, says "Here. I'm finished."

"Do you want a refill?"

"Not just now. Will you put some music on, though?"

"What would you like to hear?"

"There's blues," he says. "And you're the guest. Take your pick. Lots of blues there on the floor." He points toward the mountain of CDs I noticed earlier.

I edge my way around the bed, kneel, and flip through the huge pile. He's got everything here, three or four B. B. Kings, Muddy Waters, Howlin' Wolf, Magic Sam—it's like somebody went into a record store with the discography for a course in the history of blues.

"Where'd all this stuff come from?"

"I bought it—well, I bought some of it. One of my friends works at Sam Goody, so there were a few I didn't have to pay for." He braces his hands against the mattress and pulls himself further erect. "Do you see the Albert King one in there? That's one of the best."

"Since when have you become a blues fan?"

"I told you I was getting into it," he says, sounding hurt. "You said I should listen to more blues. But don't worry. I'm not going to ask you to let me back in your band. That's all over now." He rubs his hands over his face. "I'd better lay down again. I really don't feel so good." He lets himself slide down the headboard till he's stretched out full-length again, his feet hanging over the end of the mattress. "Maybe I'll even sleep for a little while. By the way, why did you come here?"

"Jimmy's girlfriend is dead. I thought people should know."

"Which one?" he says.

"Monique."

"The one with the streaky hair?"

"Yeah, her."

"That's an awful shame," he says.

At home, I dig a blouse for work out of the laundry. I don't even have time to touch it up a little with the iron. I shed the cowboy boots and the yellow plaid dress, pull on the wrinkled blouse and my plain black pants. Then I step into my shoes, grab my bag, and run out the door. On my way down the stairs, it occurs to me to wonder how Stan would know what any of Jimmy's girlfriends looked like.

When Julio's music works its way into my consciousness the next morning, I roll over and bury my head under the pillow. Something bad happened yesterday, and the longer I can stay asleep, the longer I can put off having to think about it. I shut my eyes tight and try to ignore the insistent voices on the other side of the wall exhorting me to dance. But they get louder and louder. Finally I give up and let my eyes drift groggily toward the clock on my dresser.

But on the way there, they pause at the flyer for the open-mike night at the Purple Snail and suddenly I'm awake. I sit up and swing my feet onto the floor. And that's when I remember. Monique is dead. The gruesome recollection of her in the tub makes me flop back onto the bed.

I wonder if the *Times* will carry something about her. Probably. It's a pretty dramatic story. I could run out to the C-Town Superette and pick up a copy. Or I could save myself the walk and borrow Leon's. By now he's probably dressed and finishing up his breakfast, about to head out to Macy's. If I'm lucky, I can catch him before he leaves.

I hurry into the bathroom to pee and brush my teeth, pull on my biking shorts and blues festival T-shirt, step out into the hall, and tap on Leon's door. He opens it looking puzzled, but the puzzled look turns into a smile when he sees it's me.

"Come in and have some coffee," he says, pulling the door open wider. "They gave me a day off." He's already dressed, but in khaki pants and a polo shirt instead of the slacks and sports jacket that he wears to work. He smells pleasantly of after-shave.

I step into the apartment, and new and equally appealing smells take over: fresh-ground coffee, fried eggs and toast. "They owed me," he says. "I clocked about seventy hours last week. Covering for vacations is lucrative, but it's exhausting. I'll be glad when my classes start, and I can scale back."

As I follow him toward the kitchen door, he points to his coffee table, where several days' worth of the *Times* are arranged in neat piles. "I'm way behind on the news," he says. "I've been getting home so late." He turns when he reaches the kitchen door. "To what do I owe the pleasure of this early visit?"

"I need to see today's paper."

"Late-breaking news in the blues world?" he says with a smile.

"No," I say. "Somebody else who I know is dead."

His face becomes serious. All that's left of the smile are two little wrinkles running from his nose to the corners of his mouth. "What happened?"

I tell him about waiting for Monique at the park, showing up at her apartment, and the sight of her dead in that tub of red water.

He listens, nodding occasionally, like a doctor listens while you're describing your symptoms. "Let's sit down," he says at last. I follow him into the kitchen where the *Times* is spread out on the table. He pulls out a chair for me on the side opposite the remains of his breakfast. "I'll get rid of this," he says, transporting the dirty plate and silverware to the counter. He turns back with a mug of coffee that he sets in front of me.

"Where do they put stuff like that?" he says. "Maybe Metro." Standing behind his chair, he shakes a section of the paper open and starts flipping through pages. "Okay," he says after a minute or two. "I guess this is it." He pauses, then begins. "Here's the headline: 'Woman Found Dead in Bathtub in Upper West Side Apartment.' Then it says 'Police responding to a 911 call early Sunday afternoon found a woman dead in her bathtub in an apartment at 105th Street and Central Park West. She apparently bled to death from cuts on her wrists. The woman, identified as Monique Lindholm, age 32, worked as a singer, doing session work and performing in clubs and restaurants. The building in which she lived was also the residence of Jimmy Nashville, who jumped to his death from his ninth-floor apartment on August 16. She and Nashville were apparently acquainted. A police spokesperson stated that, though an autopsy will be performed, evidence indicates that Lindholm took her own life.' "

Leon folds the paper into a more manageable size and slides it across the table toward me. "Help yourself," he says. "You can keep it." I stare at the words. He gives me a few minutes. When I look up again, he says, "Do *you* think she killed herself?"

"No." I tell him about the bloody box cutter on the floor next to the tub and how the last time I saw a box cutter before that, Stan was using it.

He gives me an unconvinced look. "But was there blood all over her apartment? And were there other cuts on her body? Anybody would try to fight back if somebody came after them with a box cutter. And if she was already in the tub when he attacked her, there'd be water all over the place." Leon takes a swallow of coffee, mutters "Cold," and jumps up.

I hear a splash of liquid in his mug. "Warm yours up?" he says, reaching for mine.

"Thanks." Then I say, "She *was* pretty strong. She was into Tae Kwon Do and that kind of stuff."

Back in my own apartment, I read the article about Monique again, pausing over the line, "evidence indicates that Lindholm took her own life." I picture the white sofa and the blue sheets, immaculate, and the bathroom floor, clean and dry, except for the spot of blood by the box cutter.

But she had those sleeping pills, and Friday night when we were out, she drank a lot of scotch, and it helped her sleep. What if she wanted to sleep Saturday night too, so she had a few drinks, maybe lots of drinks, and took a few pills for good measure, and then somebody showed up who wanted to get rid of her? Or maybe she took a few pills, and then they had a few drinks together? She could have been so out of it she didn't know what was going on.

Shit! Why didn't I look in the kitchen to see if there was a bottle of scotch on the counter and maybe an empty glass or two?

The autopsy—that will answer the question about the scotch and the pills. But it's too soon to call. Last time it took about three days. Instead, I punch in the number of the restaurant.

Aldo sounds annoyed, and he doesn't even know it's me yet—or maybe Norma told him when she called him to the phone.

"It's Maxx," I say, trying to sound weak.

"Yeah?" Only Aldo could cram so much suspicion into one word.

"I seem to have a relapse of that stomach problem I had last week, and I'm not going to make it in tonight."

"There's quite an epidemic going around," he says.

"It's this hot weather. Sometimes you eat things that aren't fresh. It's usually just a twenty-four hour thing, forty-eight hours tops."

"Which do you think yours will be?"

"What?"

"Twenty-four or forty-eight?"

"I'll get well as fast as I can," I say. "I hate to miss work."

Several hours later, I'm staring into my closet. The orange velour dress from the Rescue Mission Thrift Shop? No. It's too warm out for something with long sleeves, even if the skirt only comes halfway to my knees. How about the seventies prom dress from the rummage sale at the Full Speed Gospel Church? Maybe too dressy for open-mike night.

I push hangers aside, contemplating items one by one—faded jeans, black jeans, white jeans, long skirts, mini-skirts, my yellow sundress—working my way along the rod to the very end. A few last things are jammed up against the wall back where it's too dark to even see what they are. But one of them feels nice, leathery but kind of soft. I grope for the hanger and pull it out into the light. It's my suede pants and halter, dark green, with suede fringe down the side of the pants and outlining the plunging V of the halter. Just the thing.

CHAPTER 18

The Purple Snail is on Avenue B, around the corner from St. Mark's Place, a long narrow room with a bar spread out along one wall and a mural on the other that looks like extra-terrestrials having sex in a hot tub. Mismatched chairs are arranged at mismatched tables. The people are mismatched too—everything from the hippest Alphabet City dudes all in black to middle-aged folkies in tie-dye and sandals.

I grab a Bud at the bar and prowl along the edge of the tables looking for the tall guy. No sign of him, but it's only a little after eight and the place isn't nearly full yet. I settle in at a table along the wall where I can watch the room and the stage at the same time. A keyboard guy with a homely face and a nasal voice is singing about how he'd never stoop to go out with a girl who would stoop to go out with him.

But I'm not paying attention. I'm replaying that strange encounter with the tall guy, chasing him down 30th Street, hanging on his arm. "Who are you?" I'm asking desperately while a small curious crowd gathers on the corner. "Come to the Purple Snail next Monday night," he says. "Maybe you'll find out then."

When the keyboard guy gets done, delirious applause erupts at a table near the edge of the stage, his fans no doubt. Or maybe his friends. "I'm gonna do one more," he says, "then turn the stage over to my good friend, Shane Destry." He points out into the audience.

How many people are here to perform, I'm wondering, and how many just to watch? Almost every occupied table has at least one gig bag leaning against it. A couple of guys even have their guitars out, tuning up or just noodling. There's a jam-night vibe in the air, too, like everybody in the room is nervous.

The keyboard guy finishes up, and the MC—I recognize him as one of the guys who hang around Feedback—is reminding everybody that this is the weekly Feedback open-mike night and that anybody who wants to perform can sign up at the studio.

As Shane Destry, a little guy with curly red hair and freckles, takes the stage, settling himself into a chair centered in the spotlight and cradling an acoustic guitar in his lap, I make my way to the bar for another beer. I'm looking for a spot where I can push close enough to get the bartender's attention when I hear a voice at my elbow say, "Maxx?"

I turn around. It's Tony from Feedback, smiling his toothy smile, his dark hair smoothed back from his forehead. He's wearing a B. B. King T-shirt with the sleeves cut out. He's holding a bottle of beer—and he's about six inches shorter than I am. I've never seen him when he wasn't sitting on the stool behind the desk. He shifts the beer to his other hand and treats me to a handshake, damp and chilly for a change. "Hey, good to see you," he says.

"What are you doing here?"

"Helping out with the tech stuff." He jerks his thumb toward the stage. "See all that gear up there? Who do you think schlepped it?" He starts to take a sip of beer, pauses, and says, "Can I get you something?"

"No, really," I say. "I'm okay."

"You're sure?"

I look at the crowd around the bar, about four deep in every direction. The place has filled up since I got here.

"How'd you get that?" I say.

"The bartender's a buddy of mine."

"Well . . . I was hoping for a beer, if I can get close enough."

"Rolling Rock okay?"

"Bud?"

"Hold this." He hands me his beer and wades back into the crowd. From the stage comes a yearning voice accompanied by the mellow plink of nylon strings.

Tony's back amazingly soon. He hands me a Bud and says, "Wanna sit with me?"

I realize I'm drinking the beer he just bought me and let him guide me to a table.

The acoustic folk guy has finished his set and everyone's applauding. He looks happy—and relieved.

"I heard that guitar player you had before was a pretty amazing player," Tony says, settling into a chair. "What happened with the Blues from the Heart deal?"

"What Blues from the Heart deal?"

"He was supposed to back up Mississippi Slim, but then he pulled out."

"I didn't know Jimmy was involved in it at all. He never said anything to me."

"Well, he wasn't involved for very long. He was in, but then he was out—and Bart was pissed as hell too. Felt like Jimmy pulling out made a bunch of other guys pull out." He swallows a few more gulps of beer.

A woman who's going for a Joni Mitchell thing gets up and does a few songs. While she's singing, I stare around the room, looking for the tall guy. Still no sign of him. "Joni" is followed by a duo, where a guy plays keyboards and a gorgeous black woman sings some gospel-inspired tunes.

When they're done, the MC climbs up behind the mike and scans the audience. "Let's see who's next," he says, and glances away from the audience to consult his list.

A figure rises from a table in a shadowy spot near the wall, his hand clamped around the neck of a guitar. "It's me," says a not-very-confident voice. The figure edges between tables, mounts the steps at the side of the stage, and emerges into the light.

It's him, the tall guy.

He settles the strap of his guitar around his neck—an acoustic with a little pickup mounted on the sound hole—then stoops to plug himself into the amp and steps up to the mike. Even from way back where I'm sitting, I can tell he's nervous. His face looks blank, his eyes kind of desperate.

Without a word, he strums a few chords, simple chords with open strings like you'd learn at your first guitar lesson, and launches into "Don't Think Twice, It's All Right."

Halfway through the first chorus, the hand that's strumming falters for a minute, and the look in the guy's eyes becomes even more desperate. But the strumming resumes, gradually becoming more confident, and he sings another verse.

Despite the fact that he looks petrified and the guitar playing is about as rudimentary as you can get, the song is actually coming across. He's got a light voice, higher pitched than most guy voices, but the high-pitched thing makes it more intense, like the emotion he's feeling is kind of warping the sound.

He looks surprised at the applause, almost seems to be blushing. It takes him so long to collect himself, I'm wondering if he's okay. Finally, he says something inaudible.

"Step up to the mike," the MC calls.

The guy steps forward and says, "That was an old one, an old classic. Here's another one."

This one is "Maggie May," and he puts it across with a little more confidence. By the time he gets to the end, he's actually smiling a little.

"Here's my last one," he says. He's nervous again, leaning

forward, bumping his teeth on the mike, backing so far away that the first words of the song are inaudible. After a couple of lines, he settles into it, gets a little calmer. Now I can make out what he's saying—and it sounds very familiar.

"Finding my own socks, washing my own jeans," he's singing. I know exactly what's going to come next, and it does. "Mama don't love me. Mama don't love me. Mama don't love me no more."

It's "Whiskey for Breakfast." But how did he get it? Unless, of course, he's the one who wrote it.

"I've gotta ask this guy something," I say to Tony and push my chair back from the table.

"Don't disappear," he says with a wink.

I'm waiting for the tall guy when he climbs down the steps at the edge of the stage. "Nice job," I say.

It takes him a minute to focus on me. "So you came," he says at last. Then he tries to step around me. I edge sideways and plant myself in front of him. "You know everything you need to know about me now," he says. "Let me get by." The relieved look that settled over his face as he strummed his final chords has been replaced by a frown.

I stay where I am and keep talking. "That last one was a real interesting song. Where'd you find it?" He tries to step around me again. " 'Whiskey for Breakfast,' " I say. "Who else does it?"

He stops moving forward and lifts his guitar in front of him like a cumbersome shield. "Nobody," he says. "That's *my* song."

"You mean you wrote it."

"Yeah," he says, almost accusingly. "I wrote it."

"You're a good songwriter," I say. "You're a good singer, too. The audience was really into your performance."

His face softens the tiniest bit. "Thanks."

"I'm Maxx Maxwell." I stick out my hand. "What's your name?"

"I know who you are," he says, ignoring the question, grouchy again.

"I think you were a friend of Jimmy Nashville, the guy who used to be the guitar player in my band."

"I knew him. Why?"

"You gave him copies of some of your songs."

"Why would I do that?"

"I don't know. Why did you?"

"I don't know either," he says. "I wish I hadn't. He thought they were shit."

At home, I grab a Bud out of the refrigerator, put Bessie Smith on the stereo, and settle into the big chair, where I lapse into a beery daydream featuring Ray Collins.

But it gives way to a vision of Jimmy skimming the tall guy's songs with a quick glance, twisting them into a crumpled knot, and dropping them into the wastebasket—while the tall guy stands there and watches.

And what happens next?

CHAPTER 19

The next morning, even though I know it's probably too soon to call Walter Stallings about Monique's autopsy, I head for the big chair with my coffee and punch his number into the phone.

First the crisp voice that tells me I've reached the police comes on. "Detective Stallings, please," I say.

"Who's calling?"

"Maxx Maxwell. He knows me."

I wait so long that finally I stretch the cord as far as it will reach and walk over to the window to distract myself by seeing what's going on down below. Aside from the A-1 Sewer truck pulled up in front of one of the aluminum siding houses, there's not much to look at.

I'm just retreating to the big chair again when I hear Stallings's half-tired, half-bored voice say, "What are you up to now?"

"The paper said there was going to be an autopsy on Monique. Is it done yet?"

"No," he says. "Not yet. And I won't tell you to call again because I know you will anyway."

I tell him about how when I mentioned Monique to Stan, he asked if she was the one with the streaky hair—even though he'd never met her.

He gives a little snort and says, "You know what your problem is? You have too much free time, and it makes you think too much. Don't you have some songs you should be practicing or something?"

"A singer can't sing all the time. Your throat is your instrument. You'd wear it out. It's not like being a guitar player or a drummer or something."

"Yeah," he says, in that different, soft voice he uses sometimes. "There were days when I was in high school when I'd get up in the morning and sit down behind my drums, and next thing I knew my mom would be hollering into the basement, calling me to dinner."

"So when can I call back about the autopsy?"

"We'll probably have the results tomorrow." There's a silence, and I almost think he's put the phone down or forgotten about me, when he says, "Why don't you drop by if you're in the neighborhood? I've got something else you might be interested in too."

"What is it?" I say, leaning forward in the chair. It squeaks.

"She left a journal."

"You can let people see stuff like that? It's not . . . classified or something?"

"I'm about to retire. Remember? It's at the ME's right now, but I can get it back when I get the autopsy results."

"Thanks. What time should I come?"

"I'll be here eight to six, like always."

When I show up for work, Vinnie's out by the Dumpster smoking a cigarette and staring pensively across the parking lot. It's like catching an actor offstage because the minute he notices me heading for my usual space at the far edge of the lot, he turns back into Vinnie, small body vibrating with energy, rubbery face stretched into a grin.

"Maxx! How's it goin'? How you feelin'? Aldo said you had somethin' wrong with your stomach." The words rush out in one garbled breath as he scurries toward me.

"I'm better," I say. Then, "Actually, I was down at the Purple

Snail last night. I told Aldo I was sick. Ever been there?"

"No."

"You might be interested. Monday they've got open-mike night. Anybody can get up and do anything. Maybe you could find a guitar player and work up a few tunes."

"Good idea," he says. "I been goin' to those jams you tol' me about at Feedback. Lotsa good players hang out there." He looks at his cigarette, not much more than a butt, takes one last drag, and spins it off in the direction of the Dumpster. "Hey, didja hear? Cops showed up at Feedback last night and took that guy Bart away."

"They did? What for?"

"I don't know, man. Everybody was standin' around starin', but nobody knew what was goin' on."

"They just . . . dragged him off? Just like that?"

"Handcuffs and everything."

A blast of warm greasy air from the ventilating system greets me as I get near the kitchen door. Through the ancient screen, I can make out Manfred standing at the grill, his cornrow pigtails partly covered by a starched white skull cap. Vinnie holds the door for me, and I head through the kitchen to the break room.

In the break room, I pull on my Seafood Chalet vest, unclip my hair, twist the sweaty stragglers off my neck and forehead, and gather it all up into the clip again. The last step of the ritual is to deposit my bag in my locker.

"Well, well, well." Aldo is standing at the edge of the dining room as I push my way through the kitchen doors. "Another miraculous recovery." Something weird has happened to his mustache, like his razor slipped when he was shaving, but the effect is that it's undertaken some slow migration across his face.

At first things aren't too bad. Half the tables are empty, and most of the people at the other ones are picking at the remains of late lunches they ordered before I showed up. Or having a last cigarette before they ask for their checks.

I refill a few coffees, have a brief argument with a woman who wants a fresh tea bag with her hot water refill, and clean up the soda that spilled when a little kid decided to climb up on the table while his mother was tending to an even littler kid in one of those portable cradles.

When I get my break, I rush to the phone and put in a call to Tony at Feedback. "What's this about Bart getting arrested last night?" I say. "I heard the cops dragged him out of the studio in handcuffs."

"Man, news travels fast. It happened while we were down at the Purple Snail. When me and Andy—he's the guy that was the MC—got back to Feedback with the gear, the whole place was buzzin'. Bart could be in big trouble."

"What did he do?"

"Beat up a guy. With a tire iron. The guy's in the hospital, in a coma."

"Who's the guy? Did it have anything to do with Blues from the Heart?"

"Nobody knows. I mean the cops know, of course. But nobody at the studio knows."

The black guy is at the reception desk again. He recognizes me with a pleasant nod and a "How're you doing today?"

"I need to see Detective Stallings," I say. "I'm Maxx Maxwell."

"Is he expecting you?"

"Yeah, he invited me to drop by. He knows me."

"He does indeed," the guy says with a grin. "He does indeed." He turns to the phone and picks up the receiver.

I'm wearing long pants today, jeans, and a long-sleeved T-shirt, so I'm not quite frozen by the time Walter Stallings sticks his head out the door. He looks more cheerful than usual. The gravity that usually pulls the extra flesh on his face into jowly folds seems to have reversed itself, and his face looks round and gleaming.

"I sent my retirement papers through this morning," he says, as if answering my unspoken question. "Come on back to the office."

I follow him down the narrow hallway, noticing how springy his step is. At the door, he stands aside to let me enter, follows behind, and pulls one of the austere chairs up to the edge of the desk.

Taking his place behind it, he settles into his chair and looks at me with his mouth in a curious twist that I'd almost describe as a teasing smile, if it wasn't on the face of Walter Stallings. "So what can I do for you?" he says.

"You know why I'm here. You said you'd show me Monique's journal."

His fingers tap out a complicated pattern on the edge of the desk, and the curious twist to his mouth grows more pronounced. "When did I say that?"

"Yesterday on the phone."

"Are you sure it was me?" The tapping becomes louder, the pattern more intricate.

"Are you trying to torture me with suspense or what?"

"Why would I do that?"

"Because every drummer I've ever known has been a total pain in the butt."

"Really?"

"Yes, really. Are you going to go back to it now that you're retired?"

"It's been too long. Much too long." His fingers stop tapping and stiffen as he leans on the desk to pull himself erect. "I'm too out of shape besides."

He edges past me, opens the door, and steps out into the hall. I hear his footsteps gradually grow fainter. Then they get loud again, and he's back in the little room, carrying a manila folder. It's wrapped around a bulky-looking notebook. He extracts the notebook and flips through it from the back till he finds the page he's looking for. He puts the notebook into my hands.

The page I'm looking at is covered with graceful but ragged handwriting. My eyes travel over the words, which read like a transcript of one of my conversations with Monique, minus my sprightly attempts to change the subject. I look up when I get to the bottom.

"Go on," he says. "There's more."

I skim a few more pages, pausing as the handwriting becomes even more ragged, staring at a passage that reads: "OK, Monique. It's time to admit the truth. You weren't the only one. You knew it a long time before you found that lipstick. And what a pitiful, pitiful case you were. Moving into his building. Tracking him down at his rehearsals. Showing up for his gigs and sitting there worshipping him along with whatever other love-crazed women had come out to hear him play. Where did you think he went those nights he didn't come home with you? But when he wanted you to climb into bed with him after the gig, you were more than happy to oblige."

Under those words, a pen stroke divides the page like a savage slash. Under the slash are scribbled the words "I'm going to end it all."

"Where was the journal?"

"Tangled up in the sheets. She must have been sitting in bed writing and drinking. There was an empty glass down between the bed and the wall. So . . ." He shakes his head.

I'm staring at the last page of the journal. "You know what? Monique kind of rambled. This last line doesn't sound like something she'd write. Besides, the thing that leads up to it isn't even about being depressed. It's more like she's mad because it finally dawned on her that Jimmy had a million girlfriends. It's almost like something she'd write if she was getting ready to kill him, not herself." Stallings snorts and gives me a skeptical look, but I keep talking. "And check out the handwriting. Her handwriting was messy, but this looks messy in a different way."

He reaches for the journal, but I hang onto it. "The person who killed her could have added this one line to the journal entry. Made it look like a suicide note. It would have to be somebody who knew her pretty well, somebody who knew she kept a journal—or maybe it was just on the bed or something, and he got a clever idea."

"Looks like a pretty straightforward case of suicide to me. People usually put up a struggle if somebody comes after them with a box cutter—and besides, it was her box cutter. She was unpacking boxes because she recently moved in there."

"What if she was drunk when the person showed up? And I happen to know she was taking sleeping pills. She could have been so out of it that she didn't know what was going on."

Stallings snorts again. "Like I told you on the phone, the autopsy's not done yet, and they're running a fingerprint check on the box cutter. I suppose if anything out of the ordinary shows up, we could do a handwriting analysis."

By the time I get home from the Seafood Chalet that night, I'm not in great shape. I feel really worn out, and I've got a scratchy feeling in my throat. I plop in the big chair without even taking my shoes off, let my head roll back, and close my eyes.

But my brain isn't ready to turn itself off yet. First it replays the argument I had with the man who sent his surf-and-turf back three times because he said the steak wasn't rare enough, and meanwhile the lobster tail dried out because we had to keep reheating it while we made him new steaks. So then he said he'd go somewhere else and refused to pay.

Thinking about that makes we want a beer so bad I drag myself to my feet, kick off my shoes, and limp out to the kitchen where I grab two cans of Bud. I can't avoid lingering for a minute over the picture of the band stuck up on the door of the refrigerator, especially Jimmy with his sweet lopsided grin and the little straggling piece of hair falling over his forehead. I'm not as crazy as poor Monique was, but I might as well admit I was kind of obsessed with Jimmy too.

Back in the other room, I peel off my work clothes and the uncomfortable push-up bra, pull on my blues festival T-shirt, and sink back into the big chair. I pop open a can of Bud and pour a welcome stream of it down my throat.

A few sips into the second can, I drift into a kind of semi-sleep, complete with a dream, or maybe it's just a daydream, in which Ray, still gorgeous but somehow domesticated, has become the perfect, dependable, sweet, faithful boyfriend.

Nearby, someone is making strange sounds, low snorting sounds. The sounds are ruining a romantic scene in which Ray is lightly strumming his guitar and singing to me in a tuneless but adorable voice as we sit in an artistically furnished living room and sip cans of Bud.

The sounds, I realize as I open my eyes, are coming from me. I guess I was almost asleep. My neck has a crick in it from the angle of my head as it slipped lower and lower in the chair. A tap on the door pulls me back to reality. "It's Leon," says a pleasant voice. "Are you still up?"

The chair creaks as I rock forward and jump to my feet, stumbling to the door. He's holding a section of the *Times* in his hand.

"What's going on, Leon? Come in."

"You're sure it's okay? You look like I just woke you up."

"No, I was snoring, and I woke myself up."

He laughs, a mellow laugh that makes his teeth gleam white against his dark skin and his eyes crinkle up behind the tortoise-shell glasses. He offers me the newspaper. "Here's something I thought you'd like to see."

"What is it?"

"The *Times* ran an obituary for your friend Jimmy a couple of days after that first article. It was buried in that pile of newspapers on my coffee table and I just worked my way around to it." I let him stick the piece of newspaper into my hand. "Did you know his father was a big country and western star?"

"Who?"

"Bill Jenks," Leon says.

"Holy shit! That's the guy who was married to Nancy Lee Parker and then left her."

"Want me to read it to you?" Leon says, reaching for the paper again.

"Yeah, go ahead. My mind's all in a jumble—and I think I'm getting sick." I climb back into the big chair.

" 'Jimmy Nashville, Last of a Guitar Dynasty,' " Leon reads. " 'Guitarist Jimmy Nashville, son of Bill Jenks and grandson of Bob Jenks, has died. He was thirty-five. His death has been ruled suicide, pending autopsy results.' "

"The autopsy already happened," I say.

Leon goes on. " 'Nashville, who used that name profession-ally, was a fixture on the New York music scene, playing in local bands and doing session work. His roots, however, were in the city of Nashville, where his grandfather gained fame with the Grand Ole Opry in its early days, leading his band, Bob Jenks and the Tennessee Travelers, to national prominence. His father, also a bandleader, was equally noted for his songwriting. He is the author of the classics "You'll See Me When You See Me"

187

and "There's No Time Like the Present When I've Got My Arms Around You." A private memorial service will be held in Nashville, Tennessee.' "

"So does that mean Nancy Lee Parker was his mother?"

"If she was, I think the obituary would mention it. Especially since she just died too."

An hour later someone's car alarm goes off in the street under my window. My mind rises into consciousness through layers of sleep. The sounds—a series of horn blasts, like the baa-ing of an electronic sheep punctuated by bursts of high-pitched beeping—first function as part of an indistinct dream, then gradually resolve themselves into what they really are.

Somebody finally puts the car alarm to rest, but after that, sleeping becomes hopeless. I can't turn my brain off. Stan and the tall guy and Bart swirl around in a hopeless stew, mixed with Jimmy and Bill Jenks and Nancy Lee Parker. My mind jumps from thinking about the band and Ray and whether I'll ever escape from Aldo's to thinking about who killed Jimmy to thinking about what poor Monique was thinking as she dug that box cutter into her wrists—if she really did it.

By the time the sky starts to turn gray, I'm so jumpy I feel like I have ants crawling around inside my skin. And I feel like now I really am getting sick, but not that stomach thing I've been lying to Aldo about, something more like Stan's ailment with the burning throat and the dizzy spells.

CHAPTER 20

I'm standing in the bathroom staring in the mirror. My reflection is staring back at me with reddish, tired-looking eyes and a strained expression. I've been fighting off that sore throat all day, drinking tea with lemon and honey and whispering along with my rehearsal tapes to save my voice. Now whatever's been at work down in my throat has moved up to my forehead, where it's settled between my eyebrows in a dull, throbbing knot, like a medium-bad hangover.

But I can't cancel the rehearsal. This is my chance to get the band going on a whole new footing with a great new guitar player, Ray. Not to mention that if I cancel at the last minute, I'll have to pay eighty bucks for the studio anyway, and I probably won't be able to get the guys to help me out.

The thought of Ray gives me a little twinge of excitement in spite of how bad I feel and all my resolutions about not getting involved with any more guitar players. I lean closer to the mirror. There's no color in my face at all, except for the red eyes, and my lips are dry and chapped.

With hands that aren't completely steady, I stroke foundation over my face. It helps a little with the washed-out thing. Maybe some eye makeup will make my eyes look a little less like I just came off a twenty-four-hour binge. I outline them with black eyeliner and run the mascara wand over my lashes, going back and forth a couple of times while each eye dries. The effect is kind of startling. My eyes still look red, but now they look like some kind of Hollywood special effect, maybe something out of *Vampires of Death Strike Back.* I rub a lot of Vaseline into my lips, wipe it off, and color them with my reddest red lipstick.

Out in the other room, I contemplate my wardrobe. The summer is inching toward fall, and it's cooler tonight. The air coming in the windows feels different, not crisp exactly, but clean, with the faintest smell of dry leaves. What should I wear? It's only a rehearsal—no need to dress up just because Ray will be there. Besides, it's too cool outside to wear something fancy like the suede pants and halter I wore to the Purple Snail.

Maybe my black velvet jeans, though. I haven't had them out all summer and I have to paw through my whole wardrobe until I find them hanging all the way at the end of the rack, tucked up against the closet wall. I dig around in my dresser till I find my black T-shirt with the cap sleeves and the low V-neck, and from the underwear drawer I take my most lacy and glamorous push-up bra.

I like what I see in the mirror. The outfit kind of distracts from the Vampires-of-Death eyes, and I finish the look with cowboy boots, a western-style belt with a rhinestone buckle, and a pair of dangly rhinestone earrings.

I grab my bag and head out the door. As I near the end of the hall, the door to the stairwell opens and Leon emerges. "Wow," he says, stopping in mock amazement—or maybe it's real. "Where are you off to?"

"Rehearsal."

"Why the party clothes?"

"No special reason. I was a little down, and I felt like dressing up."

He gives me a knowing look. "It wouldn't have anything to do with a new guitar player or anything, would it?"

"What if it does?"

"See you later for a beer?"

"Sure."

It's totally dark outside, and it really is starting to smell like fall. I'm not in any condition to enjoy it, though. I feel light-headed as I walk toward the parking lot, despite the satisfaction of knowing that my outfit is a success.

Driving over to Manhattan, wondering why I'm even doing this when I feel so lousy, my mind wanders back to Doretta. If I hadn't met her, I wouldn't be living in Hackensack, struggling to keep my band together. I'd probably still be with Sandy, making loads of money performing at those glitzy places in Atlantic City. But I did meet her. And here's the final chapter—of that story at least.

So I show up that night for her gig. The club is just as downbeat as the other place, maybe even worse, but there are a few more people there, some brown faces mixed in with the white ones. The scrawny guitar player with the cheap guitar recognizes me, looks surprised, then goes into a little huddle with the drummer that leaves them both laughing.

The set is just about to start, so I grab a Bud and slip into a chair at the edge of what passes for the stage—a clearing at the edge of the floor.

Doretta launches into "I Love My Baby, but My Baby Don't Love Me." I don't know if it's because she knows I'm there or what. She seems in a world of her own, like the last time, reliving in her mind scenes from a life that makes her voice waver and soar. The one spotlight is focused only on her, skin already gleaming with a light film of sweat, face like a dark, eloquent sculpture.

The set could have lasted five minutes or a year. I'm so caught up in it that I have no sense of time passing, yet when it ends I feel like I'm much older than when I came in, like by living through those songs with her I've received a transfusion of her grit and power.

"How about it, honey?" she says, leaning toward me as the guitar player lets one last chord die slowly. "Wanna try one?"

"Yeah," I say, trying to ignore the quick pulse clicking away in my throat. "But I don't know the words."

"Make up your own," she says. "It's nobody's life but yours."

So I step behind the mike, give the drummer a nod, and open my mouth.

I'm not sitting in that shabby club now, drinking another Bud and trying to read the expression on the face of the guitar player while Doretta says, "Yeah, you got a chance, honey. But you gotta remember that the blues ain't pretty."

Instead, I'm circling the block endlessly, passing Feedback again and again, trying to ignore how whirly my head feels. The Stones are at Madison Square Garden, and the parking situation is a mess. The lots all have signs out advising that they're charging their special exorbitant "Garden Event" rate, and of course there's nothing left on the street.

I finally find a place way down at the corner of Ninth Avenue, slipping into it just as a van pulls out. I turn off the ignition and close my eyes for a minute.

As I step out onto the sidewalk, praying that once we get started with the rehearsal I'll forget about the whirly feeling, I look up to see the tall guy heading straight toward me.

Except apparently he doesn't know it's me. "Hello," I say, because he's looking right at me. He stops in puzzlement, smiles briefly. Recognition dawns and his face closes again. "I guess we're headed the same direction," I say, as he turns and starts walking east. "On your way to Feedback?"

"As a matter of fact, yes," he says, speeding up and leaving me behind.

I watch him hurry through the crowd. He seems different

tonight. His walk is different, for one thing—almost jaunty. If that gig bag bouncing against his back was the size and shape of an electric guitar instead of an acoustic, he could be a taller version of Jimmy.

I lose sight of him long before I even get to the corner of Eighth, but when I step inside the Feedback building, he's still down in the lobby. He's staring at the numbers tracking the elevator's slow descent. He looks over at me and grunts.

"Rehearsal?" I say.

"I'm making a demo."

"Your own songs?"

He nods, trying to hide the fact that he's pleased. As the wait for the elevator continues, he says, "A guy who heard me the other night said he'd be interested in booking me at his club."

At last the elevator comes and we ride up in silence, joined by a couple of eighties hair-band throwbacks who dashed in from the street as the elevator doors opened.

The parking space search and the wait for the elevator took up so much time that it's nine o'clock on the dot as I head down the hallway toward the Coke machine, the trashcan, and the mangy sofa that constitute Feedback's lounge. I don't see Neil, but he's probably in the john toking up. Dom and Michael are perched at opposite ends of the sofa, watching the TV, but Dom jumps up when he sees me.

"Hear about what happened to Bart?" he says.

"Oh, yeah," I say. "I did—at least up as far as him beating the guy up and the guy being in a coma. What's going on with that?"

"Self-defense, I guess. Or at least that's what he's gonna argue. The guy apparently came at him with a knife. Bart was hittin' on the guy's girlfriend, so he was askin' for it if you want my opinion. But we'll see what the lawyers come up with."

I'm wondering where Ray is, as Dom continues to talk.

Maybe inside by the desk. I feel a momentary clutch in my throat at the thought that in a minute I'll be looking into Ray's beautiful green eyes. I head through the door into the office.

But he's not in there. Stan is, though, hanging out among the nose-ring guys in one of the folding chairs lined up against the back wall. As usual he's cradling his guitar in his lap and noodling away, coaxing little un-amplified whispers from the strings. He interrupts himself in the middle of a lick to give me a cheerful wave. The tall guy bustles past me and plops himself down in the only empty seat. Neil has grabbed the armchair and looks half asleep.

Tony's sitting behind the desk, his head twisted about as far to the left as it will go, apparently watching somebody disappear down the corridor that leads to the studios. In recognition of the cooler weather, he's wearing a T-shirt under his leather vest, a black T-shirt with a Harley on the front.

After a few seconds he swings his head back around to face front again. He's got a puzzled look on his face.

"What's up?" I say.

"I'm surprised that guy showed up tonight."

"Who?"

"That Luke guy. The jazzer that was so pissed off about the noise the last time he was here."

"Yeah, he said he was going to find another place."

"Aw, he says that every time. What I mean is that his girlfriend—or ex-girlfriend, or somethin'—died a couple days ago. Killed herself, they say. I heard he's takin' it pretty hard."

"What was her name?" I ask Tony, as a weird feeling sweeps over me.

"Mona or somethin' like that. I'm not sure."

"Monique?"

"That sounds right."

Here I've been running into Monique's ex this whole time,

and I didn't know it. She never told me she was still playing gigs with the guy, that he was the guitar player who was backing her up at Lemon's that night.

Meanwhile, Tony's looking as sad as if *his* girlfriend has just died.

"Are you okay?" I say.

"I've got bad news."

"Something to do with Ray?"

"You guessed it. He got a gig at the last minute, and he's not going to show up tonight." Tony hands me a band flyer like the ones arranged in piles along the edge of the desk. It's folded in half, and in the empty space between the band's picture and a blurb about the gig, the words GIVE TO MAXX MAXWELL have been printed in big letters with a not very sharp pencil.

"I guess it was the only thing he could find to write on," Tony says. "Look inside."

Inside, on the blank back of the flyer, a message has been scrawled with that same not very sharp pencil: "Sorry I can't make it tonight. Got a paying gig at the last minute." And below, in bigger letters, "Ray," with an elaborate flourish underneath.

"He gave you this?"

"No. It was on the desk when I came in. Sorry I read it, but at first I didn't know what it was."

"That's okay."

"He's a great guitar player," Tony says, as if that explains everything. I hand the note back. "Trash?" he says and I nod. He leans over to drop it in the wastebasket.

"Do you ever run into him, Tony?"

"He's in here a lot."

"Tell him I need somebody I can depend on."

Tony nods. "That's a really nice outfit, Maxx," he says. He looks into my eyes, and I feel like he understands the whole sad thing, like he's some kind of a super-wise shrink, not a hairy guy in a Harley T-shirt and a leather vest. But in a second he turns back into Tony. "Where is that tech punk?" he bellows looking around the room.

"In the can," says one of the nose-ring guys, gesturing with his thumb toward the door in the wall opposite where the studios are, then raising his fingers to his mouth as if dragging on a joint.

Tony edges out from behind the desk and strides toward the door. "Maxx Maxwell needs her room," he shouts as he pounds on it. "Studio G."

I turn away from the desk in kind of a daze, half because of the news about Ray, half because I'm starting to feel feverish and I've still got that throbbing between my eyebrows. What am I going to tell the band, especially Dom? Maybe I should cancel the whole thing and go home and climb into bed.

As I'm standing there, a guy comes in from the hall. He's a small wiry guy, and he's wearing baggy shorts that end a little bit below his knees and a baggy T-shirt that hides about two-thirds of the shorts. He's carrying a clipboard. He surveys the row of guys sitting in the folding chairs, consults the clipboard, and says, "Which one of you is here to cut the demo?"

The tall guy says, "I am."

The baggy shorts guy slips behind the desk. "I'm gonna need some cash or a credit card imprint before we get started."

"Sure." The tall guy is trying to act cool, but I can tell he's kind of nervous. He reaches into his back pocket and pulls out a wallet.

Meanwhile, Stan is edging toward me. "I couldn't help overhearing," he says, "about your guitar player. I could sit in. Just as a favor. No strings attached."

At first I'm too amazed to even speak. The guy never gives up. Finally I say, "What on earth are you even doing here? You told me you weren't playing with the Blue Dudes anymore."

"Uh—what I'm doing here?" His gaze darts away then darts back and his head droops.

"You didn't have anything to do with Ray canceling out, did you?" A sudden image of Ray lying limp on the ground under an open ninth-floor window pops into my brain.

"No. How can you think that about me?"

"Why are you acting so nervous then?"

"Because you're getting mad at me again. It makes me nervous when people get mad at me." He lifts his chin. "I met some guys at SOS—you know, the night I got sick? They jam here on Thursday nights, but they haven't shown up yet."

"Stan, it wouldn't work. Your style just isn't—"

"It's different now," he says. "Really. I've been listening to all those things you told me to listen to." He makes a "stay there" gesture with one of his huge hands. "Wait. Check this out." He backs toward the chair he was sitting in, feeling for the guitar he left leaning against the wall, losing his balance and nearly ending up in the lap of one of the nose-ring guys.

He grabs the guitar and plants his foot on the seat of the chair, balances the guitar on his thigh, and beckons to me. "C'mere," he says. "You have to really stick your ear close to hear anything without an amp."

I edge a little closer. Stan's fingers get busy, and I hear the whispery echo of a line that's nothing like his usual frantic jumble of sounds. It's only three or four notes, placed just right, with a heart-melting touch of vibrato at the end. I half expect to see B. B. King beaming at me when I look up from his fingers to his face.

But no, it's still Stan, blinking at me through a piece of hair that's become detached from his careless ponytail, fallen over his left eye, and somehow gotten stuck on his lip. He lifts his hand from the strings and pushes it behind his ear.

Why not? I'm too sick to fight with him. And what would be

worse? To tell Dom there's no guitar player at all or to tell him Stan's sitting in just for the rehearsal?

"Okay," I say with a long sigh. "But just for tonight."

"Understood." He nods and the piece of hair comes loose again. "I know all the tunes," he says. "Don't worry about a thing." He trots happily toward the corridor that leads to the studios. "G? Like the old days?" I nod and head out into the hall to get Dom and Michael.

Dom raises his eyebrows when I tell him Stan is sitting in. "Are you sure you know what you're doing?" he says.

Michael gives me a sulky look.

"He sounds different now," I say, "and it's just for tonight."

Michael's sulky look intensifies. He stands and picks up his bass, and moves toward the door with all the enthusiasm of somebody who's about to spend the next three hours at hard labor.

I follow them into the office and let them head for the studio without me as I bend over to shake Neil's shoulder. He comes awake with a start, muttering, "What is it? What is it?"

"Let's go," I say. "The room's ready."

His eyelids flutter closed and his head sways back against the chair.

I lean over him again. "Come on, Neil. Let's get going."

As I pull myself erect again, I suddenly feel woozy. Reddish-black spots gather in front of my eyes, blanking out Neil's face and the wall behind him and the scruffy chair and everything. I feel my body start to sag and my legs give way. I grab the arm of the chair and lower myself onto the floor.

Neil's more or less awake now, and he's got a worried look on his face. "Are you okay?" he says.

"Fine," I say. "I just need to sit here for a minute. Go on in. Tell them I'll be there in a minute."

"What's wrong?" Tony says from behind the desk.

"I just felt a little light-headed. I think I'm coming down with something."

The next thing I know, Tony is kneeling at my side with a Styrofoam cup of water. "Drink this," he says, "and I'll get you some more. Want some aspirin?" He takes my hand and slips the glass into it, holds on for a minute to make sure I'm steady enough to raise the cup to my lips.

"Would aspirin help?" I say weakly.

"Couldn't hurt." He stands and heads back to the desk where I hear drawers opening and closing. He's back in a second holding out two aspirin in his hand. "Need more water?"

"Yeah." I take the aspirin and wait while he refills the cup at the water fountain in the corner.

"Here," he says, offering me his hand. "You'd be more comfortable in this chair." I let him help me up and settle gratefully into the armchair.

CHAPTER 21

A few minutes later, I'm making my way down the hall to Studio G, feeling a little bit better after drinking the water, and with Tony's assurance that the aspirin will really help. Even before I open the outer door, I can hear music, and it doesn't sound bad. A nice blues shuffle, and Stan's got some kind of a tasteful guitar part going on, adding a jangle here, a lick there.

I negotiate the doors, toss my bag on one of the folding chairs, and step up behind the mike. " 'Heeey!' " I sing, " 'baby do you want to go?' " The groove they've got going feels great, even though my voice isn't at its best tonight. But no sound at all is coming out of the PA. Shit. A roomful of musicians and they forget to tell the tech guy that there's a singer.

I pull the inner door toward me, push the outer door away from me, and make my way back down the corridor to get the tech guy. The tech guy follows me back to the studio and gets the mike hooked up. The band is still playing the "Sweet Home Chicago" groove, so I start in with the first verse again and nod at Stan when I'm done.

His solo has all the Stan chops from before, but now the frantic million-notes-a-minute stuff has a funky twang to it, and it's punctuated with sweet, leisurely lines that ooze from his fingers like honey. I can't resist a look at Dom. He's staring at Stan like he can't believe his ears.

"Take another one," I say as Stan wraps up his twelve bars.

He does, and I sing again, then Neil solos, and I let Stan take it out.

"What the hell happened, bud?" Dom says in amazement as the final chord dies away.

"Is something wrong?" Stan glances around the room with a puzzled expression on his face. "Am I unplugged or what?"

"No, no, man. I mean you sound awesome."

"Yes, indeed," Michael adds. "Fantastic."

"You been takin' lessons or what? Where'd it come from?" Dom says. He catches my eye and makes a thumbs-up gesture.

"I don't know," Stan says, scratching his head. "Like I told Maxx, I've been listening to more blues. I guess after a while you just get those sounds in your brain."

Neil is staring at Stan like he just stepped out of a spaceship. Finally he says, "Nice soloing."

"Thanks," Stan says and turns and stoops toward his amp to mess with the knobs. Just to make sure we don't forget he's still Stan, he loses his balance on the way up and whacks the mike stand with his guitar neck.

I grab the mike stand before it goes over. "Is your guitar okay?" I say.

"Sure," Stan says, running his hand down the fret board. "I bump into things all the time."

"Ready to do another one?" He nods. "How about 'Sweet Little Angel'? Go ahead and kick it off."

This time Stan's soloing is even more amazing than it was on the last tune. Notes fall from his fingers like slow drops of molten silver, till he lands on one that hangs in the air so long time seems to stop.

I step up to the mike, try to ignore my throbbing head and scratchy throat, and sing, " 'I've got a sweet little angel, and I love the way he spreads his wings.' " Stan fills in a delicate figure behind me. " 'I've got a sweet little angel—' " I let the line breathe for a few seconds, then go on. I feel a slight motion next to me and look over to see Stan swaying, hair hiding his face, bent over the guitar in kind of a trance. A few of those careful, silvery notes chime from his amp.

I pause and take a breath so I can really throw myself into the next couple of words.

At the end of the verse, I nod at Neil to solo. When he's done, I sing a couple more verses and let Stan solo a while before I take it out.

As Dom's cymbal crash dies away, Stan looks over at him. "Good, good, real good," he says. "But I wouldn't use those fills like you were doing."

Dom looks at him and his eyes get big. "What?"

"I wouldn't use the fills."

"Why?"

"It doesn't go with the tune."

"Bud, you sound good tonight, but I don't need the blues police tellin' me how to play the drums."

"No, Stan's right," Michael chimes in. "Haven't you noticed how I have to lay out right there because of what you're doing on the drums?"

Dom's voice is sarcastic. "No, bud, I can't say I've noticed."

Stan is looking earnestly at Dom. "Have you ever listened to the drums on *Live at the Regal*? It's a very cool drum part." He turns his gaze on me. "I assume you're going for the B. B. King sound."

"I said I don't need no blues police tellin' me how to play the drums," Dom says.

"You guys want to sound like a blues band. Am I right?" Stan looks at me again. I don't know what to say, so I don't say anything. "Or maybe you're thinking of the Big Mama Thornton version?" He looks back at Dom. "In that case . . ." He edges toward the drum kit, carefully because of the guitar dangling around his neck, and reaches for one of the spare sticks Dom has stockpiled on the floor. "There's a great lick her drummer uses . . ."

Dom's foot comes crashing down on the drumsticks, barely missing Stan's hand. "I don't need you tellin' me how to play the drums," he says with a snarl.

"But it could sound so much better," Stan says. Dom doesn't say anything, but his face starts to turn pink. "Don't you want it to sound better?"

Dom glares at him. "No," he says.

"How about 'She's Into Something'?" I say brightly. In my mind I'm picturing myself walking in the door of my apartment and collapsing into the big chair with a beer. I'm popping the top open and pouring the cold liquid down my poor sore throat. Or maybe I'll have a shot of Jack Daniel's. Maybe two.

I check the clock on the wall behind Dom. We've only been here twenty minutes. Will I even survive?

"Good call," Stan says. "Real good. I copped a cool intro off the Muddy Waters recording. We weren't doing a very authentic version when I was in the band before."

Dom grits his teeth.

I say, "Go for it."

Stan bends over his guitar and picks out a bouncy riff.

Things go smoothly for the next couple of hours, mostly because I keep calling tunes fast enough that there's no time for Stan to make suggestions in between. Unfortunately, with about half an hour to go, Neil announces that he's got to hit the head.

Dom frowns as he watches him leave the room. "He's getting worse," he observes as Neil disappears through the outer door. "Have you noticed? Since Jimmy died?"

"What do you mean?"

"He's stoned all the time now. What do you think he's going to the head for?"

"It's his business," I say.

"It's gonna be the band's business pretty soon, if there even is a band."

"Dom, chill out," I say. "Everything's going to be fine. There will be a band." I look around for a chair and lower myself into it, close my eyes, and let my head sink toward my knees.

"You okay?" This is Stan talking.

"Yeah, I'm fine. I'm just coming down with something. A couple days' rest and I'll be back to normal."

"Good," he says. "I hope you didn't catch it from me." He perches on the edge of his amp and leans toward me companionably, curving his lean body around his guitar. "You know, on that tune we just did, I think it would be better if we tried to add some more dynamics, start real basic and build it up. If you listen to Buddy Guy, you realize how effective that can be."

I lift my head slightly, open my eyes, and try to bring him into focus. "You don't think it has dynamics now?"

"*You* do, but you're fighting the drums the whole time. If the drums are too loud, everything else gets loud."

I close my eyes and let my head slump toward my knees again. Behind me I hear a kind of growl coming from the direction of the drum kit. It's followed by Dom's voice saying, "I'm gonna try to stay calm, bud, and I'm only gonna say one thing." He sounds anything but calm, and by the time he gets to the end, he's shouting, "Why don't you mind your own business?"

"This is a blues band," Stan says placidly. "We should all be working together."

I raise my head, fling myself against the back of the chair, and glare at Stan. "For God's sake, Stan," I say. "You are only sitting in with us. You are not a member of the band." I stand up. Usually I don't lose my temper, but when I do, it's pretty dramatic. "Where is that fucking pothead asshole?" I hear myself say as I stomp toward the double doors.

As I grab the knob of the inner door and pull it toward me, the outer door opens as well. I barely miss colliding with Neil as he steps toward me, bearing with him a drift of marijuana smoke.

" 'Scuse me," he murmurs and edges around me.

"I'm going to get some water," I say without turning around, and I head down the corridor to the office. I storm through the office, past Tony and the nose-ring guys, jerk open the door of the unisex bathroom, slam down the toilet seat, and perch on the edge of it, biting my lips to keep from crying.

I picture the big chair, the can of cold beer, the shot of Jack Daniel's. I even picture the miraculous day in the future when the band is making money and I'm telling Aldo to fuck off. I take deep breaths, trying to ignore the fact that the air I'm breathing is mostly marijuana smoke.

Finally, I get to my feet and look at myself in the mirror. The eye makeup isn't standing up too well to the tears brought on by my emotions and the acrid air. I grab a piece of toilet paper, dampen it under the tap, and try to dab away some of the worst damage.

"You okay?" Tony asks as I emerge.

"Fine," I say. "The aspirin really helped."

"You're sure?" he says, his homely face puckering with concern.

"I just have to live through the next half hour," I say and head toward the corridor.

I can hear the band even before I open the outer door. They've got kind of a Latin groove going on, like an Albert King thing, "Killing Floor" or "Crosscut Saw," and they sound great. Except there's no drums. What now? I ask myself. I pull the outer door toward me, push the inner door away from me, and step into the room.

Neil is bent over the keyboard, his fingers dancing from black keys to white keys, picking out a single note here, a cluster of notes there. Michael, looking cheerful enough, is methodically plucking away at his strings, his hand like a giant, busy spider moving back and forth across his fret board. Stan looks like he's in heaven.

Dom, however, isn't even sitting behind his drums. He's perched on the edge of the little dais that raises the drum kit about a foot off the floor, and he's chewing on his lip and staring at the wall.

I just stand there watching them. After two or three minutes, Michael stops. Stan is next. Neil carries on for about half a chorus till he realizes nobody else is playing.

" 'Killing Floor'?" I say in the most cheerful voice I can muster. "Sounds great. Let's take it from the top." I step behind the mike. Dom doesn't move. "Dom, are you okay?"

He stops chewing on his lip long enough to say, "No."

"What happened?"

"I don't need the blues police to tell me the difference between a rumba and a mambo."

I take a deep breath and try to avoid catching Stan's eye. "We've only got about twenty minutes left," I say. "Stan, you've been great to sit in with us at short notice, but . . . uh . . ." I don't know how to finish the sentence so I just stop. "Let's just play something. Come on, Dom. We need you."

He pulls himself to his feet with a scowl and climbs up behind the drum kit. " 'Killing Floor,' " he says. "And I'll play it however I damn well want to."

I beg my poor throat to rise to the occasion, but I'm basically croaking my way through it. Neil and Stan take their solos, and since I don't think my throat can handle even one more verse, I nod to Michael, and he happily jumps in with a bass solo. Then I nod to Dom. Why not throw in a drum solo? He obliges, but kind of stingily, like he's still really pissed off and doesn't even want to be playing at all.

I let him take it out. When the last flurry of drumbeats subsides, Stan looks over at Dom. "Good, good," he says. "That was much better. Much closer to what Albert King's drummer does on the *Roadhouse Blues* album."

"I wasn't tryin' to be Albert King's drummer!" Dom shouts at him.

"Well, it was good anyway. So much better than what you were going for the first time."

Dom rises. Since the drums are already on a dais, the effect is of him towering over the rest of us. "I been playin' drums my whole life," he says. "I been in at least a hundred bands. I don't need a skinny weirdo with too much hair tellin' me I'm gettin' *better*."

"We can all learn," Stan says. "I'm always trying to learn. I didn't get pissed off when you told me I sounded better." He twists his neck to the side and tugs at his guitar strap. "If I were you, I'd only do one thing different in that drum part for 'Killing Floor.' "

"That's it," Dom says. He stoops over and grabs the handful of spare sticks off the edge of the dais, plucks the nylon case he carries them in off the floor, and stalks toward the door. "Maxxie," he says on the way out, "you're a cool chick, but this band ain't goin' nowhere, and even if it does go somewhere, it's gonna have to get there without me."

CHAPTER 22

"I guess the rehearsal's over," I say. The lights are blinking anyway, so we've only got five minutes left.

Neil looks like he's trying to figure out what's going on, but Michael looks almost triumphant, like this proves Dom was bad news, and he knew it all the time. Stan is staring at the floor, his guitar still dangling around his neck; his body slumped over; his hair hiding his face.

"I'm sorry," he mumbles.

"You should be," I say. Then, "I'll be right back."

The inner door is ajar but the outer door is kind of stuck shut. Dom must have given it a good slam on the way out. I throw myself against it, and it pops open. For a second I'm off balance. When I get my footing again, I hurry down the corridor. There's no sign of Dom in the office, so I hurry past Tony, ignoring the question on his face, through the knot of guys milling around the Coke machine and the trashcan, down the long hall that leads to the elevators.

I can hear the cables creaking as I approach the corner. Will Dom still be here? If so, what will I say? My head feels like it's about to burst, enveloped in a hot haze, my fury at Stan intermingling with the throbbing behind my forehead. And my throat is on fire, partly from this flu or whatever it is, partly because a huge sob is lurking down there, waiting to explode.

I turn the corner. Dom is tapping his foot, glowering at the elevator doors, the combination of his shaved head and his intense frown making his face look like some kind of a tribal mask.

"Dom, please," I say, grabbing his arm. He shakes his head no, the frown still firmly in place. "Stan was only sitting in for the rehearsal," I say, desperately. "I know how you feel. He's still a pain in the butt—now he's just a different kind of pain." I'm tugging on Dom's arm now, like a little kid begging a parent for something, but I can't help it. "I won't have Stan back—*ever.*"

"Your band ain't goin' nowhere, Maxx. And Kenny White's is."

"Please hang on just a little longer. Everything was great when we had Jimmy. It'll be great again."

"Jimmy's gone."

"But I got Josh. He's a fabulous player."

"Yeah, and he could see it wasn't goin' nowhere, so he cut out."

"He dug the band. He just can't afford to play in bars."

"Well, neither can I, and you know what? I wouldn't take a million-dollar gig if I had to play with Stan." He spits the name out like he can't even stand to have it in his mouth.

I can hear the elevator coming closer, cables creaking like the groans of a tormented beast.

"You won't have to," I say. "I promise."

"Sorry. It's over." He shakes his head. "Oh, I suppose you'll be wantin' this." He pulls out his wallet and extracts a twenty-dollar bill. "Keep the change."

"Dom, you can't quit. It will kill the band. I worked so hard. It's so important to me. Please." Tears are popping into my eyes, the kind that burn before they overflow.

"It wasn't workin' out," he says, more gently. "And besides, Dora—she hated me bein' in your band. She's the one who canceled the gig the night Jimmy died. And she messed up my van last Saturday—killed the battery by leavin' the lights on all day. Did it on purpose. Thought I'd blow off the gig."

With a ponderous thud, the elevator halts on the sixth floor and the doors clank open. Dom starts to step in. I'm still clinging to his arm. "Let go," he says. "I'm cuttin' out."

"Say you won't quit," I hear myself wail. "Please say you won't quit."

"I gotta go, Maxx," he says, prying my fingers loose. The doors try to close on him then bounce back with a reproachful squeal. I reach for his arm again. He fends me off, steps around me, and says, "Damn, I'm takin' the stairs." He eludes my grasp and sprints away, surprisingly speedy for a guy who has twenty or twenty-five extra pounds hanging over his belt.

I head back down the hall toward the office, not sure where I'm going or what I'm going to do, my head still throbbing and my throat still on fire. Behind the desk, Tony's holding a credit card in his hand and looking puzzled. "Where'd this come from?" he says. "Somebody left it in the imprint gizmo." He scans the guys lounging in the folding chairs, squints at the card. "Bill Jenks, Jr.? Anybody here named Bill Jenks, Jr.?"

Bill Jenks, Jr.? I feel a jolt like I just saw a ghost.

A kid with a nose ring says, "I think it belongs to the guy making the demo." Just then the tall guy rounds the corner from the hall. "Him," the kid says, pointing. "He forgot to get it back before he went down to the studio."

I look up at the tall guy. His face is Jimmy's face—why didn't I ever notice that before? A wave of misery surges over me. Jimmy is dead, and my band is totally fucked up and *this* is the guy responsible. But not because Jimmy hated his songs.

"I need to book some more studio time," the tall guy says. "Got anything open tomorrow night?"

"This yours?" Tony says, handing him the credit card.

The tall guy glances at the credit card, nods, and says,

"Thanks, man. Where was it?"

Tony points at the imprint gizmo.

The tall guy tucks the credit card into his pocket, confers with Tony for a minute, and heads out the door. In a daze, I trail him into the hall.

"You killed Jimmy Nashville," I hear myself say. Through tears that make it seem like I'm watching the scene through fingerprint-smeared glasses, I can see that he's too surprised to wear the careful mask he usually wears, and behind him I can see the curious faces of the guys loitering around the Coke machine.

But I don't care who's watching or who's listening. The words come pouring out. "You're his brother, aren't you? His half brother. Your dad was Bill Jenks, and your mom was Nancy Lee Parker, and your dad left Nancy Lee Parker to marry Jimmy's mom, and you always blamed Jimmy because your mom's life was a mess. And you gave him a tape of her last album and you wrote 'Whiskey for Breakfast,' about growing up with her, and when she died last week you decided he should die too, so you went up to his apartment and pushed him out the window. And then you killed Monique because she was there and she saw you do it."

Some of the Coke machine guys have come closer. Among them is Luke, the grouchy jazz guy, staring at me like I have two heads. I must be making quite a spectacle of myself, but I don't really care. I'm running out of breath now, but I've still got more to say.

I take kind of a strangled breath and keep talking. "Jimmy's apartment was full of clues, clues only a musician would recognize, and I got the key from his next-door neighbor, a crazy old lady. At first I was confused because there were so many clues, but I have it all figured out now, and I'm going to the cops. You won't get away with it. You'll see. Because I have a friend, a cop, and now he'll really have to believe me."

I'm running out of breath again, and finally I stop and when I do, the sob that was waiting in my throat comes choking out. I bury my face in my hands and lurch forward, landing on my knees with my elbows on the sofa.

For a while all I hear is the sound of my own crying, huge gasping sobs that are almost a relief after all this time holding them in, not just tonight, but ever since Jimmy died. My face, burrowed into my hands, feels hot and slippery with tears. Red and black patterns swirl around behind my closed eyelids. As I cry, I can feel my body becoming less and less stiff, finally slumping toward the floor until only my arms rest on the sofa. I stretch them out in front of me and rest my cheek in the crook of one elbow.

Your eye makeup must be an absolute mess, a voice in my mind says irrelevantly. From above me come voices: the voice of the tall guy—I still think of him as that even though I know his name now—and a voice I recognize as Tony's.

". . . totally flipped out," the tall guy is saying. "Thinks I killed somebody. Has it all figured out like some kind of a mystery plot."

"She's been having a rough time with her band," Tony says. "The guitar player committed suicide. Jimmy Nashville. Did you know him?"

"I may have heard the name," the tall guy says.

The next thing I know, a gentle hand is rubbing my back, and Tony's voice is whispering, "How about I help you make it back to the john? Drink some cold water, splash a little on your face—you'll be yourself in no time. An' I can leave the tech punk to run things for a while, drive you home. Maybe you're a little too woozy to make it on your own."

I let him pull me to my feet and I totter unsteadily around the corner into the office, leaning on his shoulder.

"Why don't cha sit right down here?" he says as we near the armchair. "I'll get you that water."

I sink into the armchair, aware that the Coke machine guys are now bunched up outside the office door, still staring at me curiously. The tall guy seems to have disappeared.

In a minute, Tony is at my elbow again, holding a Styrofoam cup of water from the drinking fountain. I accept it gratefully and pour it down my throat, wishing it was beer.

"My bag," I croak to Tony. "I think it's still in the studio."

"Sure thing." He hurries toward the doorway that leads to the studios and disappears into the corridor.

When he returns he's being trailed by Michael, Neil, and Stan. Stan slinks toward the door without saying anything. Michael and Neil regard me with worried looks. "Are you going to be okay?" Michael says.

"Fine," I mumble. "I'll be fine."

"Are we going to have a rehearsal next week?"

"I'll call you," I say.

"Here's the money," Michael says, thrusting a handful of bills at me. "Stan put in double to cover Dom's share."

"Dom already gave me some money."

"What should I do with the extra?"

"I don't know," I say, waving him away. "I don't care."

Five minutes later, I'm feeling somewhat like myself. I've finished the cup of water, washed my face, combed my hair and clipped the loose, sweaty strands into a twist. I've even retrieved my car keys from my bag and apologized to Tony for creating a scene.

I make my way down the hall, wondering if I'll ever have the nerve to show my face at Feedback again. Why will I even need to? The band is fucked. As I wait for the elevator, I picture myself still working at Aldo's five years from now, ten years from now. Maybe my mother was right when she said I should forget about the music and stay in college and study something practical.

The elevator comes, and I step into it. Now that I've finally calmed down, I'm just tired, very tired. It's after midnight, and my car's parked way over at Ninth Avenue.

Down on the street, there aren't many people around. It's like all of a sudden it's not summer anymore, and people are home curled up in front of their TVs, not strolling the streets all night talking and laughing.

But as I start to make my way down the sidewalk, I hear a voice say, "Maxx?" I turn. It's Stan, pushing his lanky body away from the wall next to the door of the Feedback building.

"I don't want to talk about it." I continue to walk.

"Doesn't he want to learn?" Stan wails, trailing after me. "When I was at Jimmy's place, he said—" I speed up. But then I stop and turn.

"When you were at Jimmy's place? But you said you weren't at Jimmy's place. You said you didn't even know him."

Caught in the pink neon glare of the Rave sign, Stan's face looks even more confused than usual. "I lied," he says, head bowed, looking at the sidewalk. "I didn't want you to know. I, uh, went there to ask him for some pointers on my playing. Because, uh, I figured if you liked his sound so much, maybe I could learn something." His head droops even further. "I wasn't there Saturday night, though."

"How did you even find him?"

"I asked some guy at Feedback who he was, after I saw him there with you Thursday night. He's in the phone book. I called him Saturday morning, and he said to come over. He was very cool about it. We jammed for a while. He was sort of getting into my style. Then he put a CD on, Charlie Christian—Jimmy really dug him—and we talked for a while."

"Why didn't you tell me that sooner?"

"I thought you'd get mad at me." He shakes his head, still looking at the sidewalk. Then he looks up. "I'm really sorry about what happened tonight. And I know a guy who's a really good drummer. I could ask him if he'd be interested."

"No," I say. "The relationship between you and the band is over forever. There's just something about you that messes things up."

I turn and start to walk away. I hear his voice behind me, saying, "Please, Maxx." But I ignore it. I dart past a couple of lovers strolling along hand in hand and leave Stan somewhere behind them.

I make my way along 30th, past the Center for Homeless Women, with its exuberant jungle of plastic plants behind a pane of frosted glass, past the hobby store with its window full of toys, past the place that sells cheap plastic luggage imported from God knows where.

When I think I've lost Stan, I slow down, poking along like an old woman creeping home after being on her feet all day—like I'll be after ten or twenty more years at Aldo's.

At the corner of Eighth Avenue, I wait for the light, noticing how dark and deserted the stretch of 30th between Eighth and Ninth is. Thirtieth suddenly becomes residential at Eighth, with a row of low brick tenements, neighborly stoops deserted on this no-longer-summer night. There's not much traffic on Eighth. I wait for the light because I'd just as soon stand as move. No traffic to speak of on 30th. And the Stones concert must have ended in time for all those people to clear out of the city by now.

When the light changes, I make my way across Eighth, walking slower and slower. I move from one pool of streetlamp light to the next, an unbroken row of cars on my left, tenement facades on my right, all closed up for the night with barely even a glimmer of light in the windows.

Midway down the block, I cut diagonally across 30th. I can see my car down there at the end of the street, parked in front of a nondescript brick apartment building at the end of a row of dark tenements. I stay on the pavement, avoiding the sidewalk, skirting the row of parked cars. There's something creepy about those dark facades with the deep pockets of darkness at the edges of the stoops, the jumbled piles of garbage bags heaped around trash bins the size of small humans, the steps themselves in shadow unless the front door has a porch light. I poke through a pool of streetlamp light, step out of its fading rim into darkness, then into another light pool. I'm three cars away now. I've got my keys jingling in my hand, my bag slung over my shoulder.

My car's sea-foam green is neutered to an anonymous gray in the dark. I decide not to fight the lock, so I switch my keys to my left hand, slip between the front bumper of my car and the back bumper of the one I'm parked behind, edge along the fender, and reach for the passenger-side door.

It's almost over, I sigh to myself. I've made the drive home from the studio so many times I can do it on autopilot. Then what? The beer I've been dreaming of all night? Or maybe a hot shower and bed. And I won't think about the future of the band until I've had a good night's sleep.

I click the door open, throw my bag into the back, and lower myself into the car. I'm tugging the door shut, getting ready to slide across the seat and settle myself behind the steering wheel, when I feel something tugging the door back. I look through the window and all I see is a T-shirt—some indeterminate color in the dark—and the top few inches of a pair of jeans.

I feel like something's grabbing my throat, but the person— whoever it is—is still out there on the sidewalk. The feeling in my throat is coming from inside, welling up from where my heart now feels like it's pumping a few extra gallons of blood per minute.

I tug harder on the door. Even if I get it to latch, the lock doesn't work, and I can't start the car with my right hand clinging to the passenger-side door handle.

The person on the outside tugs harder too, and finally my fingers can't hold on anymore. The door flies open. I pull my hand away, fingers tingling, and the face of the tall guy appears. I grab for the door handle on my side of the car, pressing on it as hard as I can, praying for the latch to click open. No luck.

"I wanted to talk to you," the tall guy says, lowering himself onto the seat.

"Oh?" I try to sound calm. The street is totally deserted. All the tenement windows I can see are dark, and the apartment building I'm parked next to offers only a blank brick wall punctuated by a service door.

If I was outside, maybe somebody would be able to hear me yell. But here, stuck in the car with the windows rolled up . . . I reach for the knob that unrolls the window. Thank God that still works. But a large hand encloses my hand and pulls it down onto the seat between us.

"There's no reason to panic," the tall guy says. "I just want to talk."

"What about?" My whole body seems to be throbbing in time with the pulse in my neck.

"You said some pretty remarkable things about me up there in the studio," he says. "Some of them weren't true."

"Which ones?" I scan the sidewalk, praying that someone will wander by.

"You said I killed Jimmy and somebody named Monique. First of all, I've never known anybody named Monique . . ." He pauses. "Look at me," he says. "I'm going to try to explain something to you."

I turn my head toward him. He looks worried and defenseless, even kind of tender, and so much like Jimmy I can hardly stand it. He's still got my hand captured in his between us on the seat, and he's squeezing it so hard that it's starting to hurt. I feel like I'm going to faint or scream.

"Maybe Jimmy Nashville *was* my brother," he says. "And maybe Nancy Lee Parker was my mother, and maybe I'm pissed as hell that her life turned out the way it did—"

All of a sudden, his eyes leave mine and focus on something behind me, outside the window.

There's a light tap on the car door, almost no more than a scratching sound, but I'm so wired it makes me jump. I swivel my head away from the tall guy and find myself looking into the eyes of Stan, who's bent over, staring at me through the car window.

I pull my hand out of the tall guy's grasp, and he lets it go without saying anything. I grab the knob and roll the window down. Stan's face remains where it was, an inch from the opening. "You're mad at me again," he says. "And now I can see that I'm interrupting something—"

"Stan, thank God." For some reason I whisper it, even though I know the tall guy can hear whatever I say. Stan looks startled, like he can't imagine what's going on. "Stan, get me out of here." I grab the driver's side door handle again and start shaking it. Nothing happens.

"What's going on?" Stan bends over further and sticks his head in the window.

The tall guy says, "Butt out. We're having a peaceful chat. She's got some kind of a delusion that I killed her friends, and I'm trying to set her straight."

"What friends? Jimmy and Monique? You think he killed Jimmy and Monique?" I nod. "No, you're all wrong there. *He* didn't kill Jimmy—"

Stan stops in confusion and backs away from the car.

CHAPTER 23

"What are you telling me?" I scream as Stan turns and darts across the street. The condition of my throat makes the words squeeze out in a raw squawk. Stan slips between two parked cars and vanishes into the shadows, heading up Ninth Avenue.

I disentangle my fingers from the keys clutched in my left hand, switch them to my right hand, and twist the car key in the ignition, pumping the gas pedal till the car chokes its way to life.

I slam the car into reverse, back up far enough to clear the bumper of the guy in front of me, and jerk the steering wheel to the left. "Make sure that door is latched," I say to the tall guy.

"What the fuck are you doing?" he says, squirming like he's about to throw the door open and jump out.

"He's the one that killed Jimmy," I say. "I knew it all the time. We've got to go after him."

"Why?"

"Didn't you hear me? I said he killed Jimmy. And he wrecked my band and ruined my life and if at all possible, I'm going to run him down and squash him like a bug."

I'm just about to launch myself onto Ninth Avenue when I notice it's one-way in the wrong direction. So instead I roar up the middle of 30th to Eighth, ignore the light, and swing left. How fast can Stan run? How many blocks should I allow before I cut back over and swoop down on him from the north?

I speed up Eighth, ignoring the traffic lights, just slowing the slightest bit at each corner to make sure nothing's coming through. At 34th I swing left again, careening past some big entertainment complex with a zipper sign flashing a dizzying stream of words. At Ninth I have to stop. The light's red, and a cab is barreling toward the intersection, followed by a van with Chinese writing on the side.

When the van's out of the way, I lurch into the intersection, narrowly missing an oblivious guy on a bicycle who will never know how close he came to getting mowed down. The light's still red, but I make my turn anyway.

This stretch of Ninth skirts the back of the big post office and several blocks of anonymous wall shadowed by construction scaffolding. Stan would be on this side of the street, based on the last I saw of him as he headed up the block. I stick to the left lane, alternating between watching the road ahead of me and scanning the shadowy sidewalk for that familiar loping form.

But just for good measure, I glance to the right once in awhile. Is that him stepping onto the curb in front of the fancy Chinese place with the awning? No, not tall enough and not enough hair. I pass a row of anonymous storefronts and restaurants and still no sign of Stan.

Back at 30th, I pull into the same place I left ten minutes ago and slump forward with my arms crossed on the steering wheel and my head resting on them. I close my eyes and watch the red and black blotches behind my eyelids jump around in time to my heartbeats. After a while I feel a little bit calmer.

"Are you gonna be okay?" the tall guy says.

I raise my head and open my eyes. He's leaning toward me, looking worried, looking sweet, like Jimmy looked when he asked me if I'd miss him if he was gone. "Yeah," I say. "I'll probably survive. I'm pretty tough."

"You're sure?"

"I'm sure." Then, "You said maybe she was your mother. Was she?"

"Yeah."

"She was a good singer."

"I know."

"How old were you when . . . when they broke up?"

"Not even a year. He never came around afterwards. I don't have any memory of him."

"I can see why you'd be pissed off," I say. "But it wasn't Jimmy's fault. You didn't have to lay a guilt trip on him with that tape."

"I should have stayed in Nashville, but I thought a change of scene would help me push the music thing along. Then I got up here and found out Jimmy was here, and I wanted to know him. I wanted him to know about her, too. She wasn't really any relation of his, but still . . ." He sighs. "It seemed like he was too busy to bother with us. Then she died." He rubs his face with his hands. When he pulls his hands away, he looks even more like Jimmy. "So this—what's his name? The guy we were chasing?"

"Stan," I say.

"What's his story?"

"He was in my band. I fired him, and Jimmy took his place. He wanted his job back. He figured if Jimmy was out of the way, I'd have to give him another chance."

"What are you going to do now?"

"Go home to bed. And tomorrow I'm going to the cops and tell them what happened tonight. I already tried to tell them Stan killed Jimmy, but they blew me off. They have to believe me now. How could anybody act more guilty?" I twist the key in the ignition. "Can I take you somewhere?"

"No," he says. "I live a couple blocks from here. Besides, your driving makes me a little nervous." He clicks the door open and slides out. But before he slams the door behind him, he leans back in. "You gonna be okay getting home?"

"Yeah."

As the bridge comes into view halfway up the West Side Highway, I have an unnerving thought. Stan's specialty seems to be popping up when he's least expected. What if he's waiting for me as I pull into the parking lot behind my building? He gave me a ride back to Hackensack once after we played a gig in North Jersey, so he knows where I live.

But no, I tell myself. Nothing to worry about. It's silly to think about it. He probably couldn't even find Hackensack again, let alone my building. And he'd have to go back to the East Village for his car first. He usually takes the train around the city because he doesn't like to lose his parking space. So he couldn't possibly get to Hackensack before me.

I concentrate on keeping my eyes open and focused on the road, making sure there's enough of a gap between me and the taillights of the car in front of me, so I can stop in time if he stops. I'm already on the broad elevated stretch of the highway that skirts the Upper West Side, swinging past high-rise apartments, over little pockets of park—the bridge getting closer and brighter every minute.

I catch myself just in time to swerve left onto the ramp for the bridge entry. The roadway curves and spirals, narrows and constricts to a brief tunnel under the ramp leading to the upper level of the bridge. Then I'm out over the water, chugging along in the right lane while semis thunder past on my left, always more of them late at night like this, and three lanes of traffic on the upper level roar overhead.

I take Route 4 to the Hackensack Avenue turnoff, sail through Fort Lee, Leonia, Teaneck, past the bland, looming shapes of the Riverside Square Mall, under the overpass and swing south on Hackensack Avenue. In a few minutes I'm pulling into the parking lot behind my building. I feel a little shiver of fear, remembering Stan again. But he could never have made it to Hackensack before me.

Lights beam from the back wall of the building, down into the lot, making the wall a glowing screen of yellow brick. But at the wall's edges darkness takes over—darkness to the left, where a sidewalk skirts the building from parking lot to front door, darker darkness to the right, where odorous ranks of trash cans lurk in the alley. And maybe Stan lurks there, as well. I park as close to the sidewalk as possible.

I turn off the car and suddenly I'm sitting in a silence broken only by the whir of the air conditioners in a few of the nearer windows. I snap the headlights off, jerk the emergency brake on. Quickly, I twist my head this way and that. No sign of Stan in the blank brightness of the parking lot floodlights. But what about where the brightness gives way to that dark void off to the right?

I try the door handle on the driver's side, but the lock's still stuck. Otherwise I could launch myself from the side of the car nearest the sidewalk and tear along the side of the building, the key in my hand, dashing for the pool of light at the front door. Instead, I'll have to slide across the seat, let myself out the passenger door, and slip around the back of the car before I can make a run for it.

Stan. My first impression turned out to be the right one. Things got a little confusing for a while, and most of the time Stan seemed so harmless, so bumbling. But it was obvious, really. The guitar pick, the amp settings, the box cutter—and how would he have known what color Monique's hair was? I don't believe for a minute he was only up there Saturday afternoon, asking Jimmy for guitar pointers. What a classic motive. Kill the guy who took your job. Then kill the woman who watched you do it.

This time Walter Stallings has to believe me. Stan practically confessed, and surely it's not too late to check Jimmy's apartment for fingerprints. And they'll get fingerprints off that box cutter. They'll get Stan's fingerprints and compare them and the whole thing will be over.

I slide across the seat and come to rest against the passenger door, ready to fling the door open. I stare toward the mouth of the alley that leads to the trashcans. Is that a tall, ungainly guy lurking at the edge of the shadows? Or is it a floor lamp somebody put out for the trash pickup? It's not moving at all, and if it's a person, even a hairy person like Stan, it's got a funny shaped head.

I shift my body to the right and scan the parking lot. So many cars, and Stan could be crouching behind any one of them. But if I run fast . . . I glance over my right shoulder, and over my left. Nothing's moving behind me.

Time to go. My keys are in my hand, the key to the front door clutched between thumb and index finger. I click down the door handle, bump the door with my shoulder, slide my feet onto the pavement, slam the door behind me, and run around the back bumper. I thud onto the sidewalk, my mouth open, panting in the humid air. I don't even turn to look behind me for fear it will slow me down.

At the corner of the building, I spin to the right and careen into the spot of light that draws the summer bugs to circle aimlessly around the heavy glass door.

Key in lock, I lean in toward the door. I slip through the opening, and the door latches behind me with a heavy, comforting click. It's dimmer in here than out on the walk. I stop for a second to let my eyes adjust, sagging against the door, panting again but this time with relief.

I step toward the stairwell, about to reach for the doorknob, when the door opens toward me, seemingly of its own accord. I'm facing a bony chest wearing a T-shirt with a Fender guitar logo stretched across it. The last person I saw wearing a T-shirt like that was Stan, about forty-five minutes ago.

My gaze travels upward, but not before my body registers a jolt of shock that makes me stiffen like I've just touched a bare wire. My skin feels hot, then cold. It's Stan, of course, and I'm staring right into his eyes, one of them at least. The other is covered by stray wisps from the bushy thicket of his hair. I'm so frozen from the shock that my gaze is locked on his.

"The only place to sit was these steps back here," he says. "I didn't mean to scare you." One of his hands drifts up to his mouth to stifle a yawn. "Man, it's late. But I really had to talk to you." The yawn-stifling hand travels to his forehead to sweep his hair back.

I whirl around and fumble for the latch on the heavy glass door that leads back outside. A large hand grabs my right shoulder; another grabs my left. A voice I don't recognize, but I guess it's mine, yells, "Help me! Please, somebody help me!"

I'm not cold anymore, but hot again, almost burning, and my skin feels slick with sweat. Patches of warm dampness form under my arms. I can't reach the latch because Stan's pulling me toward him.

"Help me! Somebody help me! Please!" the strange, desperate voice cries again.

The hands release me. For a second I just stand there, limp with relief, long enough to hear Stan say, "There's something wrong with you tonight, isn't there? You're usually so calm."

I jerk the door latch to the right and launch myself out onto the walk, running through the patch of brightness toward the dark street beyond. He's running after me, calling my name, asking me why I'm running away.

Three blocks later, I'm standing in front of the C-Town Superette, still open, and with a reassuring pool of light around its door, a reassuring glimpse of a checker lounging behind his cash register. I'm panting so hard my lungs can't even hold all the air they're trying to take in.

Stan rounds the corner, pauses ten feet away. I can't make out his features, only his shape, silhouetted against the glow from the streetlight on the corner. "I won't come any closer," he calls. "Obviously something about me is freaking you out."

"Yeah," I say between gasps for breath. "You killed Jimmy and Monique." He says something inaudible. "You might as well come over here where I can hear you," I say. "If you were going to kill *me,* you would have done it by now."

"Why would I kill you?"

"Because I know you killed Jimmy and Monique."

"Why would I kill them?"

"Because I gave Jimmy your job, and Monique knew what you did to him."

"Maxx! I thought we went all through that before. How could you even imagine I'd kill somebody? Let alone two people?"

"But you were up at Jimmy's place the day he went out that window. You admitted it. And you stood right there tonight and looked at me and told me that other guy *didn't* kill him. How did you know that?"

"Uh . . ." He edges back a few feet and lets his head droop in the familiar Stan pose. "I've seen that guy around the studio. He just doesn't seem like the murdering type."

"No." I shake my head. "That's not good enough. Look at me!" His head snaps up. "How did you know?"

His head droops again, and all I can see is hair. A small voice emerges from the hair. "Because I was there when it happened. That guy isn't the person who did it."

I step toward him, and he cringes away from me without raising his head.

"How could you just stand there and let somebody attack Jimmy? You're a big guy. Couldn't you do something to help him?"

"I was in the closet. I didn't know what was happening until it was too late."

"What on earth were you doing in the closet?"

"Looking at Jimmy's spare amp. That lady with the streaky hair was screaming at him, and I was trying to stay out of the way."

"Monique was there? Why was she screaming?" *She was so much bigger than Jimmy,* says a voice in my head, *and she had those muscular shoulders from all that Tae Kwon Do.*

"She found some other lady's lipstick and sort of flipped out."

"And you were there the whole time?"

He looks at me and sighs. "Most of it's pretty much like I told you before. I called him Saturday morning, and he invited me over, just as nice as you could imagine. So I went there, maybe about five-thirty or so and we jammed for a while. Then he put on this Charlie Christian CD, and he's telling me that Charlie Christian always pretended he was a horn player, and that's how he got such cool phrasing." Stan's fingers twitch like they're reaching for an invisible guitar. "At first I didn't know anybody else was there, but all of a sudden the bedroom door flies open and this lady's screaming at him about somebody's lipstick in the bathroom and it's not her lipstick."

Stan shakes his head. "Didn't sound like such a big deal to me, but she was just about going nuts. So Jimmy shooed her back in the bedroom, talking real quiet and sweet, and he followed her in there and closed the door. I could hear their voices, but not too good because the door was closed. I picked up his guitar and noodled around on it a little bit.

"She was still yelling in the next room, so after a while I got up and started checking out a couple other guitars Jimmy had sitting around. The door to the closet was open and I stuck my head inside. He had more guitars in there, but they were zipped up in gig bags. Then I noticed the amp, sort of hidden behind some other stuff. I never saw a Fender that old before. Usually you see reissues. So while I was poking around, trying to get a better look at the amp, the bedroom door flies open and the voices get real loud again. And I feel like a total jackass hanging out in his closet, so I hope he just figures I took off when things were getting heavy. Then I hear her say, 'Okay, that's it,' and feet tramp across the floor and the apartment door slams so hard I'm wondering if there's going to be plaster all over the floor when I come out."

Stan shakes his head. "So I'm debating whether to step out and feel like a total fool, or just stay there till maybe Jimmy goes someplace and I can leave without him knowing that I was there, that I heard the whole scene. But then the buzzer buzzes, and I'm thinking it's her again, so I decide I better stay in the closet. But it's not her. It's some guy. I can't see him, but I hear him say, 'Charlie Christian? You've got better taste than I expected.' Pretty impressive. He knew who the CD was just like that. I'd never even heard of Charlie Christian before. Then I don't hear anything for a couple seconds except kind of a scuffling noise and something big falling on the floor."

"A person?"

"No, a chair. I stuck my eye up to the crack between the edge of the door and the door frame to see what was going on, and a guy was sliding a chair back up to that table between the windows."

"What did he look like?"

"Not too tall, kind of stocky. I only saw his back, but it wasn't that guy in the car with you. He wasn't nearly that big."

"He knew the CD was Charlie Christian?"

Stan nods.

All of a sudden I'm worried about Helen. "C'mon, Stan," I say. "You're riding back to the city with me."

CHAPTER 24

"Hurry," I say, flicking my fingers toward him in a shooing motion. "Turn around and head back to my apartment building. My car's in the lot."

"I have my own car," he says. "And why do you want to go back to the city? It's really late."

"I'll tell you on the way. Just come on along with me." I grab his arm and propel him out of the circle of brightness that leaks onto the sidewalk from the C-Town Superette. Now we're in the dark again.

"Well, okay, I owe you something," he says. "You were pretty freaked out for a while there, and I guess it was my fault. But what are we going to do? And whatever it is, why can't I drive my own car and meet you there?"

"Because you'll get lost or find some other way to mess things up." I pull him along the dark sidewalk. "And I'm going to need you once we get there."

"Why?"

"Because you're big. Now don't talk. My throat is killing me, and we've got to keep moving." In fact I'm pretty much running on adrenaline. I don't feel so great, but somehow I'm too wound up to care.

Stan gallops obediently at my side, panting slightly as he struggles to keep up with me, even though his legs are much longer than mine.

Soon we're standing under the lights that bathe the edge of

the parking lot. I sort through my keys, which I've been clutching in my hand ever since I slipped from my car and darted for the front door of my building.

I find the car key but realize the driver's side lock isn't any more likely to work than it usually is. Stan knows the drill. He's already making his way around to the never-locked passenger side.

"Let me in first," I say, maneuvering past him and sliding across the seat.

The trip to the city alternates bright and dark: the gloomy stretch of Hackensack Avenue that passes the cemetery just before the ramp, the bright oases of gas stations, and the city visible as a far-off glow that makes the night sky never really look like night.

It's dark again through Teaneck, where wide swathes of green guarantee that the fancy houses are undisturbed by Route 4 running through the town.

As we get closer to the bridge, the road grows smoother and wider, and cars seem to accelerate, as if pulled toward the city, unable to resist. I hear a funny snort from the passenger seat, and look over to see Stan's head thrown back, eyes closed and mouth open. Ahead of me, ranks of taillights glow brighter red as drivers brake in the heavier traffic backed up at the tollbooths.

On the bridge, over the Hudson, the river carves a dark channel between two bright shores: Manhattan brighter with taller buildings, the shore of New Jersey lower.

The West Side Highway is bright and dark, too, as stretches of billboards alternate with stretches of trees until I reach the exit I'll always think of as Jimmy's. Finally, I drive past the bodegas. It's too late to find a cluster of guys on the sidewalk, drinking out of bottles with paper bags pressed around them, but I see a street person pushing a shopping cart full of soda cans to be recycled.

I swing around the corner onto Central Park West. This is no time to look for a parking space. I pull into a bus zone across from Jimmy's building.

"Stan," I croak, grabbing his shoulder and shaking it. "Wake up. We're there."

His huge body heaves against the seat, but his eyes don't open.

"C'mon." My voice is barely more than a whisper. "I need you. Wake up."

"What? Where?" He lurches forward, nearly bumping his head on the joint where the windshield meets the car's roof.

"You have to get out. I can't get out till you do because I have to use your door."

He fumbles for the door handle. "I guess I fell asleep for a minute," he says. "Where are we?"

"You don't recognize it?" I squirm with impatience. "C'mon. Hurry and get that door open."

"Looks like the edge of Central Park."

"No, the building across the street. Hurry. We could already be too late."

I give him a little push. He shoves the door open and eases his huge frame onto the sidewalk. I slide across the seat. Out on the sidewalk, he bends back from the waist to stretch his back, raises his arms in the air and yawns. I grab his arm and haul him across the street, pausing in the middle to let a cab rush past.

I lead him to the door between the urns with their trailing vines. But how are we going to get in? I've always been lucky during the day, always finding somebody on the way in or out.

I don't know Helen's last name, but I know her apartment number. I push the button, but I'm not surprised when nobody buzzes back. That's what I was afraid of.

Taking a deep breath, I start pushing buttons at random.

"Those people are probably all asleep," Stan says, sounding worried. "They're going to be upset that you're waking them up."

"It's an emergency," I say. "Somebody could be dying up there."

At last somebody buzzes back, maybe somebody expecting a late-night visitor or a key-forgetting spouse, somebody who's going to be puzzled when nobody shows up at the door.

I hurry Stan across the lobby and into the little elevator, standing open and ready at this time of night.

"There's something I'm curious about," I whisper, since that's all the sound I can get out of my poor raw throat, as we sway slowly past one floor, then another. "Why didn't you tell the cops what you saw when you were up in Jimmy's apartment? Didn't it occur to you that it would be the responsible thing to do?"

He shudders, and his head droops in the familiar Stan pose, hair hiding his face. "I felt like such a fool," he says. "Hiding in the closet while Jimmy has a fight with his girlfriend. I didn't see that much of the guy who did it, anyway. And besides, I thought, what if when I tell them I was up there they think it was me who killed him?"

"Why would they think that?"

"You did."

He's got a point.

The elevator thumps as it passes one floor, then another, and I'm trying not to imagine what we might encounter when we get where we're going.

Stan is slumped in the corner, his head drooping toward his chest. Will he even be helpful? At least he's big. That's kind of scary in itself. He scared me, on more than one occasion.

I can hear myself breathing, shallow quick panting. My body leans forward, poised to rush from the elevator as soon as it

233

clanks to a stop on the ninth floor. I feel a supernormal alert-
ness, like I'll never be sleepy again in my whole life.

Finally, the elevator wheezes and shudders, and the doors
squeal as they slowly part.

"Let's go," I say to Stan. "Follow me."

I take off down the hall, half running, aware of dim light,
linoleum floor, odd smells of dinners cooked hours ago. Behind
my left breast, my heart seems to be migrating, creeping
upwards toward my throat, about to suffocate me. And I'm
aware of the shallow panting I don't quite recognize as mine.

I glance over my shoulder to make sure Stan is following.
He's keeping up with me, a brisk enough pace that makes his
shaggy mass of hair bounce in time to his steps.

We're at the door of Helen's apartment. Thankfully it's
ajar—a good sign, but a bad sign too. It means we can get in,
but it also means something's not right. New Yorkers never
leave their doors open.

Now that we're so close, I can hear a sound, a heavy, repeated
thudding. Like somebody is beating steadily on something—or
someone. Looking behind me to make sure that Stan has caught
up with me, I take a deep breath. It doesn't help much because
my heart has now reached my throat and lodged itself there
permanently. I push the door open and step inside the apartment.

No sign of anybody, just a chaotic vision of open drawers, an
antique cupboard ripped from the wall, broken crystal and china
jumbled on the love seat and the floor. A deep red satin pillow
with tassels on each corner has been incongruously plopped on
top of a lamp. The lamp's mate is lying on the carpet with its
shade askew—and still that steady thumping, deep and regular,
like a bass drum. It's only been a few seconds, but I feel like
many minutes have elapsed.

The kitchen, from which Helen brought her careful trays of

coffee, is off to the left. That's not where the thumping is coming from, but I glance in there first just to make sure she's not cowering—or worse—behind the refrigerator.

"C'mon, Stan," I say, grabbing him by the arm. "Here we go." I pull him past the love seat, stepping over the fallen lamp.

"Damn, what was that?" He pulls his foot out of the lampshade and we proceed to stand in the doorway of the bedroom.

Inside the bedroom, more drawers are open, some pulled out and piled haphazardly on the floor. The bed has been turned back, but roughly, hastily, as if by someone crazed by the need for sleep and desperate to climb between the sheets, and the pillows have been tossed on the floor.

Now I can see where the thudding has been coming from. A door leads off the bedroom into somewhere—probably the bathroom—and a man is rhythmically flinging himself against it.

Backing up, launching himself, bouncing off the door, again and again—silent, stolid, determined.

"Is that the guy?" Stan whispers. "The guy who was in Jimmy's place."

"Of course it is," I say. "Why do you think we're here?"

Now the guy leaves off throwing himself against the bathroom door and turns. He looks at me like I've got two heads, the same look he gave me as he stood by the Coke machine at the studio and listened to me tell the tall guy that Jimmy's apartment was full of clues and that Jimmy's neighbor had his key and that I had a friend who was a cop.

After he looks at me, his gaze shifts upwards and he looks at Stan. But he doesn't seem worried, just determined. Tae kwon do class, I'm remembering. That's where Monique said she met him. That's how he made such short work of Jimmy.

Quiet-voiced, calm, he looks at us. Was it Helen who made the mess out in the living room, desperately trying to defend herself as he demanded Jimmy's key? Which she didn't even have anymore because I forgot to give it back. Would she have given it up if she had it? Or held out on general principles because he didn't look like the kind of person who should be allowed free run of Jimmy's apartment? Helen is a pretty tough character, and I'd bet on choice number two.

"So you figured it out," he says, like he's not surprised. "I didn't plan things that way, you know."

What did Monique see in him? Maybe it was his eyes, knowing eyes, the eyes of a guy who can look right down into you. Eyes that make you blink first if he stares at you long enough. Monique seemed like a chick who wanted to give herself to a guy who was in control. He's got a sexy mouth too, full lips that glisten.

"I was just improvising," he says suddenly with a laugh—not a humorous laugh, though, and underlining the word "improvising" with his voice. "Going where things took me. Sometimes one line leads to another. You pick up the guitar, you start simple, but before you know it, you're blowing through the changes with ideas you never knew you had." He shrugs his shoulders and holds up his hands as if to show us that they're empty.

"I showed up looking for Monique at the place where I thought she was staying. She moved in with one of her woman friends when she left me. I'd been doing a lot of thinking, and I hoped she'd come back if I said I'd marry her. That's what you all want, isn't it? To get your hooks into a guy? But the friend let it slip that Monique had moved to be close to Jimmy. I went there, but she wasn't in her apartment, so I tried his. I didn't plan it really. Just did it. Like I said, improvised. With her, too. First I thought she'd come back once Jimmy was gone. But she wouldn't. And the box cutter was there, and the journal, and she was drunk and drugged out of her mind. But even drugged she managed to tell me she was through with me forever because being with Jimmy made her see what it was like to be loved by a human being."

He shows us his empty hands again, like now what he means is they're empty of her.

But quicker than anything I've even seen in a movie, Stan's laid out on the floor and the guy's got both my wrists gripped in his hands.

His eyes are closed. "Improvise," he's saying to himself. "F-major, that's a good key. In my mind I see red. I see red again, like I did for Monique."

Maybe Stan's not really knocked out, I'm thinking to myself. Stall for time. "You're not the first guy I've ever heard who said he saw keys as different colors," I say. "But does everybody see the same key as the same color? Blue, for instance? Would that always be a blues key? Like, let's say, B flat?"

He doesn't answer. He probably doesn't even hear me. His eyes are still closed, and he's off in some secret part of himself. I glance down at Stan, praying for any sign that he's still conscious, that at the right moment he'll spring up and rescue me.

He'll trip over something and fall down again—that's more likely, says a voice in my head that doesn't seem to understand the seriousness of the situation.

"Improvise," the guy murmurs, eyes still closed.

Is it my imagination or has a tiny crack appeared where the bathroom door meets the doorframe? Helen? But what on earth could she do to help me? She's better off staying in the bathroom with the locked door between her and Luke.

Of course, after he gets rid of Stan and me, he'll go back to his steady thudding, and eventually he'll break the door down. It will only be a matter of time.

The crack widens. Luke will open his eyes any minute now.

His back is to the bathroom door, but he'll hear a creak, footsteps. He'll whirl and that will be the end of Helen.

Now he's humming a little melody. In F major? This Luke guy is really scary.

Helen's head appears in the widening crack in the door. She doesn't look too much the worse for wear, bright lipstick still in place, bright eyes alert under carefully drawn brows, only her hair is a little tousled. She's mouthing "It's okay."

What on earth can she mean? How can things possibly be okay?

The door widens further, and she steps into the bedroom. She's carrying, of all things, a dumbbell, like the kind people use to work out with at the gym.

Luke's still in his eyes-closed-and-humming mode, but the tune is getting a little more complicated.

Helen creeps closer, brandishing the dumbbell like a weapon. The dumbbell is kind of an alarming thing. It probably doesn't weigh more than five pounds, but the bar stretches between two octagonal pods with sharp edges carving out the octagonal shape, and it's made out of a dull, silver metal.

I wouldn't like to have it land on my head, but can she possibly be strong enough to seriously slow this guy down? Or will she bring him out of his trance and make him mad?

At the very moment Helen raises the dumbbell, the phone rings.

Stan, apparently hearing the phone, gives a huge grunt and starts to sit up.

Luke opens his eyes and looks around like he doesn't know where he is. But then he catches sight of Helen behind him with the dumbbell and whirls toward her.

The phone keeps ringing.

Stan succeeds in sitting up.

Helen's machine answers the phone, and her coquettish

recorded voice tells the unknown caller that she's not available to come to the phone, leave a name and number.

Stan lurches forward, tackles Luke around the knees, and falls back, pulling Luke down on top of him.

Luke stares at the ceiling like he doesn't know what happened.

"Good work," I croak to Stan. "Keep a grip on him and don't let go no matter what he does." I look at Helen. "Go ahead," I say. "Do it."

"I can't hit a person," Helen squeals. "Not in the face."

I grab one of the pillows lying on the floor, drop it on Luke's head, and plop on top of it. His arms are flailing uselessly, but then he uses them to try and push himself into a sitting position.

"Okay," I tell Helen, "don't hit him. Drag one of those drawers over here and put it across his chest. And gather up as many of those weights as you've got and put them in the drawer, along with anything else you can find that's heavy."

Helen hurries to the bathroom and back a few times with weights, piles in some books from the night stand, heads for the bathroom again, and staggers back with the porcelain cover from the toilet tank, which she places across the drawer."

"Great," I say. "Now find something to tie him up with."

"What? What can we use?" She stands where she is, looking puzzled, her lips a narrow dash of brilliant red.

"Pantyhose," I say, feeling Luke squirm under me.

"I can't breathe down here," Stan gasps.

"Where are they?" Helen says. "My drawers are a mess. Everything's just tossed around."

"Those things," I say. "Those leggings you're wearing. They'd work great. Just peel them off. Hurry!"

A horrified look passes over her face, then she says resolutely, "Yes. I have to."

Sitting on the bed, she eases off her high heels, stands to slip the leggings over her hips, then sits again to peel them off.

"I'm dying down here," Stan moans.

Luke's legs twitch.

"Tie his legs first," I tell Helen. "Just wrap the leggings around a couple times and make a good knot."

She kneels on the floor and gets to work. Under the leggings, she was wearing pantyhose, so her narrow legs aren't completely bare.

"Now we need something for his hands," I say. "We'll have to use the panty hose you're wearing, if you can't find any other ones."

She returns obediently to the edge of the bed and strips them off, leaving a pair of lacy black panties.

"Stan," I say, "can you hear me?"

"Barely," he says.

"We've got his legs tied. Try to get out from under there so you can help Helen with his hands."

The pillow under me shifts one way, then another. It's like I'm sitting on a sack with some kind of a restless animal in it.

Stan eases himself out from under Luke as I lift my right leg out of the way to let him pass. "Take Helen's pantyhose and tie his hands."

Helen has pulled a satin dressing gown out of her closet and is slipping into it.

"Get the pantyhose knotted around one of his wrists really good," I tell Stan, "then wrap it around the other wrist and pull them together."

After Stan gets Luke's wrists bound together, I raise myself gingerly from the pillow. Luke is still squirming, but not as much as before. Wondering what I'll find underneath, I start to move the pillow but then think better of it.

"Where's your phone?" I ask Helen. "It should only take the

cops a couple of minutes to get here."

She looks embarrassed, like she should have thought of that herself, probably before she changed into her dressing gown. "Living room," she says.

Stan follows me and stands at my elbow while I make the call. As soon as I hang up, he says, "I've been thinking about the band. We can talk about it again, can't we?" He backs toward the love seat, pushes a few broken teacups to the side, and sits down. "The only problem now is that Dom doesn't like me. But there are plenty of drummers in the world. We don't need him."

"We don't need you," I say, firmly. "So don't even ask."

EPILOGUE

It's Saturday night, and the Hot Spot is in full swing. Scarcely a table is empty. Back by the bar, people are packed so tightly that late arrivals don't stand a chance of working their way to a clear view of the stage, let alone a chair. Sweat and beer smells clog the air like a greasy, odorous fog. Half the people in the place are talking and laughing, loud enough to make themselves heard over the band. The other half are focused on the stage, where a perspiring woman with too much makeup and hair that's too blond to be real is belting out the last verse of "Swing It on Home."

Her eyes are closed, her head thrown back, one hand clutching the mike stand, the other held aloft as if she's surrendering to somebody. Her body is curvy on top, trim down below, and she's dressed in leopard-patterned leggings and a black leather bustier.

The verse finished, she steps away from the mike and nods to the guitar player, a tall, skinny man in faded jeans and a shapeless T-shirt. His abundant hair is tugged back into a ponytail, but wiry tendrils frame his face with a dark corona. He bends over his guitar, a sleek black Stratocaster that glints in the bright lights. He tweaks out a soulful note that lingers like a fading train whistle, then another and another.

To the left of him, a thin man with a careful expression of concentration on his thin face methodically works the strings of an electric bass. At the far right of the stage, a small fair-haired man bends over a keyboard, his face hidden by a shaggy mop of hair, his hands hopping among the keys like dance partners retreating and advancing, retreating and advancing.

Scarcely visible behind the singer, except for the huge grin that hasn't left his face all evening, is the drummer, a stocky man with a florid face made more florid by the heat from the lights.

As the last notes of the guitar solo echo through the room, the drummer catches the singer's eye. She nods, and he winds the tune up with a drum flourish. The reverberations from the cymbals hang in the air as the crowd bursts into applause.

The singer steps back up to the mike, passes a hand across her sweaty forehead and smiles a lipsticky smile. "Thanks a lot," she says. "That was the one and only 'Swing It on Home,' a Big Mama Thornton tune, and we're Maxximum Blues. We'll do one more, and then take a short break, but first I'd like to introduce the band."

She bows toward the bass player and a strand of blond hair flops loose. "On bass we have Michael Scott. Give it up for Mike." She waits till the applause dies down then sweeps an arm in the opposite direction. "And over here we've got Neil Patterson on the keys. Neil Patterson. Let's hear it." More applause. "And on guitar—" She gestures toward the hairy guy, who looks embarrassed. "I'd like to introduce Stan Dunlap, back with the band tonight after taking a little break to pursue other projects." The guitar player's head droops in an awkward bow. "And finally, last but certainly not least, on the drums— our new drummer. Give it up for Walter Stallings. Big Walt Stallings! Let's hear it."

The drummer's huge grin gets even bigger.

The hairy guy steps up to the mike stand, leans forward, bumps his nose on the mike, then leans quickly back. "Maxx

Maxwell!" he shouts, waving his arm with an awkward flourish. "I'd like to introduce Maxx Maxwell. Let's hear it for Maxx."

ABOUT THE AUTHOR

Peggy Ehrhart is a former college English professor who lives in Leonia, New Jersey, where she plays blues guitar and writes mysteries. She has won awards for her short fiction, and her stories have appeared in *Futures Mystery Anthology Magazine,* several anthologies, and numerous e-zines. As Margaret J. Ehrhart, she has also published widely in the field of her academic specialty, medieval literature. She is a longtime member of Mystery Writers of America and Sisters in Crime. As a guitar player, she has performed with The Last Stand Band and other bands in the New York/TriState area. She is married to Norm Smith and is the mother of Matt Smith.